THE PANEM COMPANION

AN UNOFFICIAL GUIDE TO SUZANNE COLLINS' HUNGER GAMES, FROM MELLARK BAKERY TO MOCKINGJAYS

V. ARROW

SMART POP

An Imprint of BenBella Books, Inc.
Dallas, Texas

THIS PUBLICATION IS UNOFFICIAL AND UNAUTHORIZED. IT HAS NOT BEEN PREPARED, APPROVED, AUTHORIZED, LICENSED, OR ENDORSED BY ANY ENTITY THAT CREATED OR PRODUCED THE WELL-KNOWN BOOK OR FILM SERIES THE HUNGER GAMES.

The Panem Companion copyright © 2012 by V. Arrow

All rights reserved. No part of this book may be used or reproduced in any manner whatsoever without written permission of the publisher, except in the case of brief quotations embodied in critical articles or reviews.

BenBella Books, Inc.
10440 N. Central Expressway, Suite 800
Dallas, TX 75231
www.benbellabooks.com
Send feedback to feedback@benbellabooks.com

Printed in the United States of America

Library of Congress Cataloging-in-Publication Data is available for this title.
978-1-937856-20-5

Copyediting by Debra Kirkby, Kirkby Editorial Services
Proofreading by Michael Fedison and Rainbow Graphics
Cover design by Nora Rosansky
Text design and composition by Cape Cod Compositors, Inc.

Distributed to the trade by Two Rivers Distribution, an Ingram brand (www.tworiversdistribution.com)

Special discounts for bulk sales are available.
Please contact bulkorders@benbellabooks.com.

Contents

Introduction	v
1. Mapping Panem	1
2. How Panem Came to Be	21
3. Race, Ethnicity, and Culture in Panem	27
4. The Socioeconomics of Tesserae	43
5. The Curious Case of Primrose "Everdeen"	57
6. Family Life in Panem	65
7. The Games as Exploitation, Exploitation as Entertainment	77
8. Gender Roles and Sexuality in Panem	93
9. District 4	113
10. Mythology and Music in Panem	127
11. District 11	135
12. The Architects of the Rebellion	145
13. Truly, My Name Is Cinna	157
14. District 13 and the Capitol: Two Sides of the Same "Coin"	165
15. Accountability for Acts of War in the Hunger Games	175
Final Notes: Capitol Viewers and the New Panem	185
The Hunger Games Lexicon	189
A Note on District Names	193

CONTENTS

Acknowledgments 239

About the Author 241

Endnotes 243

Introduction

The Hunger Games trilogy, by Suzanne Collins, is arguably the most significant Young Adult literary work of the last few years; it has certainly been the most visible. It has also been lauded for its accessibility to a wide audience, from students reading it as an assignment in schools to adult men and women reading it for its literary value—or to see what all the fuss is about.

What is that fuss about? What makes the Hunger Games so compelling as to have become an international phenomenon? On first blush, the synopsis of the series does not exactly sound like the kind of pleasant, jaunty read that most casual readers would seek out—the story of a girl trying to survive a gladiatorial battle to the death in a televised competition, which ends with a war that kills most of the beloved characters—and its status as a young adult novel would seem, unfortunately, to disqualify it from many intellectuals' "Must Read" lists. Yet somehow, the series managed to bridge that gap between scholarly critics and casual readers in a way that few books, much less series, have managed.

Perhaps it's not so surprising that the Hunger Games bridges that gap, given that bringing different groups together is one of the key themes of the series: bridging class divides, ideologies, and political schism. As Katniss' awareness of her world grows and opens, so does our own as readers; as her outlook matures, so does Collins' literary voice—and so do we. It is Katniss, in her role as our conduit to the horrors of Panem, who makes the series palatable. The story is told so closely from her point of view as to be inextricable from it: the story of Panem becomes Katniss' story, and as Katniss takes her place as the Mockingjay figurehead in the war, Katniss' story drives and shapes the story of Panem.

INTRODUCTION

Countless fan guides have been written for the Hunger Games series already, and most have focused specifically on Katniss and her tale: Katniss and Peeta, the boy with the bread; Katniss and Gale, the boy with the bombs; Katniss and Prim, the sister who could not survive. But Katniss and her personal narrative are only a part of the story of the Hunger Games, and the tantalizing gaps that Katniss leaves for us as she tells her story attest that there are as many stories in Panem as there are tessera slips. *The Panem Companion* looks at these stories, and it looks at Panem itself: the country's relationship to Katniss and her story, but also how the other characters in the novels shape and are shaped by the world they share—as well as by our own world, and of the way we engage with media like the Hunger Games.

In Panem, viewing the Hunger Games is mandated as a way to bend the populace to the Capitol's will and remind them of their low status and lack of freedom. In the Capitol itself, the Hunger Games are a phenomenon, spawning fanatic aficionados, glitz, glamour, speculation, and excitement. In our world, millions of us have freely chosen to read the Hunger Games series—and it has become a phenomenon involving fanatic aficionados, glitz, glamour, speculation, and excitement. Perhaps the truest reason, then, and the simplest, for the Hunger Games trilogy's popularity in our own world is that it is the most effective mirror of our own culture that has been produced since the advent of reality television and celebrity social media coincided with the mainstream practice of fandom: the transformative interactions (from "meta" discussion of canon and the creation of "headcanon"—extrapolated, unconfirmed, precanonical or postcanonical "facts"—to fanfiction and fanart) among an engaged community of a particular piece of media (in this case, the Hunger Games series). The Hunger Games is a story about public interaction with mainstream media. It's a story about what happens when media content and consumption become tangled—when interpretation becomes reflexive or bidirectional (in which the media and the analyst are able to affect each other) rather than reflective (in which the analysis is more unilateral and impersonal).

Of course, reflexivity is the core of both academic inquiry and fandom. Academic inquiry of the Hunger Games seeks to find the instances of social criticism in Collins' text and demonstrate their effectiveness to the books' audience in a way that inevitably becomes a deeply personal critique of the readers' own relationship to both the Hunger Games series and society in general. If we see the Hunger Games as a scathing examination of how Big Media and the government in our world entwine to create and maintain the socioeconomic status quo, then we are forced to consider this question: Can anyone enjoy a mainstream media phenomenon—like the one the Hunger Games has become—from an unbiased position outside of the system the series itself exposes? The world we live in necessarily depends on understood societal values and class assignments reinforced by stereotype and superficiality, just as in Panem. An analysis of the way Panem's government and media combine to reinforce social perceptions of race, class, gender, sex, and morality necessarily fosters recognition of our own—either by divorcing Panem from us and critiquing it as an independent culture or by viewing it as an extension of the contemporary world and a critique of contemporary American culture.

Fandom is also a deep reading of the text, but the focus is intrapersonal (each individual on how or why the media is so resonant to the self), not interpersonal (despite the communal nature of fandom), and based more on extrapolation and the fulfillment of reader desire than scholastic research. More than passive enjoyment, the practice of fandom—the verb form of which, at least in Hunger Games fandom, is "fangirling," regardless of the sex or gender of the fan—is *an active consumption of media* and the creation of derivative and transformative works through deeper analysis. Academic analysis looks at the overall scope of the Hunger Games; fandom analysis focuses on what outsiders may consider trivialities (Mags needing "translation," Cinna's lack of Capitol accent, Peeta's observations of Katniss' parents) to try to build a deeper understanding of the characters' lives and the country they live in as its own place—outside of, or even unrelated to, the canonical text and authorial intent. Fandom strives constantly to wring additional information out of the canon Hunger Games text, often in an effort to "give justice" to characters who are seen as receiving unjust fates or to open new avenues of transformation. They craft scenarios for pre-series Hunger Games, question whether there were truly no other chances for rebellion. In short, fans explore, expand, justify, and transform actions or words in the text that are often overlooked by even the most stringent academic annotation—and explore, expand, justify, and transform scenes implied by, but outside of, the text as well. Hunger Games fandom is more than fanatic enjoyment of the series; it is an almost compulsive need to extract (or to create) from the main text *more* of Katniss, more of Peeta, *more* of Cato and Clove, *more of Panem*.

In *The Panem Companion*, I have tried to incorporate both broad-scope academic analysis and the minutiae of fandom concerns in order to provide a fuller, richer, and more complete picture of the nation of Panem and the people who live (or, in the case of most characters, lived) there. When I say "broad-scope" academic analysis, I mean that the overall goal of this guide is to place Panem within the context of the Hunger Games series' resonance as a pop culture phenomenon today, as well as place Panem in its own context as a nation that is not our own, not part of our culture, and therefore does not share our understanding of ethics or morality or etiquette. But because this book has its origins in my own desire to understand more, more, more about Panem, I would be remiss if I did not also employ fandom-style analysis to inform that academic analysis of Panem's systems and institutions. To this end, I've also incorporated the thoughts and work of many of my fellow fans in the Hunger Games fandom community.

One final note before we jump into that analysis itself: I've looked here only at the Panem of the novels, given that the Panem of the movie is quite different and, in some places, directly oppositional. In large part, this was a choice based on continuity, because at the time of this writing only one film has been released, whereas the complete series is available in novel form. The Hunger Games film series and the Hunger

INTRODUCTION

Games novel series exist in different spheres of audience interaction, as well; while the novels require of us active participation with the text to consume the story and idea of Panem, the movies let us passively consume it as a viewer if we so choose . . . adding an additional parallel between us, as fans of the Hunger Games series, and the citizens of Panem's Capitol, as fans of the Hunger Games.

How we view and consume media is a major aspect of Suzanne Collins' series and it is one that follows us on our journey through Panem, from the mines of District 12 to the ocean of District 4, and the vast fields of District 11 to the secret tunnels of District 13. I hope that exploring the more hidden geographies of Panem through *The Panem Companion* will make Katniss' journey in the Hunger Games an even more thrilling one to travel.

1

Mapping Panem

A significant part of what makes the Hunger Games trilogy unique within the genre of dystopian sci-fi is not its plot (which is both based in real history and a common trope within the genre, an oppressive political regime forcing the disenfranchised to become citizen–gladiators) or its characters (many of whom serve largely as archetypes and allegories) but the nation of Panem itself.

Like many other fictional dystopian nations, it is North America—But Not: recognizable to us as our own culture but different enough that it should not be held to the same cultural or sociological standards. Panem, like any other culture, has its own structure of values and standards based on its history, ethnic make-up, economy, and geography. Although Katniss lives in the coal-mining shadow of the Appalachian Mountains, she does not live in West Virginia or Pennsylvania or Virginia: she lives, very particularly, in District 12's Seam, and every decision she makes is a product of that place and its culture. So, as a fan of the series, what I wanted to know was—just where, and what, is District 12? And how does it fit in to Panem as a whole?

For me, involvement in the Hunger Games fandom really began with the creation of a map of Panem, and that's the most logical place for this guide to begin, too.

We see very little of Panem over the course of the Hunger Games trilogy. But what we do see during the Victory Tour in *Catching Fire* really drove home for me the idea that Panem is not, in fact, one nation, but instead is made up of autonomous, isolated nation-states. I also realized slowly, as Katniss did during the Quarter Quell, that the lives of each of those nation-states' residents are affected as deeply—at least—as Katniss' life has been affected by the mines in District 12. And that the Capitol, too, shapes its citizens, for better or worse. In other words, despite how little time the books spend in most of the country, Panem itself plays a central role in the story.

Panem seems to take on a character of its own even from the first scene of the series:

> I can feel the muscles in my face relaxing, my pace quickening as I climb the hills to our place, a rock ledge overlooking a valley. A thicket of berry bushes protects it from unwanted eyes . . . Gale says I never smile except in the woods . . .
>
> From this place, we are invisible but have a clear view of the valley, which is teeming with summer life, greens to gather, roots to dig, fish iridescent in the sunlight . . . With both of us hunting daily, there are still nights . . . when we go to bed with our stomachs growling.[THG6-9]

In looking more deeply at Katniss' world, the nation of Panem should be front and center; it shapes everything in the series, from the horror of the Games themselves to Katniss' family's dynamics, from why Rue knew what night-vision goggles were to why Mags' language is "unintelligible."

So, armed with frosting, ice cream, and overflowing love for Finnick Odair—as well as a mountain of research—a fellow Hunger Games enthusiast and research geek friend of mine, Meg, and I started mapping Panem. We began with an image of modern North America:

FIG. 1

The first question we had to ask, in order to map the country, was about Panem's origins: When did Panem begin? Suzanne Collins has kept fairly mum on the subject but did tell Scholastic in 2008 that Panem was not a prediction for the lifetime of any of the Hunger Games' contemporary readers!

> Q: *How long would it take for North America to deteriorate into the world depicted in the books?*
> A: You'd have to allow for the collapse of civilization as we know it, the emergence of Panem, a rebellion, and seventy-four years of the Hunger Games. We're talking triple digits.[i]

Given the grand scale of cultural collapse, anywhere from 200–999 years seems absolutely believable for a nation like Panem to arise.

However, the changes that have taken place by the start of *The Hunger Games* aren't just cultural. They're physical, too. Katniss herself recounts geological catastrophe as a major part of the fall of North America, as she narrates Mayor Undersee's recitation of "the history of Panem, the country that rose up out of the ashes of a place that was once called North America. He lists the disasters, the droughts, the storms, the fires, the encroaching seas that swallowed up so much of the land."[THG18]

Panem, then, is likely best seen as its own continental island nation, like Australia is today, with North America as its precursor. It would take at least 300 years, according to the best estimates of ecologists, meteorologists, and other global warming scientists, to see a major disaster or chain of disasters extensive enough to change the topography of North America drastically. Therefore, in terms of the creation of the Panem map, Meg and I were more focused on the geological cataclysm than on social change—and it turns out that even "triple-digit" years is a pretty short amount of time for the earth literally to fall apart!

When Suzanne Collins signed the three-book deal for the Hunger Games with Scholastic in 2006, the world was still reeling from the effects of Hurricane Katrina in Louisiana, a tsunami in the Indian Ocean, record-low fatal freezing temperatures in Canada and the northern United States, and a massive Pakistani earthquake. It's easy to imagine our real-world events being woven into Katniss' story. But there's a piece still missing: "the encroaching seas," which is a common trope in sci-fi literature that takes place on Future Earths. One possible origin is the urban myth that California is sinking or will "break off" into the ocean—and that, admittedly, is what Meg and I used in making our first draft of the map. However, it's more likely that a combination of tectonic shifts in California causing tsunamis, global warming affecting the Atlantic, and continued erosion in Louisiana and the Gulf would have been responsible for the seas "encroaching" on North America.

Either way, we needed to collapse the coasts of the United States, Mexico, and Canada an adequate amount to reduce landmass enough to result in "the brutal war for what little sustenance remained."[THG18] We chose to reduce Mexico significantly to create the futuristic border crisis we saw as the likely cause of Panem's racial tensions (which will be explored further in both chapter two and chapter three), and theorized that the polar ice melt would take care of much of Canada.

Given that the "Sinking California" theory is actually pretty much science fiction—which is okay, because so is the Hunger Games—we had a fair amount of leeway in how we wanted to pursue the various avenues of geological cataclysm.

First, we pinpointed a specific assumption about the time frame of Panem: 400–500 years from the present. That allows not only for the minimum 300 years necessary for the large-scale geological catastrophes but, overlapping that somewhat, also the 74 years of the Games–tesserae system and, before that, time for a pre-existing Panem to develop a full culture and go through the kind of sociological and socioeconomic transformation that could lead to the First Rebellion—most likely, at minimum, another 60–100 years. At least three to four generations of social programming would be necessary to create the kind of district identity separation that would foster the distinct and hegemonic cultures that make up the districts; however, the genetic homogenization Katniss describes in the Seam would require at least six. If you assume that one factor contributing to the fall of North America is the depletion of oil reserves worldwide, and extrapolate from estimates that, at the current depletion rate, oil reserves will be emptied by 2054,[ii] that sets Katniss' Panem in at least the late 2400s.

~2054 (approximate depletion of oil reserves)
~300 (approximate time for widespread geographic and cultural change)
~60 (time before the First Rebellion)
+ 74 (time after the First Rebellion)
2488 (start of *The Hunger Games*)

Then we looked at actually sinking the continent. Here's some of that encroaching seas theory Meg and I looked up: between 1900 and 2000, the ocean rose six to eight inches due to global warming (a global temperature rise of half a degree celsius, according to the United Nations Population Fund). Supposing the same rate for those 300 years—until shortly before the First Rebellion, in our estimation—that's another eighteen to twenty-four inches of oceanic rise. Think that's a crazy estimate? Some experts estimate a twelve-inch rise just by 2050![iii]

At that rate of rise, coastal cities all over North America and the world would be at risk of sinking—kind of like Venice is sinking now, by a few inches each decade—with southernmost Florida, the Louisiana coastline at the Gulf, North Carolina's Pamlico-Albemarle Peninsula, along Chesapeake Bay, and the Texas–Mexico shoreline east of Galveston being most at risk.[iv] Other threatened U.S. cities include New York-Newark, New Orleans, Boston, Washington, Philadelphia, Tampa-St. Petersburg, and San Francisco.[v]

Part of the problem in those areas is that many millions of years ago, during the Ice Age, "around the periphery of where the glaciers sat [in] places like Chesapeake Bay and the south of England—the land was actually squeezed upward . . . by the downward pressure nearby."[vi] These areas of raised land have been slowly sinking ever since (just a few millimeters a year but still sinking), which makes the sea level rise greater than average in those regions. In some coastal areas, most notably along the Gulf of Mexico in Louisiana, the land is *falling* as well; thanks to massive oil and gas extraction, the continental shelf is collapsing "like a deflated balloon,"[vii] which would significantly diminish the available land for districts that require access to the ocean or southern climate (like District 4 and District 11, respectively). Plus, if we conjecture that the economic and political climate in Panem was indeed partially caused by the depletion of oil and gas, major problems to the Gulf area seem inevitable.

The Great Lakes region, too, is heavily at risk from flooding. However, given what we know about District 12 and District 13's location along the Appalachian mountain ridge and District 11's location in the Deep South, some adjustments had to be made for purely canonical reasons. If all of the geological theories were taken as absolutes, Panem simply isn't possible. The falling of the Gulf area and the flooding of the Great Lakes region would split North America into two smaller subcontinents, and train travel from District 12 to the Capitol would be impossible. So we endeavored to come up with the most accurately sunken map we could with canon still taken as, well, canon.

This was our first attempt at deciding where to set the geological boundaries of Panem:

FIG. 2

Although feasible, it wasn't really jelling for me. Meg brought up that there would be a natural flood break at the Sierra Nevadas and, likely, the Grand Canyon, creating new ocean/land borders for the country.

So we decided to look up some more "factually accurate" scenarios. A professor of geology at the University of Wisconsin–Green Bay actually spelled out his ideal sci-fi approach to Sinking California on his departmental website. Although his approach isn't precisely how we chose to utilize fault lines, it's still worth noting. He argues that the western provinces of Canada have a higher chance of survival than California because the San Andreas Fault and East Pacific Rise join up near Baja California,[viii] which is a significant distance from the Pacific Northwest region. He also notes that the "slippage" of the California coast would cause devastating tsunamis that would "demolish the whole Pacific Rim and possibly [even] cause damage in the Atlantic. They might well make two or three circuits of the earth before dying out."[ix] In our subsequent attempts, this contributed to our decision to flood parts of the Atlantic coast east of the Appalachians, which helped to place District 12 and District 13.

Rising sea levels along the 3,500-mile-long barrier island shoreline extending from Montauk Point on Long Island to the Mexican border would easily allow for higher land elevations to respond naturally, geologically, to the sea rise and become "floating island" cities.[x] So I chose to center part of "the Cataclysm" in the Gulf of Mexico as a tectonic shift and moved the Yucatan Peninsula, rather than sinking it. Although this was done, admittedly, for mainly aesthetic reasons, there is precedent: Madagascar originally broke free from the megacontinent of Gondwana, which later became Africa.

FIG. 3

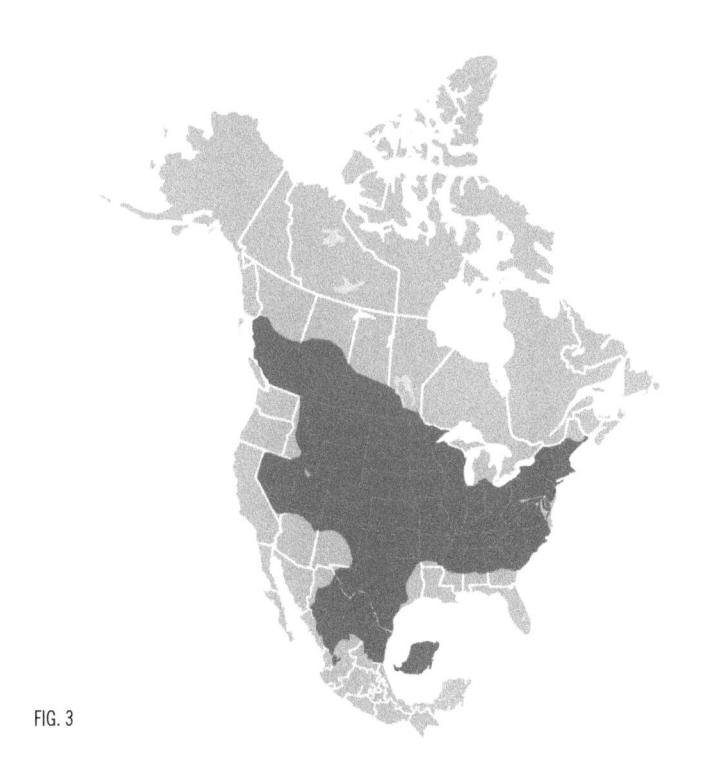

I ended up keeping more of the Eastern Seaboard than might be feasible, given the likely effects of the melting Greenland ice shelf, but Panem needed some land for District 12 and District 13.

From there, placing the districts meant taking an anthropological and geoethnographic look at what they each produce. The assumptions used for *The Panem Companion* are as follows and are based on the text canon of the Hunger Games series. The film's canon diverts from what is stated in the series in several instances regarding district specialties, most notably for District 11, District 3, and District 2. But given that the original map was made before the movie was released—and because this is an analysis of the Hunger Games novels and not films—those differences in specialties are ignored here.

DISTRICT	SPECIALTY	NOTES
District 1 (D1)	Luxury goods (goldsmithing, silversmithing, diamond mining, gemstones/precious metals)	Specifically stated in the series.
District 2 (D2)	Weaponry and Peacekeepers, some mining	Specifically stated in the series. Given their location in or very near the Rocky Mountains (which we know from the Nut in *Mockingjay*), I assume their mining is more like railroad blasting—breaking a way through the Rocky Mountains so that supply trains and tribute trains can more easily reach the Capitol, or perhaps even filling in tunnels and causeways that carried over from our own time to better fortify the Capitol's position—than goods mining, like the diamond mining of D1 or the coal mining of D12, or even the fictitious graphite mining of D13.
District 3 (D3)	Electronic goods, hardware, software	Specifically stated in the series.
District 4 (D4)	Fishing and luxury seafood, pearls	Specifically stated in the series.
District 5 (D5)	Science (DNA, muttations, experimental sciences)	Extrapolation based on Foxface's Games strategy, as well as unserved needs of the Capitol.

MAPPING PANEM

DISTRICT	SPECIALTY	NOTES
District 6 (D6)	Drugs and medicine (morphling, tracker jacker venom, medicines)	Extrapolation based on information about the D6 tributes and victors—Titus' hallucinations and the morphlings' addiction, in particular—as well as unserved needs of the Capitol.
District 7 (D7)	Lumber, logging, and forestry	Specifically stated in the series.
District 8 (D8)	Textiles	Specifically stated in the series.
District 9 (D9)	Food processing (pasteurization, preservatives, sorting/shipping, rationing; no *production* of food items)	Long-standing pre-movie fandom interpretation; extrapolation based on unserved needs of the Capitol and description of "smelly factories" in *Catching Fire*.
District 10 (D10)	Ranching, slaughterhouses, dairy products	Specifically stated in the series.
District 11 (D11)	Agriculture (grain fields, cotton fields, fruit orchards, vegetables)	Specifically stated in the series.
District 12 (D12)	Coal mining, of course!	Specifically stated in the series.
District 13 (D13)	Nuclear power	Specifically stated in the series. Propaganda informed the other districts that D13 existed to mine graphite, however.

11

So, knowing all of that, the most logical organization for the districts was not straight slices across the continent, which would allot equal land but not necessarily the type or amount of land necessary for each district's specialty. We chose to arrange the districts based on a phi spiral instead.

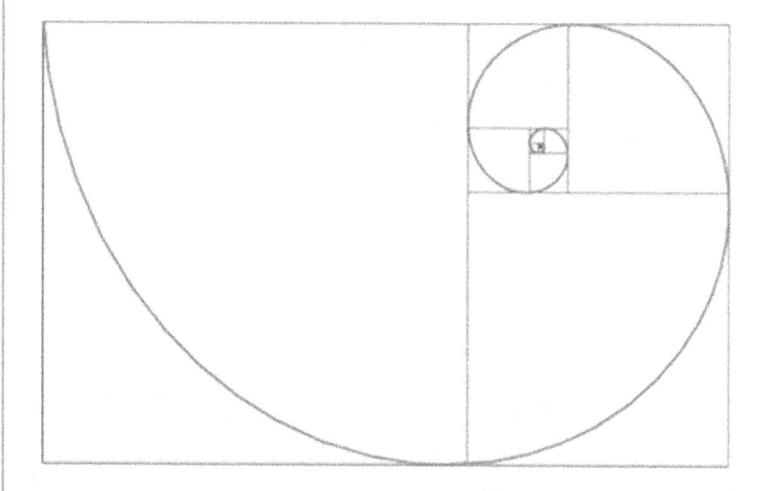

Straight slices would arbitrarily force large-scale specialties like agriculture and ranching to fit into the same landmass as indoor/small-scale specialties like electronics or drug chemistry. The phi spiral would allow for varying district sizes, as well as better organize the country for central Capitol control because it would allow for a more controlled flow of communication and travel than if districts were allotted land in randomized cookie-cutter chunks.

Given the immense difference in geography and political landscape in comparison with the present, Panem would most likely not have based its districts on modern state/province/country borders. Katniss' narrative suggests that the Capitol has had unilateral control of governmental and political decisions since the inception of Panem, which means it would have needed to re-create its entire infrastructure to accommodate its needs. The phi spiral would give each district the unique amount of space it would need to cultivate its specialty, without giving them so much room that pockets of dissent could form in "off-the-grid" communities. (This is also why we did not leave massive amounts of space between the districts. Like Katniss' forest in District 12, there are clearly fenced-off "forbidden areas" within the districts themselves, not between them—a.k.a., not outside of Capitol jurisdiction. Think of modern-day North America, where all of the land is held accountable to both state and government law, even if it is not inhabited or even inhabitable.)

Just so you don't think that this organization idea is too crazy, some believe that the phi spiral—also known as the golden spiral because it is based on a ratio called the golden mean—was commonly used in ancient Greek architecture, including in the design of the Acropolis.[xi] And Richard H. Carson, former regional president of the American Planning Association, a professional organization for city and regional planning, has proposed the use of the phi spiral as a way to alleviate problems with overcrowding and resource disbursement.[xii]

With the plan all set, it was time to place the districts! We started with the places that Katniss describes most concretely: the locations of District 12 and the Capitol.

> In school, they tell us the Capitol was built in a place once called the Rockies. District 12 was a region known as Appalachia. Even hundreds of years ago, they mined coal here. Which is why our miners have to dig so deep.[THG41]

We placed the Capitol in the Rockies—originally at what is now Denver, Colorado—and created the curve of the phi spiral around it so that, as it fanned out, the outermost curve would reach West Virginia, Virginia, and Pennsylvania (or the general Appalachian Mountains region) for District 12 and Virginia-Maryland for District 13, assuming that it incorporates either Arlington, Virginia, and the former Pentagon site or Three Mile Island, applicable for their specialty of nuclear power.

FIG. 4

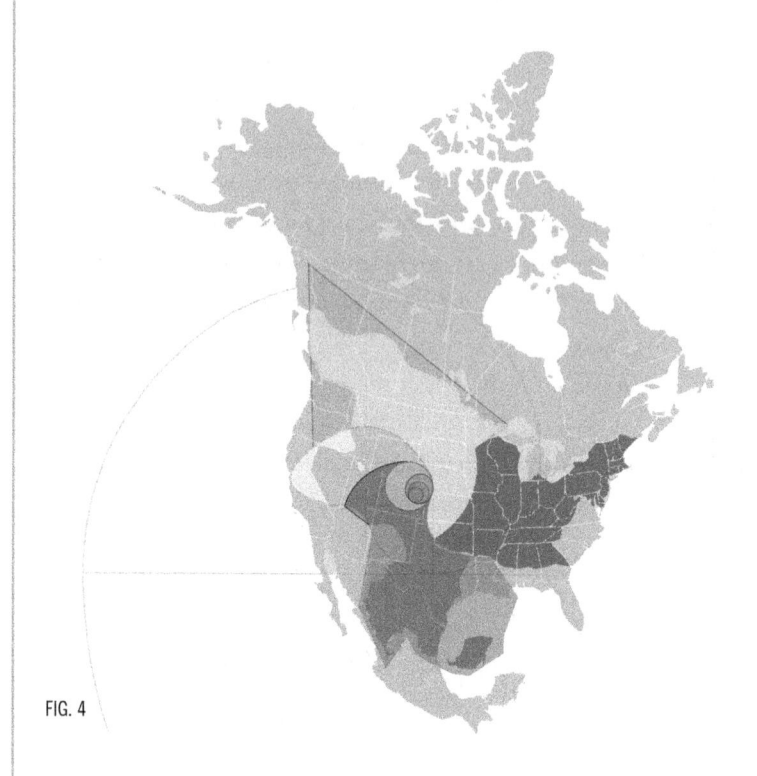

    This was our first attempt at District 1 through District 7 (and the Capitol). District 7 works well along the former United States-Canada border; it makes sense that national lumber production would require a large district, and this area reaches north towards the boreal forest. However, the issue with this placement of District 7 is that it does not leave room for District 9 to border with District 4—necessary, given that District 4 produces seafood for sale to the Capitol, and that seafood would need fairly immediate processing. This configuration also places District 8 incorrectly in the phi spiral in regard to Katniss' description of its location in *Mockingjay*, and it cuts off way too much of the landmass District 10 and District 11 would need for cattle ranching and agriculture, respectively.

Our next attempt:

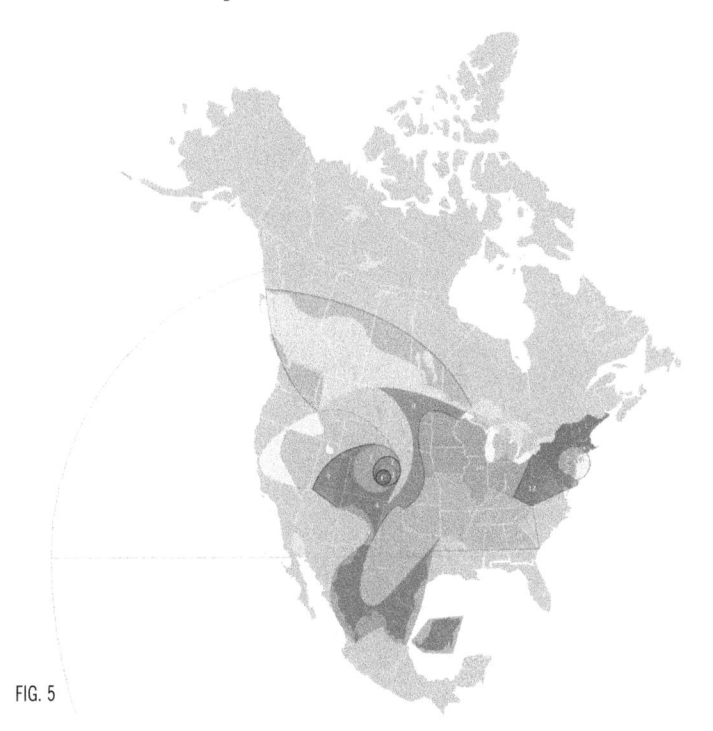

FIG. 5

Taking landlocked area away from District 4 was a major help. District 9, the district where food processing takes place, now properly borders all food production districts (District 4, District 11, and District 10). District 11 is the largest in landmass (plenty of room for lots of crops!), District 10 has room to raise a nation's worth of livestock, and District 7 is a more manageable size for Peacekeeping. And everything still lies along the intended phi spiral!

Unfortunately, a few tweaks were needed to make things adhere to canon. It makes more sense for the Nut in District 2 to be at the present-day location of NORAD because it's a pre-existing military fortress that Suzanne Collins is likely familiar with, given her family's military background.[xiii] The Capitol needed a little shift westward, from Denver to Aspen, to be better protected by the mountains.

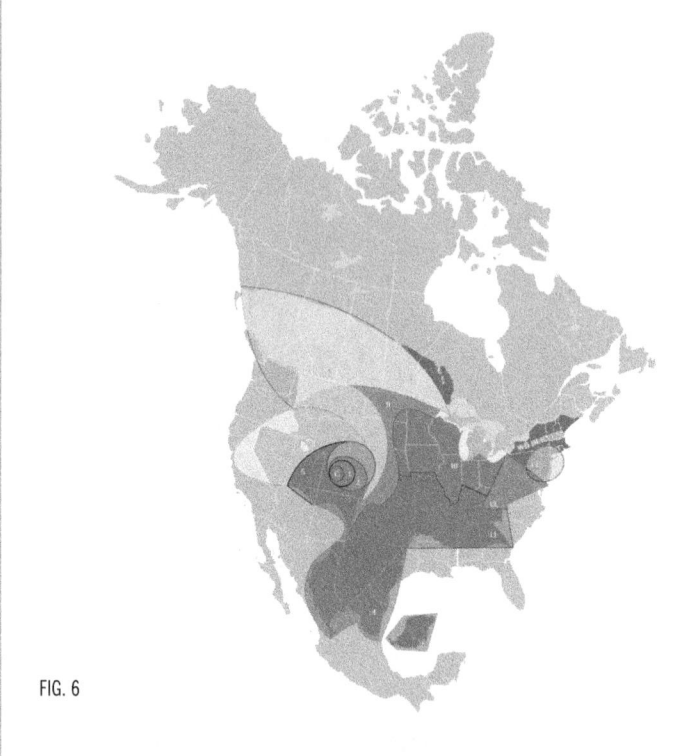

FIG. 6

There are as many interpretations of Panem as there are Hunger Games fans, and in fact, as of this writing, an officially licensed version is in the works. But the one you see here is the one we'll be using for this guide. The extrapolated locations of the districts on our map inform some of the anthropological, historical, geoethnographic, and economic assertions made in the rest of the text, although all are also supported by canonical evidence from Katniss' narrative.

So let's start by taking a look at those 400–500 years that turned our North America into Panem's—not physically but politically and culturally.

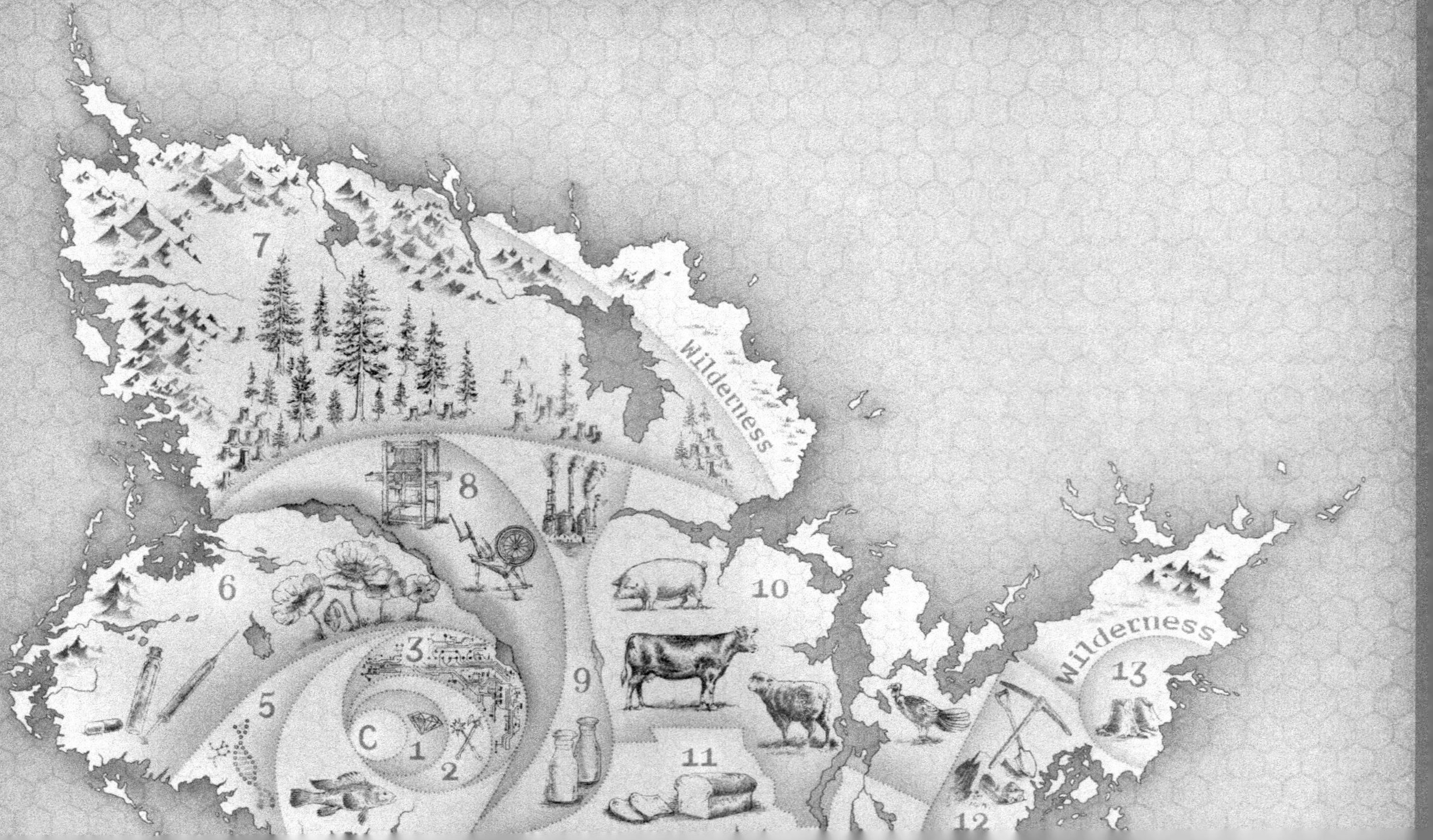

7
Wilderness
8
6
10
3
9
Wilderness
13
5
C
1
2
11
12

An Unofficial Map of Panem from The Panem Companion

How Panem Came to Be

Although conjectures about geological cataclysm would explain the physical borders—perhaps even the provincial organization—of Panem, its true dystopian horror comes from a cataclysm of a more anthropogenic nature. Panem is post-apocalyptic because of the end of our known world geography, but it is dystopian because of its political, socioeconomic, and cultural collapse and the ways it is dealt with by the Capitol. After all, it isn't centralized government like the Capitol's or geographically disparate states that is frightening; it is the operation of the Hunger Games, a system that targets its disenfranchised for death. Although employing the Hunger Games as reparations for civil war is unjust enough, the Games' enforcement of a society built on institutional classism—and, we can infer from the text, racism—is truly horrifying. (Racism and classism will be discussed in chapters three and four.) Shifting geography alone could not cause this kind of catastrophic change in ideology—so what happened in Panem to cause so much fear and violence?

One of the most realistic explanations for the strict divisions of the districts and the depth of the Capitol's institutional prejudice against district citizens would, however, stem from that geological shift. Specifically, a predictable aspect of the downfall of North America as we know it and the rise of Katniss' Panem would be the reaction of the United States to a massive influx of immigrants as a result of cataclysmic flooding.

Nobel Prize recipient and former vice president Al Gore considered this kind of scenario in his global warming documentary, *An Inconvenient Truth*. He used Asia as an example:

> The area around Beijing is home to tens of millions of people. Even worse, in the area around Shanghai, there are 40 million people. Worse still, Calcutta and, to the East Bangladesh the area covered includes 50 million people. Think of the impact of a couple hundred thousand refugees when they are displaced by an environmental event and then imagine the impact of a hundred million or more . . .[xiv]
>
> Adding insult to injury, in many parts of Asia the rice crop will be decimated by rising sea level—a three-foot sea level rise will eliminate half of the rice production in Vietnam—causing a food crisis coincident with the mass migration of people."[xv]

It's a problem that we face here in the United States as well, Gore explains, and one for which we aren't prepared.

With the seas encroaching in Mexico and Canada, as well as on the coasts of the United States, tens of thousands of people would be displaced and forced to move inland (a population increase that would later be thinned out by the First Rebellion, epidemics, and the Hunger Games). The sudden population growth may have contributed to anthropogenic disasters: epidemics, the depletion of resources, civil violence. In fact, this mass migration could have contributed to the founding of the Capitol as such a controlling entity in the first place.

Historically, the United States has reacted to waves of migration by imposing immigration caps. In 1921, Congress passed the Emergency Quota Act, virtually cutting off legal immigration from "cultures dissimilar to the United States" (as described by the Act itself).[xvi] During the Cold War in 1965, with the United States grappling with xenophobic tensions, we restricted the number of legal visas on a nation-of-origin basis. The United States has also responded to migration by passing laws that discourage specific immigrant groups, particularly nonwhites—as in 1917, when laws requiring a minimum level of English literacy led to the exclusion of virtually all immigrants of Asian descent. On a cultural level, the waves of immigration that prompted congressional action were greeted with mass xenophobia and racial hatred; segregation, both legal (as in the South) or socially enforced (as in the North), was common, from "Whites Only" water fountains to "No Irish Need Apply" job opening signs. Despite the cultural myth of America as a land of equal opportunity for all, the United States has as much history as any other country of responding to an influx of outsiders with prohibitive laws that institutionalize racism and classism.

The same is true today. When Suzanne Collins was writing the Hunger Games trilogy, the news (and "news-like" political commentary) was dominated by the United States–Mexico "border crisis." The commanding dialogue of the debate encouraged racism against Mexican, Puerto Rican, and Cuban immigrants in the United States by endemically grouping all Latin American peoples together as an entity to be feared. As Glenn Beck put it: "Every undocumented worker is an illegal immigrant, a criminal and a drain on our dwindling resources."[xvii] Even those born in the United States who share an ethnic background with many illegal immigrants have been treated as criminals without burden of proof; the racial profiling of the mainstream media has given rise to sanctioned governmental action against an entire racial/ethnic group.

Given the level of immigration that Panem's geological collapse would cause, it is easy to extrapolate that a true chaos of racial targeting and interpersonal distrust would emerge on both civilian and governmental levels. The Capitol might have reacted to this tension as the former USSR did after the Russian Civil War: by organizing its administrative units by race, ethnicity, and/or culture. Although the USSR encouraged and enforced "Russification" or the promotion of Russian language and culture as dominant across all republics, its people represented more than 100 distinct ethnic groups. And although some ethnicities were represented faithfully by the USSR's administrative divisions, others were subject to forced assimilation with larger, more favored groups within their region—somewhat similar to how Seam residents and merchants are both labeled simply "District 12" by the Capitol, even though they have very different social experiences.

Within Panem's districts, it's no surprise that a merchant class, likely marked by racial alignment with the Capitol, would rise. It's a development parallel to the racial make-up of contemporary US suburbs, which do not legally enforce higher social positions or economic status for whites but do culturally reinforce white privilege through ethnic nepotism (a sociology term for scenarios in which people unconsciously prefer to provide job, housing, or relationship opportunities to people who share their race or ethnicity). Capitol media would also play a role in the devaluation of the specialty classes of nonwhite recent immigrants. In essence, even before the First Rebellion—which canonically we know nothing about beyond its existence, and for even that, Katniss is an unreliable narrator, given that her knowledge of the event comes from propagandist schoolbooks—Panem was uniquely organized for acts of institutional violence . . . and socioeconomic genocide.

In the First Rebellion, what caused the downfall of the districts is likely what helped them to prevail in the Second Rebellion: their organizational setup as isolated nation-states. Although Panem is located on the former site of the United States (as well as Canada and Mexico, both of which have their own provincial states), it is inherently not a united nation, as Katniss reveals early in *The Hunger Games*.

> [T]ravel between the districts is forbidden except for officially sanctioned duties.[THG41]

[I]n fact enclosing all of District 12, is a high chain-link fence topped with barbed-wire loops. In theory, it's supposed to be electrified twenty-four hours a day.[THG4]

Instead of one interdependent and homogenous nation dependent on Capitol culture cues, the fencing in and separation of the districts essentially created thirteen unique nation-states with various levels of independence and one main similarity—being preyed upon by the Capitol, stripped of resources, gaining nothing, and victimized at their most basic level, their children. The Capitol created its own enemies and had no control over their individual cultures and the ways that they retained pre-Panem or non-Capitol-approved traditions.

By segregating the districts so staunchly, the Capitol essentially prevented any kind of pro-Capitol assimilation. Evidence of these insular cultures from the books includes the persistence of words with foreign origin—names in particular, such as Mags, Annie, Johanna, and the naming customs of District 11 and the Career districts (see chapters nine and eleven, as well as the lexicon)—and disparate district marriage customs, such as District 12's "toasting ceremony" and the District 4 practice of touching the lips with saltwater and wearing a veil of nets.

A similar phenomenon in real-world history of the development of such insular cultures is that national delimitation of the Soviet Union, which divided areas in what had been known as the Russian Empire into republics, autonomous provinces, and autonomous national territories based on ethnicity and language. Each of these areas retained their own languages outside of the enforced national language of the central government, and created their own social patterns to the point that "the Soviet Union became increasingly worried about a possible disloyalty of diaspora ethnic groups with cross-border ties . . . which eventually led to the start of Stalin's repressive policy towards them,"[xviii] much like the Capitol's policy towards the districts in the lead-up to both the First and Second Rebellions.

Despite these small nation-state cultures flourishing in the districts, the white-preferential Panem culture still marginalized the specialty-class cultural elements, turning them into markers of lower class and loss of privilege. Nonwhites were displaced, even within the geographical boundaries of each district—if our own history is our guide, through the systematic rise in rent/land prices, incidental costs, and overall cost of living. It's an all-too-familiar process, seen in everything from the rise of the Colonies/United States and the takeover/elimination of Native Americans to England and India, and Australia and its aboriginal population.

Many years later, this is the Panem we are introduced to at the beginning of *The Hunger Games*: a society built on and structured by institutional racism and classism, under the thumb of an all-powerful central government.

Race, Ethnicity, and Culture in Panem

"[Gale] could be my brother. Straight black hair, olive skin, we even have the same gray eyes. But we're not related, at least not closely . . . That's why my mother and Prim, with their light hair and blue eyes, always look out of place. They are. My mother's parents were part of the small merchant class"[THG8]

The question of race in the Seam is the subject of a long, bitter, multifold debate within the Hunger Games fandom. Because Katniss' racial make-up is intentionally vague, those who believe that she is white, those who believe that she is categorically any race except white, and those who believe she is biracial can, and do, claim ownership of Katniss and the rest of the Seam. They often support their belief in her racial make-up by citing personal experience—"I'm Portuguese and have olive skin, but I'm definitely white," "I'm biracial and I look like Katniss but my sister looks like Rue," "I always saw Katniss as Native American, like me." The internet is flooded with posts— some undeniably racist to anyone's understanding and some more subtly informed by cultural conditioning—that argue all sides of the issue.

Suzanne Collins, after the first Hunger Games film was cast, told *Entertainment Weekly* that she saw Panem as "a time period where hundreds of years have passed from now. There's been a lot of ethnic mixing."[xix] From that small nugget of official information, only one true fact of Katniss' race can be determined: however far in the future the Hunger Games is set, whatever the darkness of Katniss' skin, however many races truly mixed to create the Seam skin tone, the Seam is "not white"—in either the modern understanding of skin tone or in societal privilege. As YA author Shannon Riffe phrased it, "[W]e don't know what [Katniss] is, but we know what she's not. She's not blonde haired and blue eyed like her mother and sister and Peeta. She's dark, like Gale."[xx]

The inclusion of Gale in both Katniss' and the readers' understanding of Katniss' racial make-up is important because it creates a specific identity that is uniquely "Seam" in the world of Panem. Katniss, and Gale even more staunchly, views Seam people as inherently different from merchants or the people of the Capitol, and it would be irresponsible to dismiss her understanding of their genetic similarity and the physical appearance of race as a root of that understanding. People who are racially "Seam" share the physical traits of olive skin, gray eyes, and black hair—whether that olive skin is evidence of Mediterranean roots (which themselves are the result of centuries-old racial mixing) or the popular Hunger Games theory that the residents of the Seam descended from Appalachia's tri-racial Melungeon community. "Melungeon" is a term traditionally applied to any of the distinct multiracial groups that help to make up the Cumberland Gap area of central Appalachia, the approximate location of Panem's District 12. Through centuries of "ethnic mixing" (to appropriate Collins' terminology!) between freed slaves (some biracial), Latino settlers (from Spain, Portugal, or ports in the Caribbean), Native Americans, and Anglo/white settlers, Melungeon groups today are described in terms extremely similar to Katniss' description of the "typical Seam look" of black hair, olive skin, and gray eyes.

Is Katniss Melungeon?

An essayist at *Dead Bro Walking*, a community for commentary on the representation, imagery, and narrative arcs of characters of color in sci-fi, fantasy, and horror genre works, detailed the literary evidence for Katniss' likely Native American or Melungeon roots in an article in March 2011:

> I keep seeing this call that "Katniss is racially ambiguous!" ... Yes, Katniss is described as having olive skin, dark hair, and gray eyes, which is pretty generic as far as physical descriptions go, but ... race is about far more than how you look and/or appear. The text goes on to expound upon several pertinent details:

- Collins chose to set District 12 in what was once Appalachia. Coal-mining Appalachia. If coal was the active reason for the setting, she could have chose another setting where coal is mined, a setting where there is not a distinct racial history of intermarriage since the 1500s (if not before, but I am citing popular texts). Check out just about any family in this region and you'll find interracial marriage (or relationships because our marriages were not legal until various points in history) and interracial families. Check out the Native nations whom still live on our original land like the Eastern Band Cherokee and Lumbee. Once in a blue moon, a "real-looking Indian" will show up in a family; our looks vary beyond the scope of Natives presented on TV or in Hollywood.
- Katniss is the name of a plant [a plant that's common name is arrowhead]. In many families where mother tongues were lost due to genocide, English equivalents are substituted. In browsing the social security name records for the last century, several plant and animal names pop up frequently for children born in Appalachia and the south east ... Familial and communal oral history from as far back as Reconstruction (as well as a family bible started in 1887) show that many racially mixed families chose plant and animal names, or used them as nicknames if the child had to have a "Christian name."
- Katniss is not only a hunter but she uses a bow and arrows as her father before her did. Is this slightly stereotypical? More than a little stereotypical? Yes, but it is an interesting choice when pieced together into the whole. Gale uses snares and traps and he is described as a hunter who is just as skilled as Katniss. Katniss

CONTINUES

needed a skill that helped her feed her family as well as help her in the arena, but there were several choices that Collins could have gone with as she mentions spears, snares, knives, etc. as weapons of the other tributes.

- [In real-world Appalachia,] the merchant and ruling classes [are] white and the rest of [the residents aren't]. In Collins' world, District 12 is set up the same way. It's a small district of 8,000 people and all of the Seam (coal miners and their families, the poor) are described as Katniss is described, so much so that when Capitol tells people Gale is Katniss' cousin no one questions it because they look very much alike. This is problematic for the obvious reasons—we don't all look alike—but I do think Collins is consciously playing with race and ethnicity even as she does so in a way that conflates race and class, but it's conscious all the same . . . There is very little integration, in fact, it seems limited to school and reapings with the occasional interaction during business hours.
- And last but certainly not least, the use of 'The Hanging Tree' in the third book. The above components, even synthesized, could be argued via a simple . . . textual interpretation. However, when Katniss' childhood song is introduced, well, as they say, [!@#$%] just got real . . . I assume that Collins wrote the song, but it is obviously inspired by coded songs from American South used by slaves to communicate messages and warnings. Plainly, it's a song about lynching; that much cannot be disputed . . . [I]t's hard to believe that 'The Hanging Tree' is an innocuous song included as a motivator so that Katniss thinks about her potential lovers and losing them.
- Actually, several fellow readers who read Katniss as white were very irritated and cited cultural appropriation when they read the song lyrics in *Mockingjay*, whereas I saw it as the ultimate confirmation that I had just read three books starring a heroine who was someone like me.

In conclusion . . . Collins did not come out and write "Katniss is mixed race: black, Native and white." She didn't do so because she didn't need to do so—she leaves the reader enough concrete clues throughout the three novels to figure it out.

However, from the way that Katniss notices the world around her—and how she is treated by those who are not Seam, such as Mrs. Mellark and Effie—it's clear that even if the Seam skin tone is a "dark-skinned European," which we would view and identify as "white" in modern-day America, Katniss' *ethnic* understanding of herself and her subsequent self-identification is "not white." She understands that as a person of the Seam, who looks Seam, she is not viewed the same way as her mother or Prim or Peeta, with their fair skin, blonde hair, and blue eyes.

This difference in definition of white and nonwhite between our time and the time of the Hunger Games is well within the realm of possibility. Dr. David Freund, a historian at the University of Maryland who focuses on racial politics and public policy in the United States, says of the mutability of "not-white Caucasian" racial identification:

> [I]t's really important to remember [that] both ethnic and racial identities have changed a lot throughout history . . . "[E]thnic" groups that suffered from severe discrimination were usually labeled, at the time, as "racial" groups as well. Consider the history of discrimination against the Irish, Italians, and Jews, for example [who are now recognized as "white" in 21st-century America] . . . Italians, Jews, and Slavs were considered non-white in popular political discourse of the late 19th and early 20th century [due to their olive skin], and this discourse grew very influential in the anti-immigration movement, leading eventually, in the 1920s, to severe restrictions against entry of supposedly "non-white" groups to this country . . . I think we call these groups an ethnicity and not a race now, because those categories have actually changed. This is due in large part to a series of policy decisions that gave some groups certain advantages in the 1930s, '40s, and '50s, allowing them to be part of an ever-expanding "white" race. The political context and the power context changes. Ethnicity, like race, takes on different meanings.[xxi]

What is the difference between race and ethnicity? The easy answer to that question would be something like *race is what your physical markers say you are, ethnicity is what you see yourself as*, but that disregards culture and cultural identity, which can inform self-identification as much as race and ethnicity. Think of a dark-skinned Southeast Asian person adopted into an ethnically Anglo-Saxon family in infancy, who then grows up squarely identifying with "white" culture—ethnically, they are likely to self-identify as white, while racially self-identifying as Southeast Asian. The race of one's parents may not make a difference in one's identity. Though Katniss herself is biracial according to Panem and District 12 culture, since her father was Seam and her mother was a merchant, she *looks* like she belongs in the Seam, and clearly identifies ethnically and culturally with the other Seam residents. The complicated answer to the question of race versus ethnicity is that there is no infallible answer. However, NYU Sociology Chair Dr. Dalton Conley believes that:

> While race and ethnicity share an ideology of common ancestry, they differ in several ways. First of all, race is primarily unitary. You can only have one race, while you can claim multiple ethnic affiliations. You can identify ethnically as Irish and Polish, but you have to be essentially either black or white. The fundamental difference is that race is socially imposed and hierarchical. There is an inequality built into the system. Furthermore, you have no control over your race; it's how you're perceived by others. For example, I have a friend who was born in Korea to Korean parents, but as an infant, she was adopted by an Italian family in Italy. Ethnically, she feels Italian: she eats Italian food, she speaks Italian, she knows Italian history and culture. She knows nothing about Korean history and culture. But when she comes to the United States, she's treated racially as Asian.[xxii]

Katniss understands her *race* to be Seam, basically, because she identifies *ethnically* as Seam and because the Peacekeepers, merchants, and others in the Seam identify her as Seam. Katniss denotes herself as similar to Gale with as much ease as she notes herself as different than her mother—from whom she first feels separated at the same time in her life that she becomes fully aware of the societal difference between the Seam and the merchants: after her father's death. Katniss' negative feelings about her mother began at the same stage in her life that she saw firsthand the extent of cruelty and racial/ethnic hatred of the merchants towards Seam people, like Katniss herself.

> There was a clatter in the bakery . . . [Peeta's] mother was yelling, "Feed it to the pig, you stupid creature! Why not? No one decent will buy burned bread!"[THG30]

Katniss, with her olive Seam skin and black Seam hair, was just found starving and picking for food in the bakery's trash by blonde, blue-eyed, fair-skinned Mrs. Mellark. Mrs. Mellark is aware of Katniss' presence but would still rather have Peeta feed the burnt bread to their pigs than let Katniss have it. Her phrasing attacks Katniss' "decency" as an ethnic girl of the Seam, and implies Katniss' worth is less than even a pig's. At this moment in her life, Katniss, who looks nothing like her merchant-class mother or her well-loved and blonde, blue-eyed, fair-skinned sister, has been left to fend for herself in her time of extreme need by her merchant-class mother and now, as she realizes the gravity of her situation, is being abandoned again by another merchant-class woman: told by her mother to starve out of circumstance, and told by Mrs. Mellark to starve because she lacks "decency." It is no wonder that Katniss self-identifies so passionately as Seam and dwells on the marked differences between herself and her merchant-class mother, who, even after four years, she has difficulty trusting:

> My mother's parents were part of the small merchant class . . . My father got to know my mother because on his hunts he would sometimes collect medicinal herbs and sell them to her shop to be brewed into remedies. She must have really loved him to leave her home for the Seam. I try to remember that when all I can see is the woman who sat by, blank and unreachable, while her children turned to skin and bones. I try to forgive her for my father's sake. But to be honest, I'm not the forgiving type.[THG8]

Prim, in contrast, has no issue trusting Mrs. Everdeen—and incidentally, Prim also does not share Katniss' outward markers of being Seam. Prim, like Mrs. Everdeen, appears to be of the merchant class, with her blonde hair, blue eyes, and fair skin. She is also, by Katniss' repeated admission, the better-liked of the Everdeen sisters by the other residents of District 12, particularly—or perhaps only, because Greasy Sae and the Hawthornes seem so partial to Katniss—the merchants.

It's easy to say, "Of course Prim was better-liked; she was sweet and kind and tenderhearted!"

But.

Katniss could have kept her hunting spoils for her own family; instead, she traded in the Hob and sold to other families—which allowed them to eat when perhaps they couldn't feed themselves, either. She brought home an injured goat for the sister she loved and didn't kill Buttercup the cat (against her own better judgment) because he made Prim happy. In *Mockingjay*, we even see Katniss bonding with him to please and entertain the other refugees in District 13.

Katniss is, despite her—and Haymitch's—assessment of herself, fairly sweet. Her quick wit and wry sense of humor, as well as her genuine praise for Cinna's work and grudging fondness for Haymitch in her interviews with Caesar Flickerman, more than endear her to the Capitol public (not to mention us as readers). Why should District 12 be different?

Katniss ends up in the Hunger Games out of a desire to protect her younger sister even in a place where it wouldn't be expected ("family loyalty only goes so far on reaping day"). When in the arena, she allies only twice: with the youngest contestant, whom she sings to sleep, and with Peeta, a boy who has been so grievously injured that, without her, he would have succumbed to gangrene. Katniss performs every action she undertakes in the entire series for the benefit of someone else.

Katniss is kind. Her devotion to others, especially those who appear less fortunate than herself, is indicative of a genuinely kind nature, even if she views herself in supremely negative terms when comparing herself to Prim or to Peeta (who is actually merchant class, in addition to being blond and blue-eyed).

And as she says herself, people have a way of worming their way inside her and taking root there. Katniss is tenderhearted. Katniss Everdeen is a marshmallow. (A marshmallow that will kill you six ways from Sunday, but . . . still.) Her consistent, fond notice of Greasy Sae's disabled granddaughter and relief at her continued survival is a small, touching example of this motif.

So if both Everdeen sisters behave in ways that show them to be sweet, kind, and tenderhearted, why is Prim the better-liked sister?

Because she is blonde, blue-eyed, and fair-skinned, ostensibly seen as more similar to those from the merchant class than those from the Seam due to her physical appearance. But beyond that, likely because Prim engages in District 12 life outside of the Seam culture in a way that Katniss does not.

Katniss and Prim's interactions with the rest of District 12 are, from the outside, not all that different. Prim goes to school; she admires the cakes in the window of the bakery; she nurses animals back to health; she apprentices herself to her mother, a healer, and helps to care for injured and ill residents of District 12. Katniss, too, goes to school; she walks her sister home and allows her to window-shop at the bakery; she hunts for and sells or trades meat and pelts on the black market; she has a working relationship with many of the District 12 community adults, from Seam residents like Greasy Sae and Hazelle to Darius the Peacekeeper and Mr. Mellark in the merchant class. But although Katniss exemplifies the same positive personality traits as Prim in her daily interactions, she displays them within the context not only of her Seam race and Seam ethnicity but of the very particular Seam culture.

What is a culture, and how does it differ from race or ethnicity? Dr. Nancy Jervis, a researcher and speaker from the China Institute who commentates on the integration of multicultural inclusion in school curricula, believes that culture is:

> something material you can touch . . . something immaterial, such as values and beliefs . . . [and] our customs and traditions, our festivals and celebrations[.] While anthropologists have vacillated between material and nonmaterial definitions of culture, today most would agree with a more inclusive

definition of culture: the thoughts, behaviors, languages, customs, the things we produce and the methods we use to produce them."[xxiii]

Basically, culture is a way of life that is learned and passed down through generations. Anthropologist John Bodley posited in 1994 that "culture . . . is made up of at least three components: what people think, what they do, and the material products they produce."[xxiv]

The Seam is a clear example of a fully formed culture within the larger culture of Panem. By Katniss' accounts or in her purview:

- *Think:* In the Seam, the value of reciprocation is highly prized. Katniss struggles hugely through the trilogy with her feeling of "owing" Peeta, even after he's made it clear that in his culture—the merchant-class culture—the need for reciprocation is not so overt; he tells Katniss, point-blank, that she does not owe him anything anymore in exchange for the bread or protection during the Seventy-fourth Games and Quarter Quell. The people of the Seam also seem to place a high value on nature, even if they aren't going out into the woods themselves the way that Katniss and Gale do. Mrs. Undersee medicates with chemicals synthesized and distributed by another district, but Mrs. Everdeen (now culturally Seam even if she is merchant class by birth and appearance) relies on herbs and plants to create similar anesthetic effects for her patients.
- *Do:* Although "coal mining" is a hit-you-over-the-head example of "what Seam people do," there are other, subtler examples as well: the passing down of clothes from parent to child and sibling to sibling; trading and barter on the honor system (possible due to the cultural emphasis on reciprocation); the iconic three-fingered funerary salute.
- *Produce:* Again: "coal" is the obvious answer, but what else does the Seam produce? Wild dog stews and, perhaps most impor-

tantly in a place called Panem (which itself means *bread*), tesserae-grain biscuits.

Tesserae-grain biscuits are an integral part of the formation of Seam culture as distinctive because, as we learn in *The Hunger Games* and expand on in *Catching Fire*, every district in Panem has its own unique, isolated culture, and unique breads are a carefully crafted narrative element of those cultures. In District 3, where the specialty is electronics and technology, which depend on precision, the bread is small, white squares[CF349]—reminiscent of electrical circuitry.

The bread from District 4 is green, salty, and made from seaweed, further demonstrating the overwhelming importance of the ocean to District 4's people. In District 12, where life is hard even for the merchants and where they have almost never gotten the benefit of a year's supply of luxuries and rations after the Games, the signature bread is made of tesserae grain—Katniss describes it as "rough." The tesserae-grain biscuits aren't the only bread made in District 12. The breads she describes made in Mellark Bakery are "fragrant" and "delicate," and Peeta describes making a multitude of different breads, cakes, and even pastries, which not only demonstrates the merchant class' greater financial stability (they are able to purchase a variety of goods beyond those required for mere subsistence) but also illustrates a difference in value assessment: merchant-class products are simply worth more than those made in the Seam. In *The Hunger Games*, Peeta recalls a goat cheese and apple tart—noted by both Katniss and Peeta as "too expensive"[THG309]—made in his family's bakery. The description "too expensive" would suggest that its ingredients were rare and precious, yet it is also reminiscent of Katniss and Gale's breakfast of goat cheese and blackberries at the outset of the series, which was free—that it was the cache of the merchant bakery and not the actual economic value of the ingredients that drove the Mellark Bakery tart's price.

This highlights an important point in understanding the relationship between the merchant class and the Seam. Race does not exist in a vacuum, whether in our world or Panem: it affects, and is affected by, socioeconomic class. Although all residents of District 12 are poor in comparison to the Capitol and even the other districts, within the socioeconomic structure of the district itself, there are clear haves (the merchants) and have-nots (the Seam), divided along racial lines. And this disparity of resources creates discord and tension within the district.

Of all of the characters, Gale is the most affected by this, as shown by his early interactions with Madge in *The Hunger Games*—despite his recognition of the institutional forces that drive the socioeconomic disparity between the merchants and the Seam. He is strongly resentful of Madge; his interactions with her are underscored with tension from the first time we see them speak ("Pretty dress").[THG12]

Some Hunger Games readers show a similar pattern of prejudice. Many fans mistakenly ascribe Madge with the negative values of the Capitol—even though she demonstrates none of their vapidity, lack of empathy, or overt racism. This is because it is at times hard for us, like Gale, to see Madge beyond the veneer of her privileged class as the District 12 mayor's daughter. Her actions, though, in bringing Mrs. Everdeen contraband morphling for Gale after his whipping and in helping smuggle Katniss Capitol newspapers in the time before the Quarter Quell show that she is aware of the unfairness of the system and willing to break the rules, at least in small ways, to help. In addition, Madge's usual dress in what Katniss describes as "plain clothes"[THG12] illustrates her lack of interest in taking advantage of her class or holding it above others.

Though Katniss and Madge are friends, Katniss is not immune to this sort of negative bias either. She has also internalized a prejudicial hatred of Panem's socioeconomic upper classes and their corresponding races/ethnicities/cultures, though this is more overt in her automatic—though eventually unlearned—hatred of everyone from the Capitol and Career districts than it is in her automatic dismissal of District 12's merchants.

Katniss learns over the course of the three novels that all people, regardless of race, ethnicity, culture, or district, suffer under the current political system. By the beginning of *The Hunger Games*, she had already seen Peeta, a merchant, beaten by his mother; Haymitch, a rich victor, succumb to alcoholism; her own mother, a merchant by birth, incapacitated by depression—and yet Katniss still jealously thinks of merchants' lives as irresponsibly easy ("it's hard not to resent those who don't have to sign up for tesserae"[THG13]).

Katniss' understanding of the merchants as "Other" is clear from a young age, as when she recalls the Boy with the Bread incident at the bakery:

> I noticed him, a boy with blond hair peering out . . . I'd seen him at school. He was in my year, but I didn't know his name. He stuck with the town kids, so how would I?[THG30]

Clearly, Katniss' life in District 12 is severely segregated. Her only contact with merchants (aside from her mother) comes from semi-polite business transactions, her silent camaraderie with Madge at school, and the reaping ceremonies each year.

This alienation between the classes, the mutual "Other-ness" of the Seam and the merchants, is a theme that continues through Katniss' interactions with many of the series' characters even outside of District 12; the same dynamic is writ large between district and Capitol citizens. This type of social conditioning, which institutionally reinforces negative stereotypes of racialized groups, is common in segregated societies. Grace Kao of the Department of Sociology and Population Studies Center at the University of Pennsylvania conducted focus groups of adolescents of three different minorities (Latino American, black American, and Asian American) and determined that "[stereotyping] images maintain racially and ethnically segregated . . . activities that reinforce segregated peer groups . . . Socialization with same-race peers promotes comparable conceptions of success within racial groups."[xxv]

Katniss' sense of being "other" is bound up with the dominant group's system of valuation in which she, as a member of the racialized lower class, is considered to be "less": less worthy, less individual, and less valuable. This is, arguably, what drives a lot of Katniss' negative view of herself—the reason Katniss sees herself as consummately unlikeable, and as unattractive in comparison to (fair-skinned, blonde-haired) Glimmer.

This social conditioning is so internalized by Katniss that she acknowledges, but does not recognize, its effects during her interaction with Mrs. Mellark just before the scene with Peeta and the burnt bread:

> Suddenly a voice was screaming at me and I looked up to see the baker's wife, telling me to move on and did I want her to call the Peacekeepers and how sick she was of having those brats from the Seam pawing through her trash. The words were ugly and I had no defense.[THG29]

Mrs. Mellark refers to her as a Seam "brat"; Katniss acknowledges that the words are "ugly" but that she "has no defense"—meaning that, on some level, she believes it to be true that her Seam-ness makes her less than Mrs. Mellark and the other merchants.

The same kind of prejudice that Mrs. Mellark demonstrates is also at work in the Capitol. It's arguably a big part of what allows the Capitol residents to enjoy the Hunger Games: to them, the district tributes are so Other, and so subjugated, as to be barely human. Although some people of the Capitol, like Cinna and Octavia, ultimately reject their own prejudice, others display the full magnitude of racial hatred:

> "At least, you two have decent manners," says Effie as we're finishing the main course. "The pair last year ate everything with their hands like a couple of savages. It completely upset my digestion."
> The pair last year were two kids from the Seam who'd never, not one day in their lives, had enough to eat.[THG44]

The deep-rooted racism of the Capitol brings Katniss' popularity in the Seventy-fourth Games and the Quarter Quell into chilling question. How exactly did a Seam girl garner the favor of the racist Capitol? Cinna's skillful styling and Caesar's vote of camera-friendly camaraderie helped, but previous Seam tributes had the benefit of Caesar and a styling team—even if they were neither as invested nor as talented as Cinna and Portia! What did Katniss have in her favor that no other Seam tributes had?

"Peeta has made me an object of love . . . And there I am, blushing and confused, made . . . desirable by Peeta's confession . . . and by all accounts, unforgettable."[THG49] Peeta—fair-skinned, blond, blue-eyed, merchant-class Peeta—is placed as a buffer between the Capitolites and Katniss; he is their "understood entity," a fair-skinned, broad-shouldered, well-spoken tribute who speaks their language and essentially assures them that it's alright to support Katniss, to want Katniss, because he—with his "pure white" face[THG124]—does, too. He creates an empathetic construct between the Capitol and Katniss that serves as a mediator of "Otherness" that allows the Capitol to view Katniss as desirable enough to sponsor.

Katniss and Peeta's relationship can also be seen as a parallel of the slow opening of Panem society to reintegration. Peeta—as a baker and as someone whose name is a homonym for a type of bread, pita—is bread and Panem is bread, so what happens to Peeta happens to Panem; as Peeta crosses racial lines and breaks out of his class mold, so does Panem, resulting (eventually) in the creation of a new generation unfettered by such strict socioethnic lines. Katniss herself was born to interracial parents; she is the second generation of her family to engage in a positive interracial relationship, despite coming from a culture of such isolation that both the Seam and merchant classes have fairly static appearances. Given that Katniss and Peeta's children are born with appearances representative of both the merchant class and the Seam—a "girl with dark hair and blue eyes" and a "boy with blond curls and gray eyes" (*Mockingjay*)—it's clear that Katniss and Peeta's joint family is meant literally to represent the racial/ethnic/cultural reintegration of Panem that is a root cause, and a massive effect, of the Second Rebellion.

When Posy Hawthorne tells green-skinned Capitol citizen and prep team stylist Octavia that she would be "pretty in any color" in *Mockingjay*, it emphasizes the idea that judging worth by skin color isn't automatic or natural—and suggests the potential for change that rebellion represents.

Though Panem does not seem to have the same racial markers (or ethnic, cultural, or religious markers) as we do, that *does not mean* that these differences don't exist, and *does not mean* that they should be ignored when we are given the distinctions between Panem's races in the text. We don't know how dark the Seam's skin is, and indeed to our twenty-first-century understanding of race versus ethnicity, Katniss could well visually appear "Caucasian" to us. However, we do know that her skin, and Gale's skin, and the skin of the Seam populace, is pointedly darker than the merchants' and that has made a significant, significant difference in how people are raised, married, treated, and receive job placement in District 12—and their odds of being reaped and surviving the Hunger Games.

The Socioeconomics of Tesserae

The racially fueled class differences outlined in chapter three, both between districts and within District 12, are more than just a legacy from our world. They also perform an important function in maintaining the Capitol's rule: separating and differentiating the country's citizenry. Race, ethnicity, and culture provide a source of discord and tension that the Capitol relies on to suppress any organized rebellion in the districts. (If the residents of a district do not trust each other, they cannot work together to fight against the Capitol.) In fact, the sociopolitical system of Panem—the tesserae and the extra chance it brings of being selected as Hunger Games tribute—seems specifically designed to intensify this tension, by targeting the (darker-skinned) lower class:

> I've listened to [Gale] rant about how the tesserae are just another tool to cause misery in our district. A way to plant hatred between the starving workers of the Seam and those who can generally

count on supper and thereby ensure we will never trust one another. "It's to the Capitol's advantage to have us divided among ourselves," he might say if there were no ears to hear but mine.[THG14]

In Panem, just as in the contemporary world and throughout virtually all of human history, race justifies social inequalities as natural through the role it plays in determining societal privilege. As the concept of race evolved, it provided a reason for the extermination of Native Americans, the exclusion of Asian immigrants, and the seizure of Mexican lands. And it did so in part through institutional means. Racial practices were—and are—institutionalized within government, law, and social practices. When it comes to Panem, this means the Games–tesserae system.

Peggy McIntosh, the founder and co-director of the National S.E.E.D. Project on Inclusive Curriculum, explains privilege like this:

> Privilege exists when one group has something of value that is denied to others simply because of the groups they belong to, rather than because of anything they've done or failed to do. Access to privilege does not determine one's outcomes, but it is definitely an asset that makes it more likely that whatever talent, ability, and aspirations a person with privilege has will result in something positive for them.[xxvi]

In Panem, that is tantamount to the idea that a person with privilege doesn't necessarily avoid being reaped, but they are more likely either to avoid the reaping or survive the arena due to their racial, ethnic, and/or cultural status. And that means, of course, members of the Capitol—who do not face a reaping and the arena at all—but also people like the mayor's merchant-class daughter, Madge, in District 12.

The distribution of tesserae between people who identify as Seam and those who identify as merchants is inherently unequal—and of course, those who identify as Capitol do not take any tesserae at all, and live in a world predicated on the belief that the (predominantly darker, predominantly lower-class) children who are killed in the Hunger Games are receiving a just punishment. After all, the annual reaping ceremony in each district is begun with a reading of the "Treaty of Treason" that automatically stipulates the superiority of the Capitol class over both the merchants and district specialty classes.

That the system institutionally favors the wealthier—and fairer-skinned—higher classes is implicit in Katniss' narrative, and is best examined by looking at District 12 as an example.

Because the Hunger Games is written from the perspective of a first-person narrator, the only perspective that we get on Panem in the books is that of Katniss, who lives in District 12 and knows—or at least conveys—very little about the demographics or make-up of other districts, sometimes even leaving out their specialties. However, given the Capitol's heavily structured hierarchy of control, the assumption that all of the districts were originally formed with similar basic planning doesn't seem unwarranted; using District 12 as a model is the most reliable way to extrapolate information about Panem as a whole.

If one takes Katniss' description of District 12 economics at face value, then the residents of the Seam (who we've established are, in the world of Panem, racially nonwhite) work in the district specialty profession—mining—and are all below the poverty line, requiring all Seam children to take multiple tesserae. Both the Everdeens and Hawthornes, for example, took out the maximum available tesserae every year, and both self-identify as "nonwhite" in the context of Panem. The merchants work in more specialized, educated, high-yield professions—and may be independent business owners—requiring fewer tesserae per child. Gale assumes that Madge's name has only been entered once for each year she's been eligible, and she doesn't contradict him. Taken together, this suggests that specialty-class families—who are largely of darker skin or considered as the ethnic/racial Other in Panem—as a whole take more tesserae than merchant-class and therefore have a higher likelihood of being drawn in the reaping.

The third sentence of the entire series sets up the reaping as something to fear—before we even know what the Hunger Games are or, other than their use as the title, that they exist.

> [Prim] must have had bad dreams and climbed in with our mother. Of course, she did. This is the day of the reaping.[THG3]

Shortly after, within the first third of *The Hunger Games*, there is a slew of information that is meant to impress on us, the readers, that the Games–tesserae sociopolitical system is unfair, biased, only masquerading as punishment for all district citizens, when in fact, it unequivocally targets families of lesser economic means, living in the specialty classes. Katniss tells us this directly at the outset of *The Hunger Games*:

> The reaping system is unfair, with the poor getting the worst of it. You become eligible for the reaping the day you turn twelve. That year, your name is entered once. At thirteen, twice. And so on and so on until you reach the age of eighteen, the final year of eligibility, when your name goes into the pool seven times. That's true for every citizen in all twelve districts in the entire country of Panem.
> But here's the catch. Say you are poor and starving as we were. You can opt to add your name more times in exchange for tesserae. Each tessera is worth a meager year's supply of grain and oil for one person. You may do this for each of your family members as well. So, at the age of twelve, I had my name entered four times. Once, because I had to, and three times for tesserae for grain and oil for myself, Prim, and my mother. In fact, every year I have needed to do this. And the entries are cumulative. So now, at the age of sixteen, my name will be in the reaping twenty times. Gale, who is eighteen and has been either helping or single-handedly feeding a family of five for seven years, will have his name in forty-two times.
> You can see why someone like Madge, who has never been at risk of needing a tessera, can set him off. The chance of her name being drawn is very slim compared to those of us who live in the Seam.[THG13]

THE SOCIOECONOMICS OF TESSERAE

The division that this causes in Panem society between the merchant class—the "haves"—and the specialty classes—the "have-nots"—is clear from Gale, Katniss, and Madge's early conversation about the impending seventy-fourth reaping ceremony. Madge is used explicitly as a way to contrast Katniss' situation and the situation of merchant-class children:

> "You won't be going to the Capitol," says Gale coolly. His eyes land on a small, circular pin that adorns her dress. Real gold. Beautifully crafted. It could keep a family in bread for months. "What can you have? Five entries? I had six when I was just twelve years old."
> "That's not her fault," I say.
> "No, it's no one's fault. Just the way it is," says Gale.
> Madge's face has become closed off. She puts the money for the berries in my hand. "Good luck, Katniss."[THG12]

Although the previous quotes illustrate masterfully the premise and the execution of the Games–tesserae welfare system, and the resentment it breeds, it's Gale's "ranting" in the woods that conveys its nefarious purpose and effects:

> I've listened to [Gale] rant about how the tesserae are just another tool to cause misery in our district. A way to plant hatred between the starving workers of the Seam and those who can generally count on supper and thereby ensure we will never trust one another. "It's to the Capitol's advantage to have us divided among ourselves," he might say if there were no ears to hear but mine. If it wasn't reaping day. If a girl with a gold pin and no tesserae had not made what I'm sure she thought was a harmless comment.[THG14]

Gale is not wrong. Taking Katniss' perceptions of Panem at face value, there is a distinct social class missing from the nation: a middle class. There are those living in abject, starving, governmentally-sanctioned-physical-aid-dependent poverty—which does include the merchant class, because though they take fewer tesserae, they are still required to put their names once into the reaping—and those who live in absurd, Gilded-Age-and-then-some levels of wealth in the Capitol. The reasons for this are most succinctly summed up in a sentence from a speech given by US president Barack Obama in December 2011: "A strong middle class can only exist in an economy where everyone plays by the same rules."[xxvii]

Panem is a nation that, as far as Katniss relays to the reader, is fully predicated on the notion that its citizens do not all have to play by the same rules. Those in the Capitol are treated to sheltered lives of luxury, courtesy of the exploitation of laborers in the districts. In the districts themselves, those who work in the jobs that support the high-cost lifestyles in the Capitol see none of the financial returns from their work, but instead—if District 12 is an accurate model—live as institutionally second-class citizens to those whose jobs don't directly benefit the actual wealthy class at all, but who share the same skin color as the Capitol citizens (when the Capitol citizens aren't dyeing their skin for fashion!). Although the specialty class' jobs in every district directly provide goods to the Capitol citizens, the merchant class' vocations are largely for the benefit of the merchant class within their own districts: bakers, cobblers, butchers, apothecaries, etc. Despite being of less economic benefit to the Capitol, the Games–tesserae system still heavily favors them. Katniss' take on the system is as succinct as Obama's statement about the necessity of a middle class for healthy economic function: "It's hard not to resent those who don't have to sign up for tesserae."[THG13]

Obviously, Panem is an exaggerated case of class warfare, designed to fit within the paradigms of dystopian science fiction; however, the disparity of wealth and wealth distribution in Panem is not a far cry from the wealth distribution in the United States at the time of *The Hunger Games*' writing. When *Mockingjay* was released in 2010, 85 percent of American wealth was held by only 20 percent of its citizens, with 40 percent of Americans holding only 0.3 percent of the nation's wealth.

In the United States, wealth is highly concentrated in a relatively few hands. As of 2007, the top 1% of households (the upper class) owned 34.6% of all privately held wealth, and the next 19% (the managerial, professional, and small business stratum) had 50.5%, which means that just 20% of the people owned a remarkable 85%, leaving only 15% of the wealth for the bottom 80% (wage and salary workers). In terms of financial wealth (total net worth minus the value of one's home), the top 1% of households had an even greater share: 42.7%.[xxviii]

We don't know Panem's specific statistics—and it's unlikely that Katniss cared, because knowing numbers doesn't put food on Prim's plate—but given the vastness of the districts in comparison to the small size of the Capitol and its almost-total control over Panem's wealth, we can infer that it was, at best, along the same lines; at worst, it would have been more akin to Mexico, whose wealth distribution is vastly unequal (as of 2010, the top 10 percent of the nation's wealthy control 42.2 percent of all income, and the poorest 10 percent control only 1.3 percent).[xxix]

One of the results of such a vast disparity in wealth is the need for a welfare system. I described tesserae as welfare previously, and that's exactly what it is: a government program (ostensibly) put in place to subsidize basic living costs or needs for those at the poorest level of economic society. At the time that the Hunger Games series was being written, according to G. William Domhoff, a research professor in sociology at the University of California–Santa Cruz, in the United States "welfare (mainly AFDC [Aid for Families with Dependent Children]) dole[d] out humiliating relief primarily to poor single mothers. Welfare recipients [were] stigmatized as shiftless and irresponsible, their personal lives [were] scrutinized by government workers, and they must conform to behavioral rules in order to receive their benefits."[xxx] Unlike District 11, which has a specialty more specifically designed to reflect slavery, in which citizens begin work in early childhood, District 12 has a specialty that has historically precluded women from employment—making the majority of Seam families dependent on the male wage-earner as the primary, if not the only, source of income. There are female miners in District 12, such as Bristel, but even from what little detail Katniss gives us about the miners, the numbers seem to be overwhelmingly male (Gale, Thom, Mr. Everdeen, Mr. Hawthorne are all male miners, whereas Bristel is the only female miner mentioned). That automatically limits the ability of Seam families to provide for themselves economically to the same level as merchant families such as the Mellarks or Cartwrights, in which both heads of house can earn an equal salary. It also ensures that in the case of a mining accident, the Seam families are certain to be beholden to the state for tesserae grain/oil to survive.

The Games–tessera system is smartly designed. Unlike our present-day welfare system, it is predicated on making its beneficiaries state-dependent, creating a nation of "pauperism."[xxxi] It is only with this dependency that the Capitol can control its most oppressed class at its most basic level and assuage the doubts of any potential thinkers in the wealthier classes/districts by demonstrating that the specialty class take disproportionate tesserae only "because they need it." In addition, the tesserae is set up as something to avoid, because it increases one's chances of being reaped—which may serve as encouragement for district citizens to work harder at their specialty-class professions: *If you work hard enough, you can protect your children from taking tesserae (and allow more of your product to make its way into Capitol hands, to boot).* But the Capitol actually *wins* when its citizens take the tesserae—so long as they aren't allowed to take too much.

If tesserae serve as a monthly aid package, then ideally, the specialty-class citizens of Panem should not be in the fiscally tragic state they are in. After all, the purpose of government at its most basic level is to provide its citizens with their fundamental needs in order to ensure their full participation in national affairs,[xxxii] and Katniss' account of what life is like in the Seam does not seem to lead to the idea that she (or Gale, or most of the Seam) is able to function as a "citizen" despite her "government aid"—at least if a "citizen" of Panem is defined as someone who puts full participation into the society.

However, the Seam's poorest citizens do still make important contributions to the Capitol's way of life, by mining. Had Gale and Katniss not been able to hunt, neither of them would have been strong enough to work in the mines—if they even survived to adulthood. (Katniss says starvation is common in the Seam, especially among "older people who can't work. Children from a family with too many to feed. Those injured in the mines."[THG28]) It's in the Capitol's best interest to keep its citizens alive—alive but hungry. And so it must balance its poorest citizens' need against the threat of the Games, keeping them fed enough to serve the Capitol residents' needs but hungry enough not to rebel.

> [W]e were slowly starving to death. There's no other way to put it. I kept telling myself if I could only hold out until May, just May 8th, I would turn twelve and be able to sign up for tesserae and get that precious grain and oil to feed us.[THG27-28]

Notably, the two most personal examples we have of this disenfranchised Seam lifestyle are the Everdeen family and the Hawthorne family, both of which are single-parent households headed by single, widowed, self-employed mothers. Because both Mr. Hawthorne and Mr. Everdeen died—as far as the books specifically state—due to their work in the mines along with many other miners, it can be inferred that most of the highest tesserae-takers in District 12 are also the children of single mothers. And because they are Seam, we know that they are also darker-skinned. Using District 12 as a model for the workings of every district, this suggests that an overwhelming number of tributes are the children not only of lower-class families but of single-parent households. Because the Games–tesserae socioeconomic system of welfare specifically targets these groups, the Hunger Games would classify as, really, the definition of class warfare.

We see this system truly at work only through the eyes of a character who lives in the sort of family most harmed by it; although it can be argued, rightfully, that Rue led a worse life than Katniss because her livelihood mirrors antebellum slavery, the Everdeens became specific targets of this "pauperism" agenda the moment that Mr. Everdeen died. Even if Mrs. Everdeen had not lapsed into a state of catatonic depression, Katniss would have been required to take out the maximum number of tesserae each year. After all, Mrs. Hawthorne continued working consistently, and Gale had among the highest amounts of tesserae in D12—possibly in Panem.

The socioeconomic welfare system, at least in District 12, inherently favors two-parent households and/or households led by a male wage-earner. Simply by being female, widowed, and having multiple children, Mrs. Everdeen and Mrs. Hawthorne are inescapably tied into requiring state assistance to survive. Katniss herself even recognizes this as she heads out of the Justice Building and onto the train bound for the Capitol, even if she doesn't explain it in the same terms:

> Prim is not to take any tesserae. They can get by, if they're careful, on selling Prim's goat milk and cheese and the small apothecary business my mother now runs for the people in the Seam.[THG34-35]

Only with Katniss gone is the Everdeen family small enough to subsist on a female wage-earner's salary. When Katniss and Peeta win the Seventy-fourth Hunger Games, it is not just Katniss' stunt with the berries that is a rebellion against the Capitol. It's that Katniss should never have won at all. She is everything that the entire system, of which the Games are the zenith, literally wants to kill: specialty class, the child of a widowed mother, self-identified as culturally and ethnically "not white," and from the poorest and most state-dependent district of all.

In present-day America, the breakdown of families receiving Aid for Families with Dependent Children welfare, for the age group that roughly correlates to those eligible for reaping in Panem, is:

THE SOCIOECONOMICS OF TESSERAE

RACE/ETHNICITY	% OF WELFARE DOLLARS DISTRIBUTED	TOTAL % OF US POPULATION PER 2009 CENSUS DATA	% OF TOTAL RACIAL POPULATION RECEIVING WELFARE DOLLARS
HISPANIC	28.8	16.3	22.9
WHITE	31.2	61.6	6.3
AFRICAN AMERICAN	33.3	13	35.4
NATIVE AMERICAN & NATIVE ALASKAN	1.3	0.9	24.1
ASIAN	2.1	5	5.8
NATIVE HAWAIIAN	0.6	0.2	38.9
MULTIRACIAL	1.8	3	15.9

The racial densities of welfare receipt are even more skewed in density in Panem, thanks to tesserae being required for all district citizens in the first place, and the tiny size of the Capitol in comparison to the large sprawl of its twelve tesserae-applicable districts (the population of District 13 doesn't count, of course, because they have seceded from Panem and are not part of the Games–tesserae system).

> Suddenly I am thinking of Gale and his forty-two names in that big glass ball and how the odds are not in his favor. Not compared to a lot of the boys.[THG20]

If the contemporary United States instituted a reaping system with parameters similar to those in Panem, the odds would not be in Gale's favor in our world, either.

Calculating "The Odds"

In early 2011, Hunger Games fan Shylah Addante of DownWiththeCapitol .net and Mainstay Productions' Finnick/Annie short films did an in-depth analysis of tesserae distribution:

In a bowl full of "thousands of slips," Katniss has her name entered twenty times, Gale forty-two.

Let's do some math.

Katniss says that the population of District 12 is about 8000. Let's say for the sake of argument that the average family size is 5 (two parents and 3 children, typified by the Mellarks, Hawthornes, and Everdeens when averaged out): 8000/5= 1600

Meaning that there are roughly 1600 families in [District 12]. (This is only an estimate as some families (like Gale's) have more than three children; some (like Katniss') have less; and some people have no family unit.)

These 1600 families include 3200 adults (if we assume 2 adults/family) and 4800 children (assuming 3 children/family). Divide 4800 in half, and we have approximately 2400 female and 2400 male children of [District 12].

But not every child is eligible—only those ages 12-18 are entered into the reaping (out of the wider range for childhood which is 0-18). So only seven of the nineteen years of childhood are entered into the reaping. If we assume that the birth rate is constant, and that children are evenly distributed in each year, then there are only about 252 children (126 female and 126 male) born each year in [District 12].

Multiply 252 by 7 (the number of eligible childhood years entered into the reaping) and you get 1764.

Divided by 2, and you get approximately 882 males and 882 females eligible for the reaping each year.

Now to account for the Tesserae.

After consulting with some other Hunger Games fans, I am going with the idea that the Seam makes up 80% of the District 12 population and that the Merchant class makes up 20% [per popular polling consensus of Hunger Games fans]. In the first chapter of the book, two things are apparent: the merchant children do not have to take out Tesserae, and that Seam children are . . . forced into taking the Tesserae. It also seems to be a trend (at least from the example set by Gale and Katniss) that the eldest children take the Tesserae to protect their younger siblings.

THE SOCIOECONOMICS OF TESSERAE

So if there are 126 females in a given year, 100 of them will be Seam children and 26 will be merchant children. If the average family size includes three children, then we can assume that one third of the children will be the eldest and take extra Tesserae (+5 slips). Each age year breaks down as follows:

12-13 Year Olds
26 Merchant Children (No Tesserae; +1 Age Entry): 26 Entries
34 Seam Children—Oldest Sibling (+5 Tesserae; +1 Age Entry): 204 Entries
66 Seam Children—Younger Sibling (No Tesserae; +1 Age Entry): 66 Entries
Total (12-13) Entries: 296

13-14 Year Olds
26 Merchant Children (No Tesserae; +2 Age Entry): 52 Entries
34 Seam Children—Oldest Sibling (+5 Tesserae x2; +2 Age Entry): 408 Entries
66 Seam Children—Younger Sibling (No Tesserae; +2 Age Entry): 132 Entries
Total (13-14) Entries: 592

14-15 Year Olds
26 Merchant Children (No Tesserae; +3 Age Entry): 78 Entries
34 Seam Children—Oldest Sibling (+5 Tesserae x3; +3 Age Entry): 612 Entries
66 Seam Children—Younger Sibling (No Tesserae; +3 Age Entry): 198 Entries
Total (14-15) Entries: 888

15-16 Year Olds
26 Merchant Children (No Tesserae; +4 Age Entry): 104 Entries
34 Seam Children—Oldest Sibling (+5 Tesserae x4; +4 Age Entry): 816 Entries
66 Seam Children—Younger Sibling (No Tesserae; +4 Age Entry): 264 Entries
Total (15-16) Entries: 1184

16–17 Year Olds
26 Merchant Children (No Tesserae; +5 Age Entry): 130 Entries
34 Seam Children—Oldest Sibling (+5 Tesserae x5; +5 Age Entry): 1020 Entries
66 Seam Children—Younger Sibling (No Tesserae; +5 Age Entry): 330 Entries
Total (16–17) Entries: 1480

17–18 Year Olds
26 Merchant Children (No Tesserae; +6 Age Entry): 156 Entries
34 Seam Children—Oldest Sibling (+5 Tesserae x6; +6 Age Entry): 1224 Entries
66 Seam Children—Younger Sibling (No Tesserae; +6 Age Entry): 396 Entries
Total (17–18) Entries: 1776

18–19 Year Olds
26 Merchant Children (No Tesserae; +7 Age Entry): 182 Entries
34 Seam Children—Oldest Sibling (+5 Tesserae x7; +7 Age Entry): 1428 Entries
66 Seam Children—Younger Sibling (No Tesserae; +7 Age Entry): 462 Entries
Total (18–19) Entries: 2072

Grand Total of Entries: 8288
Total of Female Entries: 4144
Total of Male Entries: 4144

Katniss' Odds (+3 Tesserae x5; +5 Age Entry) 20/4144 or .48%
Gale's Odds (+5 Tesserae x7; +7): 42/4144 or 1.01%
Peeta's Odds (No Tesserae; +5 Age Entry): 5/4144 or .12%
Prim's Odds (No Tesserae; +1 Age Entry): 1/4144 or .02%

Although a more cynical view may look at the math and say that the odds of both Prim and Peeta being reaped for the Seventy-fourth Games are so astronomically low as to render the plot of the series unrealistic, a true Hunger Games fan might suggest that, despite the math, the odds were simply not in their favor.

The Curious Case of Primrose "Everdeen"

On the first day of kindergarten for Katniss and Peeta, when Prim was between six months and one year old, Mr. Mellark told his five-year-old son that he had been in love with Mrs. Everdeen, but that she "ran away with a coal miner" and he "had to" marry Mrs. Mellark.

Why was this still so salient and so fresh in his mind that he shared it with his *five-year-old child*?

It's easy to extrapolate that the reason for his confession was in the schoolyard that morning, being kissed good-bye by the girl in a red plaid dress. However, it's not the only reason fans have considered.

The question of Prim's parentage is a significant point of analytical fandom debate. Is blonde-haired, blue-eyed Prim really the "passes"-for-merchant biracial daughter of dark-haired Mr. Everdeen? Or should Prim really be Primrose *Mellark*? There are staunch supporters on both sides of the issue.

Katniss does not at any point overtly suppose that someone else could be Prim's father, aside from noting the differences between her and Prim's coloring, much less that Prim's father is Mr. Mellark. But Katniss, as a first-person narrator, is unreliable; our understanding of Panem is limited by what Katniss herself knows and feels.

Katniss is the consummate "Daddy's girl" and loved her father deeply, which colors much of her narrative regarding her family. And Mr. Everdeen died when Katniss was young enough that Katniss does not seem to have a sense of her parents' relationship independent of their relationship to her. Her mother "must have" loved Mr. Everdeen very much, Katniss notes at one point, but she has never spoken to her mother about their marriage. Katniss' own feelings about her father inform her opinions about her mother's feelings.

However, despite Katniss' control of the narrative, there are details about her world that can be seen through her unconscious, or incidental, narrative: the details she sees and conveys to readers but does not question or otherwise remark upon. On those, readers are left to draw their own conclusions . . . and we do!

After Katniss volunteers in Prim's place, Mr. Mellark visits her as she waits to leave for the Capitol. He seems moved to the point of silence, and presents Katniss with a gift, cookies:

> Someone else enters the room, and when I look up, I'm surprised to see it's the baker, Peeta Mellark's father. I can't believe he's come to visit me. After all, I'll be trying to kill his son soon. But we do know each other a little bit, and he knows Prim even better. When she sells her goat cheeses at the Hob, she puts two of them aside for him and he gives her a generous amount of bread in return. We always wait to trade with him when his witch of a wife isn't around because he's so much nicer. I feel certain he would never have hit his son the way she did over the burned bread. But why has he come to see me?
>
> The baker sits awkwardly on the edge of one of the plush chairs. He's a big, broad-shouldered man with burn scars from years at the ovens. He must have just said goodbye to his son.

He pulls a white paper package from his jacket pocket and holds it out to me. I open it and find cookies. These are a luxury we can never afford.

Why?

Perhaps just out of affection for Katniss' mother or appreciation for Katniss' sacrifice. But perhaps because, unwittingly, Katniss has just spared him from having to watch *two* of his children die in the arena.

"Thank you," I say. The baker's not a very talkative man in the best of times, and today he has no words at all . . .
We sit in silence until a Peacemaker summons him. He rises and coughs to clear his throat. "I'll keep an eye on the little girl. Make sure she's eating."THG37-38

Some of the most compelling pieces of evidence for Prim's potential Mellark lineage come from the subtle ways that the Mellarks have become integral to the Everdeens' family life and the similarities between Prim and the Mellark men (but not Mrs. Mellark, with her unspeakable cruelty; it could even be inferred that both Prim and Peeta got their gentle natures from Mr. Mellark for precisely this reason: both Mrs. Everdeen and Mrs. Mellark are written very negatively, as emotionally distant and, in Mrs. Mellark's case, physically abusive).

On the morning that opens *The Hunger Games*, Katniss and Gale, of course, go to the woods to hunt for their daily provisions to trade. However, before they get to work, they enjoy a meal provided for them by two like-minded people: Prim, with her cheese, and Mr. Mellark, with his bread.

On the table, under a wooden bowl . . . sits a perfect little goat cheese wrapped in basil leaves. Prim's gift to me on reaping day.THG4

It's real bakery bread, not the flat, dense loaves we make from our grain rations. I take it in my hands, pull out the arrow, and hold the puncture in the crust to my nose, inhaling the fragrance that makes my mouth flood with saliva. Fine bread like this is for special occasions . . . "[Mr. Mellark traded it for] just a squirrel. Think the old man was feeling sentimental this morning," says Gale. "Even wished me luck."[THG7]

Given that Peeta, the youngest Mellark son, is almost old enough to age out of the reaping and his two older brothers have already completed the process, why would Mr. Mellark be "feeling sentimental" on the morning of the seventy-fourth reaping ceremony?

Could it be because of whose first reaping it happens to be—Prim Everdeen?

The squirrel could also represent a clue about Prim's parentage. Because squirrels are so identified through the Hunger Games' narrative with Katniss and the Seam, the fact that Mrs. Mellark hates them but Mr. Mellark enjoys them and "will trade for them if his witch of a wife isn't around"[THG52] could suggest, metaphorically, a dalliance between Mr. Mellark and Mrs. Everdeen (resulting in Prim) as much as it does Mrs. Mellark's deeply ingrained hatred for all things Seam.

Although Katniss revered her father, her understood and understated respect for Mr. Mellark—via her appreciation and awareness of his breads—is evident in the text. And Katniss' description of the meal planned for the evening after the seventy-fourth reaping ceremony serves to tie together the Everdeens—foraged food, strawberries, stew—and the Mellarks—bakery bread: "We decide to save the strawberries and bakery bread for the evening meal, to make it special we say."[THG16]

Further evidence for Prim being Mr. Mellark's daughter comes from oversimplified fictional-world genetics. And I want to put a caveat here: this is grossly oversimplified pseudoscience. I'm employing it not to erase the immense complexity and nuance that goes into genetics but because the majority of the storytelling in the Hunger Games is accomplished through foreshadowing, foils, parallelism, extended metaphor, and symbolism, rather than scientific or nuanced economic reality. (Think of the simplistic "Sinking California" theory most likely used in determining the geography of Panem and the not-so-rigorously-scientific details like near-magical healing ointments and muttations.) Given that, an oversimplification of genetics does not seem out of the question.

We know from Katniss that she and Prim do not share the same coloring. Katniss looks like Mr. Everdeen and the other residents of the Seam. Prim looks like Mrs. Everdeen and other members of the merchant class; Katniss describes her as looking "out of place" in the Seam with her blonde hair, pale skin, and blue eyes.

If intermarriage between the Seam and the merchants is as rare as the evidence of Panem's racial segregation would suggest, then one can assume that both Mrs. Everdeen and Mr. Mellark's genes are homozygous recessive (blonde/pale/blue), stretching back between (roughly) ten and thirty-six generations, and that Mr. Everdeen's genes are homozygous dominant (black/dark/[gray]). Here are simple Punnett squares for the children of Mr. and Mrs. Everdeen:

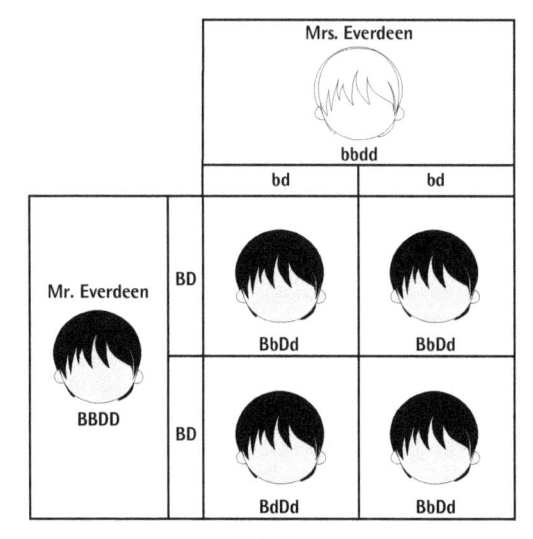

	Mrs. Everdeen bbdd	
	bd	bd
Mr. Everdeen BBDD — BD	BbDd	BbDd
BD	BdDd	BbDd

All Children
BbDd

The odds of Mr. Everdeen and Mrs. Everdeen giving birth to a blonde-haired, blue-eyed, pale-skinned child are almost 0 percent.

In contrast, the odds of Mr. Mellark and Mrs. Everdeen giving birth to a blonde-haired, blue-eyed, fair-skinned child are nearly 100 percent.

	Mrs. Everdeen bbdd	
	bd	bd
Mr. Mellark bbdd — bd	bbdd	bbdd
bd	bbdd	bbdd

All Children
bbdd

> That's why my mother and Prim, with their light hair and blue eyes, always look out of place. They are. My mother's parents were part of the small merchant class.[THG8]

> Peeta Mellark . . . I watch him as he makes his way toward the stage . . . Ashy blond hair that falls in waves over his forehead . . . Blue eyes.[THG25-26]

The odds (no pun intended) are pretty overwhelming that Prim is half-Mellark—or at least not half-Everdeen.

Because real-world genetics is more complicated, although it's not *likely* for a many-generation dark-haired, dark-skinned father and a many-generation light-haired, light-skinned mother to give birth to a light-haired, light-skinned child, it's still *possible*. We don't know for sure that Mr. Everdeen doesn't have any recessive genes for blond hair and light skin, and in fact, in our world, such strictly homogenous genes are deeply implausible. Although there are other species that have homozygous genes—Siamese cats, true-bred Dalmatians, many varietals of flowers—human beings' genetics are not so pure without horribly extensive inbreeding.

In reality, a race like the Seam's, in which (per Collins) "many races" have mixed, would always have a breadth of natural variations in skin tone, eye color, hair color, and facial structure. A set of biracial sisters like Katniss and Prim could—not with a huge degree of likelihood, but certainly plausibly—look as different from one another as they are described. British twins James and Daniel Kelly and Marcia and Millie Biggs prove that natural-born, naturally conceived siblings of mixed parentage can present visually as two different races. However, in Panem, the people of the Seam are described as a unified race with singular presentation: olive skin, straight black hair, gray eyes. It is Katniss and Gale, not Katniss and Prim, who "could look like siblings." The merchants are described with similar consistency: blonde-haired, blue-eyed, fair-skinned.

Katniss may tell us that "[her mother] must have really loved [her father] to leave her home for the Seam."[THG8] And Mrs. Everdeen may have spent years in a heavily depressive state, including a year of what Katniss describes to be near catatonia after Mr. Everdeen's death, lending credence to her feelings for him; her love must have been strong for her to feel such grief. But it's important to note here that it is Katniss who ascribes Mrs. Everdeen's withdrawal to depression; it could just as easily have been caused by guilt.

This is an issue that will draw supporters on both sides of the fandom forever, and that's *wonderful*.

6

Family Life in Panem

The most important things in Katniss' life are survival and family, perhaps not in that order. The entire journey of the Hunger Games series begins because of Katniss' devotion to Prim and her sense of duty to (and love for) family. However, as she tells the reader, "family devotion only goes so far for most people [in Panem] on reaping day."THG31

A total of 1,776 children (73 Games × 24 tributes each, plus an additional 24 tributes in the Fiftieth Hunger Games) have been a part of the Hunger Games before Katniss volunteers in Prim's place, and from the way Katniss tells it, very few—if any—have been spared their fate by family members before. Indeed, most of the nuclear families that we as readers encounter through the series are deeply dysfunctional and unhappy, and it's hard to imagine them sacrificing so much for each other. What do we know about what other families in Panem are like? How have they adapted to the threat of the Hunger Games? What do other families value, and what does Panem value in its families?

As we saw in chapter four, family structure in District 12—and, by extrapolation, in Panem as a whole—seems to be related to socioeconomic class, with the specialty-class families more likely to be single-parent households and merchant-class families more likely to include two parenting units. (We are shown no examples of Capitol families, and know very little save that Snow has a granddaughter and, per Finnick's secrets, many high-ranking Capitol families commit incest.) In looking at the four main families we encounter over the course of the series—the Everdeens, the Hawthornes, the Mellarks, and the Undersees—we get a deeper window into life in Panem, especially the role that tesserae and status play on its families.

The Everdeens

Katniss spends the majority of her pre-Games life (and much of her life between and after the Games, even into the epilogue of *Mockingjay*) angry at her living situation. She is—rightfully—angry that her father was killed by the job that their race and class forced him into and that there is no way for her family to receive compensation or even independently livable welfare. She is angry with her mother for withdrawing. She is angry that she had to become the sole provider for her family: "At eleven years old, with Prim just seven, I took over as head of the family. There was no choice."[THG27]

Despite her anger, the concept of family is Katniss' primary motivator and is present in all of her actions and decisions. From the first sentence of *The Hunger Games*, Katniss' sole concern is for her family's—specifically, Prim's—welfare:

> When I wake up, the other side of the bed is cold. My fingers stretch out, seeking Prim's warmth but finding only the rough

canvas cover of the mattress. She must have had bad dreams and climbed in with our mother.[THG1]

Katniss' first instinct is always to check for Prim's "warmth"—her presence, her safety and security.

Family—taking care of Prim—is the source of Katniss' meaning and positive sense of self. Although Katniss views herself very harshly in most respects, she does seem to acknowledge her capacity for tenderness when it comes to Prim and expects for that tenderness to function as something of a saving grace regarding the humanity she views herself as missing in other respects—especially in her relationships with people.

This is heavily reflected in regard to Katniss' feelings about her mother. Because Katniss views her status as Prim's caregiver as a function of her love for her sister, she interprets her mother's lack of caregiving in parallel; because Mrs. Everdeen withdrew and was not able to provide functional care for Katniss, Katniss perceives her as being unloving. To Katniss, at least at the beginning of the series, the subversion of those roles is tantamount to betrayal. (This may illustrate a Seam cultural value regarding parent/child relationships and the boundaries of them; perhaps adults in the Seam rarely live long enough to require their children's care. Katniss and her mother's relationship could also be intended as a foil for the relationship subversions within another family group in the Hunger Games series: Finnick caring for Annie and Mags.)

There's one other important member of the Everdeen family who sheds (no pun intended) some light on Katniss and her relationship with her mother: Buttercup the cat. Although Katniss loathes him at the outset of the series, he is the only reminder of her pre-Games life she accepts into her new post-rebellion life, after Prim has died and her mother has moved to District 4.

Buttercup functions as a symbol for Katniss throughout the series, most notably in the "Crazy Cat" scene in *Mockingjay*, in which Katniss actually explains the symbol as it is being used: Katniss explains full-out that she feels like she is engaged in a game of Crazy Cat with the Capitol, and she is Buttercup trying to reach the elusive light that is Peeta while the Capitol dangles him out of her reach. But Katniss' views of Buttercup most often seem meant to mirror her perception of herself and her role in her family, particularly how her mother views her and her correlative duty to provide food and service.

> Sitting at Prim's knees, guarding her, is the world's ugliest cat. Mashed-in nose, half of one ear missing, eyes the color of rotting squash. Prim named him Buttercup, insisting that his muddy yellow coat matched the bright flower. He hates me. Or at least distrusts me. Even though it was years ago, I think he still remembers how I tried to drown him in a bucket when Prim brought him home. Scrawny kitten, belly swollen with worms, crawling with fleas. The last thing I needed was another mouth to feed . . . [Buttercup]'s a born mouser. Even catches the occasional rat. Sometimes, when I clean a kill, I feed Buttercup the entrails. He has stopped hissing at me.
> Entrails. No hissing. This is the closest we will ever come to love.[THG3-4]

Contrast the instinct that Katniss has towards Prim with her learned reaction to her mother. When Prim feels pain, "I protect Prim in every way I can, but I'm powerless against the reaping. The anguish . . . wells up in my chest and threatens to register on my face."[THG15] However, Katniss' reaction to her mother's psychological pain is that even years after Mrs. Everdeen's recovery, "I kept watching, waiting for her to disappear on us again. I didn't trust her. And some small gnarled place inside me hated her for her weakness, for her neglect, for the months she had put us through."[THG52-53] Although Katniss took it upon herself to provide for both of her remaining family members, it is only her mother she feels is a burden.

This provides evidence that, although Katniss fully understands the necessity of caring for her mother, she doesn't equate it to taking care of a child, like Prim. It is clear that in Katniss' mind, family members have set roles and that her mother, with her disability, has compromised the integrity of those roles. For Katniss, despite the extreme sense of duty that she feels towards Prim, the distinction between "parent" and "child" is strict.

Katniss' resentment of her mother also suggests that she sees familial love as being predicated on the fulfillment of perceived duties. She has taken over as head of the Everdeen household, and appears to see her taking on the parental role in their family as both the most applicable way for her to show love and the only way for her to earn love in return. And because Katniss is the one performing the adult role in the household, she rather than her mother makes the rules of the Everdeen home: "I wouldn't let [Prim] take out any tesserae."[THG15]

Despite blaming Mrs. Everdeen fiercely for a perceived lack of contribution to the household, Katniss does not seem to want any help taking care of their small family. She does not expect her mother to find work outside of their home, and she does not seem to expect financial contributions from Prim, either, viewing her sale/trade of goat's milk and cheese with gratitude and some pity rather than as provisional support. Further, she will not allow for Prim to take any tesserae, despite being of age and despite their home situation remaining precarious even after Mrs. Everdeen's recovery. Katniss is unwilling to share the parental role with her mother or anyone else because to allow someone else to take care of Prim would, in Katniss' mind, mean that Katniss might no longer be able to earn, through her caretaking, the same "right" to receive love.

The Hunger Games trilogy would be vastly different—or just not exist—if family weren't so important to Katniss. We can see its impact in more than just her volunteering in place of Prim. She survived the arena, the Quell, and the war because of advice given to her by her father before his death and becomes renowned for a nickname that recalls his revolutionary ideals and love of the woods: the mockingjay, a bird that the Capitol never expected to exist, born out of the will to survive.

The Hawthornes

Though Katniss points out the limitations of family ties when it comes to the reaping, family does seem to be especially important in the Seam. Though perhaps in part a response to the fragility of life in the Seam—because their primary vocation is highly dangerous and the chances of their children being reaped are so much higher compared to merchant children's—Seam families, at least in Katniss' perspective, take their roles and duties seriously. Those who are caregivers remain caregivers for as long as needed: Greasy Sae, for example, seems to be her "simple" granddaughter's primary guardian. Greasy Sae, like Katniss, Gale, and even Haymitch—as illustrated by his lifelong sense of guilt and mistaken responsibility for his family's deaths—display a deep-rooted need to provide for and protect their families.

The definition of family in the Seam doesn't seem to be limited just to immediate blood relations. In fact, it's likely that Katniss learned her belief in family-above-all, blood-above-nation from non-nuclear family member Gale, her slightly older "cousin" and the person to whom she is closest. (Although Katniss/Gale shippers argue that their close friendship and like mindset make them a more believable endgame than Katniss/Peeta, Katniss/Peeta shippers are likely to point out that Katniss thinks similarly to Gale because she spent her formative years in his tutelage, listening to his opinions and beliefs out in the woods. As Katniss states in *Catching Fire*, "Gale is mine. I am his. Anything else is unthinkable.")

The Everdeens and the Hawthornes appear to have been a merged family unit since not long after the mine explosion, despite Gale and Katniss' lack of romantic entanglement. We know that Gale and Katniss share food, look after each other's siblings, and consider themselves mutually obligated to each other. Despite being distrustful of each other at first, and then for some time seeing the other only as a business partner, by the time the Hunger Games series begins, Gale and Katniss are reliant on each other for emotional sustenance, as well as physical necessities like food and medicine.

Given that this definition of family—a communal unit brought together by trauma and circumstance, as well as affection—is mirrored by Finnick, Annie, and Mags, as well as by Beetee and Wiress, this non-nuclear family structure seems to be common in Panem. Why? One reason may be to compensate for the loss of natural-born family members (to the Games, to death in specialty professions, etc.). Although Gale could have provided for his family without Katniss, the aid of her hunting prowess with a bow and arrow proved highly beneficial. For Katniss, knowing that Gale was taking care of Prim and her mother while she fought in the arena helped keep her centered and focused on her own situation, ultimately aiding her survival. Finnick relied on Mags to help him make sure that Annie was safe from the Capitol while he was away from District 4, and Mags' sacrifice in volunteering in Annie's place for the Quell saved Annie's life (and, given his mental state while Annie is missing in *Mockingjay*, likely helped prolong Finnick's life as well).

However, although the blended family model helped the Hawthornes and Everdeens alike to survive, only the Hawthornes seem to display full emotional health as a nuclear family unit. After all, Katniss and her mother live on opposite sides of an emotional chasm.

As such, Katniss' feelings about having her own children someday are—until the epilogue of *Mockingjay*—highly negative. Gale, despite coming from the same socioeconomic and cultural circumstances, looks favorably on the idea of marriage and children. (Family might actually be the only thing that Gale is optimistic about in the series, all things considered.) Although Katniss spends the majority of her time figuring out ways to keep Prim from having to participate in the reaping, Gale is unconcerned enough to be thinking about having children of his own someday—even as the seventy-fourth reaping is only a few hours away:

> "I never want to have kids," I say.
> "I might. If I didn't live here," says Gale.
> "But you do," I say, irritated.[THG9]

It's wholly possible that Gale's ability to hope enthusiastically for a domestic future comes down to gender rather than his stronger emotional bond with his mother. Because Gale is a man, even if his spouse were to die, he would be more likely able to support children on a miner's salary, whereas Katniss, as a widowed mother, would be left further open to needing tesserae. In Panem, as much as family is a source of pride and happiness, it is in equal measure a burden to fear.

The Mellarks

Because he grew up in the District 12 Bakery, Katniss assumes that Peeta has led a life of leisure. However, both she and we, the readers, learn that, although Peeta may never have been starving, his living situation was, like Katniss', still predicated on weighing food's relationship to need and need's relationship with pain. Peeta is the most detailed example we have that having two living, employed merchant-class parents does not mean your family life is functional or loving. Peeta's home situation was better than the Everdeens' only in that there was more food available for consumption.

Yes, Peeta is a baker, and may well be the best baker in his family. But he is still the youngest son of three in a nation-state where, per Katniss' inference that her mother learned the apothecary trade from her own merchant parents and per the Seam's coal-mining tradition, we can assume jobs are handed down from parent to child. Peeta will probably never own Mellark Bakery, and he probably feels as much responsibility to be an asset to his family—so they keep him on at all and he doesn't have to become a miner—as Katniss feels to be the sole provider for hers. Peeta is as much a "family man," as invested in his family's welfare, as Gale; it's just expressed within a different familial structure.

Families in both District 12 and District 11 are almost solely written as multiple-child homes, and fandom assumes that, although

Capitol citizens have easy access to reliable birth control, the districts would be prevented from access either actively or via financial means. If you don't have a reliable income source for food, clothing, and/or shelter, birth control would be—if known about at all—seen as a luxury good. Some have suggested, too, that family planning methods may be less available in the poor districts—even to merchants—as a way to force families into needing more tesserae and becoming more dependent on the Capitol. If birth control had been available, it seems unlikely that spendthrift Mrs. Mellark would have chosen to have more children than could be easily supported or were necessary in order to ensure someone would take over the bakery. Because Peeta is the youngest Mellark, it could be assumed that his birth was accidental—and that resentment is part of the motivation behind Mrs. Mellark's verbal and physical abuse.

Peeta's lifelong abuse at the hands of his mother is, of course, a very large aspect of the unfortunate Mellark family dynamics. It's very telling that in *Catching Fire*, Peeta immediately recognized the sound of whipping despite its unpopularity as a sanctioned punishment in District 12:

> I've been so consumed with my own worries, I haven't noticed the strange noise coming from the square. A whistling, the sound of an impact, the intake of breath from a crowd.
> "Come on," Peeta says, his face suddenly hard. I don't know why. I can't place the sound, even guess at the situation. But it means something bad to him.[CF103-104]

When we combine this with the overt beating Katniss remembers hearing Peeta receive at twelve after he burned the bread for her, it's obvious that Peeta's family life was, in some ways, more difficult to endure than Katniss' despite his outward economic privilege.

> There was a clatter in the bakery and I heard the woman screaming again and the sound of a blow, and I vaguely wondered what was going on . . . It was the boy . . . His mother was yelling, "Feed it to the pig, you stupid creature!"[THG30]

Katniss also remembers seeing Peeta the next day at school:

> At school, I passed the boy in the hall, his cheek swelled up and his eye blackened . . . The boy never even glanced my way, but I was watching him . . . Because of the red weal that stood out on his cheekbone. What had she hit him with? My parents never hit us. I couldn't even imagine it.[THG30-32]

The fact that Mrs. Mellark had no qualms about so obviously bruising Peeta's face also suggests that battered children are a common sight in the merchant quarters of District 12, whereas Katniss "could not even imagine" being hit by her parents, implying that it is not very common in the Seam.

Furthering the idea that the Mellarks' family life is dysfunctional, Peeta seems to have developed his idea of love not from his own family, but by watching the Everdeens, and especially the relationship of Mr. Everdeen and Mrs. Everdeen (which is deeply ironic if Prim is, indeed, his half sister). In each book of the Hunger Games trilogy, Peeta does something else that suggests he may be modeling his concept of courtship on observations of the Everdeens. In *The Hunger Games*:

> I reach out to touch his cheek and he catches my hand and presses it against his lips. I remember my father doing this very thing to my mother and I wonder where Peeta picked it up. Surely not from his father and the witch.[THG264]

In the second book, Peeta immediately recognizes Katniss' mother in old reaping footage from twenty-five years ago, and in *Mockingjay*, Peeta remembers Katniss' father singing "The Hanging Tree" even while mentally impaired by his hijacking. As YA lit blogger Sue at *Forever Young Adult*, a blog dedicated to young adult novels, words it: "To an abused, sensitive little boy, the Everdeen home—happy children, joyful father, loving mother—must have looked like heaven. Heaven with extra hugs and cinnamon on top."[xxxiii] Peeta, in the face of his mother's abuse, turned to another family model for comfort and example.

Although Katniss sees merchant life as exponentially easier than Seam life—and it is, unarguably, more privileged—the Mellark family is a stark portrayal of how life at all levels in Panem is hard and unfair. Despite Mrs. Everdeen's depression, she loves her daughters. Despite the Seam's poverty, Katniss and Gale and their siblings and Greasy Sae's granddaughter have homes where they are safe physically, if nothing else. Perhaps symbolically, Katniss and Gale have mothers who survive the series, although Peeta does not—nor does Madge Undersee.

The Undersees

Rounding out the unhappy families of District 12 are the Undersees, a downtrodden, Capitol-controlled mayor, a drug addict haunted by the system her husband represents, and their quiet daughter, Madge.

Despite having the most luxurious house in District 12, and despite the nearly inconceivable odds of daughter Madge being reaped, the Undersees' home life follows the same unhappy pattern as the Everdeens and Mellarks, one largely defined by a dysfunctional mother. "Mayor Undersee's wife," Katniss tells us, "spends half her life in bed immobilized with terrible pain, shutting out the world."[CF196] Mrs. Undersee is described as not just depressed (reminiscent of Mrs. Everdeen) but a drug addict dependent on morphling. (This is the same drug that, although ostensibly similar to morphine or heroin, "addled" the District 6 tributes in the Quarter Quell and which causes hallucinations.)

Of course, there is another member of the Undersee family whose role holds as significant a place in the narrative of the Hunger Games as Mr. Everdeen does in Katniss' personal narrative: Maysilee Donner, the now-Mrs. Undersee's twin sister, whose death in the Fiftieth Hunger Games is a contributing factor in Mrs. Undersee's continuing dysfunction.

Maysilee was the original owner of Katniss' mockingjay pin. But her impact is further reaching than that. It is perhaps because of Maysilee's demise in the Hunger Games, and the effect on Mrs. Undersee, that Madge shows a more nuanced understanding of the evils of the Capitol and empathy for the residents of the Seam than would be expected of a girl of her social standing, and is in a position to give Katniss the pin in the first place. Despite her father's status as mayor, Madge's life is deeply impacted by the Games. She is the proof that no one in the district—no family, no matter how intact or well-off it might appear—is untouched by the Capitol's tyranny. Despite never being reaped herself, Madge still loses her family—and later, her life—to the Hunger Games.

7

The Games as Exploitation, Exploitation as Entertainment

"It feels like we're in a Roman theater watching gladiators duke it out."

—Alex Guarnaschelli, *The Next Iron Chef* [xxxiv]

People have always found entertainment in stories of others faced with danger or trauma. This is true whether those stories are framed as fiction, as with Shakespeare's tragedies; as reality, as with the violent footage in grisly newscasts; or as "reality," as with doctored and fictionalized personal melodramas of glitzy celebutantes. Whether we're watching Kim Kardashian's divorce proceedings on modern scripted reality television, atrocities of war on sensationalized news programs, or athletes beating each other senseless on Ultimate Fighting, real turmoil and real violence have become as much a part of our modern entertainment culture as the real turmoil and violence of the Hunger Games is a part of Panem's. This universal acceptance—even hankering—for violent entertainment is a part of the rhetoric of entertainment in the Western world, as

Guarnaschelli's quote at the start of this chapter shows. Referencing gladiatorial games to describe a cooking show feels not only natural but apropos and expected; we have no problem seeing the contestants in *The Next Iron Chef*, whom we are ostensibly rooting for, as fierce competitors in a battle to the death.

This reverence for battle violence is what a reference to the Hunger Games would convey equally in Panem's theoretical future, when knowledge of the Roman theaters would be even more ancient history. Of course, the Games themselves (even in their name, as "games") are a pointed allusion to the gladiatorial games of Rome, in which socially marginalized slaves or venerated volunteers, trained to engage in armed combat against each other, wild animals, or condemned criminals, fought in hugely promoted shows for audiences of Roman nobility. Just as the gladiatorial games did for Rome (gladiators were usually prisoners of war, conscripted soldiers, or Roman criminals), Panem's Hunger Games demonstrate the nation's poor martial ethics and barbaric justice system.

Plenty of novels and films have used Rome's gladiatorial games as inspiration. What makes the world of the Hunger Games different in structure from that of other dystopian works (most notably *Battle Royale*) is how Collins presents her subject matter as being excused by the population not because it's custom or because of the fear of reprisal but because it is *entertainment*. Suzanne Collins has stated that her initial inspiration for the Hunger Games series came not from those games themselves, but from flipping between "reality" show programming and sensationalist news coverage of war on television.

The lush costumes entice sponsorship, like votes on *Dancing with the Stars* or *American Idol*; the short interviews outside of the main action given by the escorts, mentors, and Caesar Flickerman parallel the structure of countless reality dating programs. Claudius Templesmith fills the role of a futuristic Jeff Probst or Ryan Seacrest. And of course, the Gamemakers' obstacles are seen by Panem's general citizenry as little more than deadly Quickfire Challenges (sometimes literally, as with the fast-moving fireballs that chase Katniss across the arena in the Seventy-fourth Games).

The reality television narrative only gains traction in *Catching Fire*, when the Quarter Quell gives the Capitol citizens the "Hunger Games: All-Stars" edition they've been waiting three-quarters of a century for. It's the perfect opportunity for placing bets, discussing in the streets, saving up to sponsor, and even—as in the case of the mockingjay fashion fad Katniss sees on the train—buying merchandise for their favorite contenders.

In *Mockingjay*, the rebellion uses the same "All-Stars" technique in their propos. Even while fighting the Capitol's system, the rebels still rely on Finnick's heartthrob status and Gale's "camera-ready" face to sell their message, proving that the importance of entertainment media in Panem culture rivals our own. They trust that a celebrity endorsement from Finnick Odair, or a cute boy on a television commercial, will sell the ideals of the rebellion better than unadulterated footage of a hospital bombing, and Suzanne Collins demonstrates that masterfully. The rebels don't resign themselves to using the Capitol's technique of entertainment as social control; they revel in it.

The trilogy's scathing critique of reality television culture is not unprecedented, but it is unique to the Hunger Games in its execution. By focusing on Katniss, a participant in the medium who grew up as a spectator to it, the books are able to cast not only the reader, but the characters, into audience roles. In doing so, they subtly and successfully reflect our own enamored reading experience back to us—and show us the power that media can have over us.

Panem's Hunger Games as a Media Spectacle

"The Treaty of Treason gave us new laws to guarantee peace and, as our yearly reminder that the Dark Days must never be repeated, it gave us the Hunger Games."[THG18]

The Hunger Games began in Panem as a form of war reparations, but by Katniss' entry in the Seventy-fourth Games, it is little more than a massive media spectacle on par with our own *American Idol* (there were 132 million votes cast for the 2012 finale, compared to 131.2 million in the 2008 presidential election), celebrity weddings (Kim Kardashian and Kris Humphries' wedding in 2011 cost approximately $10 million and recouped more than $18 million in ad revenue), or the Super Bowl ($245 million in advertising revenue in 2012). The Hunger Games in Panem are a showcase for haute couture fashion, including the debuts of fresh new designers like Cinna and Portia; an occasion for outings for all of the Capitol's elite society, including President Snow himself and favored courtesan Finnick Odair; and, of course, a huge source of bookmaking revenue and sports betting.

By the seventy-fourth anniversary of the first rebellion's conclusion, the Games are a spectacle of shock-and-awe entertainment, with the shock of children killing children nearly supplanted by the awe of the surrounding events' scientific and visual brilliance, like the arena, designed anew each year, or Katniss' fiery mockingjay wedding gown. However, through that spectacle, the Capitol reinforces its own position as the privileged leader of Panem and the true victors of the Games; while the districts must forfeit their children and watch the Games in fear and poverty, the Capitol citizens enjoy the same events in wealth, leisure, and safety. The Games have become something much more subtle than straightforward punishment; they have become entertaining television.

Television as Representation

It seems fair to assume that Collins' background as a television writer (for *Clarissa Explains It All*; *Little Bear*; *The Mystery Files of Shelby Woo*[1]; *Generation O!*; and *Wow! Wow! Wubzy!*, almost all of which aired on the

---

[1] Notably one of the only sitcoms ever to feature an Asian American in a leading role, suggesting a previous engagement on Collins' part with the importance of racial/cultural/ethnic presentation in media.

Viacom-owned Nickelodeon children's media channel) hugely informed her depiction of the proceedings of the Hunger Games in Panem. This influence is especially evident in Plutarch Heavensbee and Caesar Flickerman, as representatives of the media culture in the Capitol.

Plutarch and Caesar are both concerned with creating appearances for the camera that forge an emotional connection between the viewer and what's on their screen. Plutarch approaches this task as a producer, creating scenarios, manipulating opportunities for character interaction, and using special effects, scenery, and pacing to build a bond between viewer and performer. Caesar, however, encourages that sense of connection in a different way. He acts as a stand-in for the viewer, equivalent to the role of hosts of today's "audition episodes" or reunion specials of reality shows, or talk news programs like *The View* or *60 Minutes*, in which the viewer's bond is dependent on the perception of a bond between the interviewer and interviewee.

Although the Gamemakers are cast as villains in Katniss' world (oddly casting Collins' own job as a media creator as being a cultural negative), Plutarch and Caesar provide contrasting humanitarian ideologies within the framework of mass media production. Plutarch is considered by many readers to be the "better person" because he helps to organize and lead the Second Rebellion. However, it can be argued that he did so for reasons that had more to do with power and personal freedom than the good of Panem. Plutarch did not use his influence as a Gamemaker to make the arenas any less deadly for the tributes—and his comment in *Mockingjay* that among the first broadcasts to start again after the war should be a singing competition suggests that Plutarch is more interested in the entertainment and submission of his audience than in improving the state of the media or the lives of its participants. In contrast, although Caesar Flickerman sides with the Capitol on political and sociopolitical levels, which many readers see as "evil," even Katniss acknowledges that Caesar's primary goal seems to be helping the tributes to gain sponsors— essentially, helping them gain a better chance at survival for not only themselves, but for their entire district if they are deemed the victor.

Caesar is a consummate man of the Capitol—coiffed, dyed, and heavily made up—but uses his position of influence in the media for the aid of others, as well as for his own benefit. Plutarch, despite being a rebel and a "good guy," uses the media expressly to peddle his own ideas and promote his own well-being even at the dire expense of the less fortunate.

Still, the important thing about the Games, here, is not the intent of the individuals within the system, but the effect the Games have on viewers—and how the political gamemakers use the Games as a tool. And to understand that, we have to go back to where, for individual citizens of the district, participation in the Games begins.

The Games as Exploitation

Although we, as readers, generally see Katniss' experience as a tribute as beginning with her volunteering at the seventy-fourth reaping ceremony, her participation as a contestant in the Hunger Games actually began when she was twelve years old and first signed up for tesserae. Besides being a form of welfare, taking tesserae can be seen as a television contract of sorts: in return for receiving grain and oil, Katniss must literally sign over her life and rights to her home, family, friends, and life story.

Yes, the name of every district citizen is entered between the ages of twelve and eighteen, once for every year of eligibility. But the "voluntary" nature of tesserae means Katniss is effectively increasing her chances of her own free will, signing up for the Games rather than being forced into participation. It's just one more example of Panem's systematic class warfare masquerading as a numbers game: everyone is being punished, but if you please the Capitol, your family may be punished less. The core of this idea—that the appeasement of the Capitol is tantamount to survival—informs the way the tributes and their mentors "play" the Hunger Games at every level. When the Capitol can do whatever they want to you without parameter or repercussion, what can a tribute do to make sure that "whatever the Capitol wants" is for them to survive?

Once Katniss is selected as tribute, we see several very overt references to reality TV in the Games, most obviously the opening ceremonies and interviews before the Games themselves. But there is one reality show staple echoed in the Hunger Games that's less overt: the all-encompassing, wholly binding television contract required by networks such as MTV and VH1 of their reality show participants. Even now, in the United States, contestants on reality programming are presented with stringent contracts that those contracts themselves acknowledge "under ordinary circumstances . . . would be considered a 'serious' invasion of privacy."[xxxv]

> Joseph Melillo, a 24-year-old general assignment reporter for WENY-TV in Elmira, was offered a role in Real World XXIII: Washington D.C., but declined once he read the contract. "My image, my life story—all that was theirs," the Trinity College grad recalls. Melillo also has Crohn's disease, and if he had agreed to the paperwork, he would've lost his HIPAA privacy rights. MTV would've had complete freedom to exploit his medical history . . . Under the original proposal, the crew could enter Melillo's childhood home and take memorabilia for the show at any time.[xxxvi]

In both *Catching Fire*—under the Capitol—and *Mockingjay*—under the rebels—Katniss' home and personal effects are treated as fodder for the audiences, both within and outside of the Games. She is expected to allow the camera crews into her home in the Seam, and then her home in the Victor's Village. Her Victor's Village home is bugged, as well—ostensibly to monitor for any potential rebellion but also reminiscent of the "night vision" cameras that are part and parcel of modern reality shows such as *Jersey Shore* and *Big Brother*. Further, in *Catching Fire*, the open access to her friends and family that she is required to afford the camera crew becomes a major plot point when one of the segments of the clock arena is full of jabberjays crying out in pain . . . using the voices of "Prim, Gale, my mother, Madge, Rory, Vick, even Posy, helpless little Posy."[CF344]

What Katniss learns from this escapade is that despite not being in the arena, the people in her life have become characters in the Hunger Games spectacle as well—something Johanna highlights in her reassurance to Katniss that Prim is okay:

> "The whole country adores Katniss' little sister. If they really killed her [to record the jabberjays], they'd probably have an uprising on their hands," says Johanna flatly. "Don't want that, do they?"[CF346]

No doubt the Gamemakers thought that making Prim into a character, one who is innocent and relatable to Capitol viewers, would create an empathetic link to Katniss, even as she's fiercely killing other tributes. For the viewers in the districts, though, Prim serves another purpose entirely, one unintended by the Gamemakers: a reminder that the fearsome tributes in the arena are sisters or brothers or daughters or sons, and that their own children could be next—unless the Games are stopped.

Obviously, the depiction of the Hunger Games in Panem is an exaggerated version of our own reality shows. But judging by the contents of the contracts participants are required to sign, it's less exaggerated than one might think. It's not just shows in the "life-threatening situations" genre (*Survivor*, *I'm A Celebrity . . . Get Me Out Of Here!*, *Fear Factor*) and popularity contest shows (*American Idol*, *The X-Factor*, and *Dancing with the Stars*) that require complicated contracts. Even "lifestyle" and dating-based reality television programs require releases that spare their networks from any culpability in the case of injury to contestants—even in the case of rape, disfigurement, paralysis, or death. *The Real World*'s contract, for example, stipulates:

- You may die, lose limbs, and suffer nervous breakdowns. (Stipulation 1)
- If you undergo any medical procedures while involved in the show, they carry the risk of infection, disfigurement, death. (4)

- You may be humiliated and explicitly portrayed "in a false light." (12)
- Producers are under no obligation to conduct background checks on your fellow cast members. (7)
- Interacting with other cast members carries the risk of "non-consensual physical contact" and should you contract AIDS, etc. during such an interaction, MTV is not responsible. (7)
- If you get kicked off the show, it will be filmed. (14)
- You grant the Producer blanket rights to your life story. (49)
- The Producer can do pretty much anything they want with your life story, including misrepresent it. (49)
- Your email may be monitored during participation. (20b)
- You promise not to hide from MTV cameras in establishments where they can't film. (20a)
- The production crew can show up at your personal house at any time to film and/or to take anything they want, as long as they return the objects once production has ended. (20a)[xxxvii]

The MTV contract seems like it would scarcely need to be changed to cover the risks in the arena in Panem—except in replacing a few "you may"s with "you will"s.

Exploitation as Entertainment

> "There's almost always some wood," Gale says. "Since that year half of them died of cold. Not much entertainment value in that."
> It's true . . . It was considered very anticlimactic in the Capitol, all those quiet, bloodless deaths. Since then, there's usually been wood to make fires.[THG39]

In Panem, of course, the aim of the show is to kill off the majority of participants—creating an environment where, for their audience, the deaths themselves have become the entertainment. But although people like to think that Panem's entertainment is far more gruesome than anything we'd allow today, there have been instances of rape, serious injury, and death shown on our own television screens . . . and they, too, have been branded "a part of the entertainment" and exploited as such.

In 2010, right around the release of *Mockingjay*, Capt. Phil Harris of *Deadliest Catch* suffered a stroke and died on-screen. Of the event, Salon.com reported:

> Even a sensitive documentarian might look at the "Deadliest Catch" camera crew's post-stroke footage and think, "This is a motherlode," then set about repackaging pain as entertainment . . . in a genre that has captured endless humiliation, violence and other human suffering, here was reality TV's first [on-screen] death.[xxxviii]

In 2002, while filming *The Real World: Chicago*, cast member Tonya Cooley of Washington was object-raped on camera by two male castmates and, as reported by *TMZ*, "producers not only knew about the rape, they even replaced the toothbrush but never told her what happened."[xxxix] The idea of Capitol citizens taking pleasure in viewing the brutal murders of tributes (and/or the sexual display of them, as in Katniss and Peeta kissing in the cave or Finnick in general) is not so far-fetched. After all, just look at our own societal acceptance of the death and degradation of reality TV participants because "it's what they signed up for."

In Panem, the Capitol citizens understand the events of the Games as punishment for the districts; the tributes "deserve" their fates, ostensibly because of their great-grandparents' roles in the First Rebellion, but reflexively because of where they are born, their families' incomes and vocations, and the color of their skin. Some of our justifications for the sadistic enjoyment of reality TV aren't far off. Consider the "guido" Italian Americans of *Jersey Shore*, who some viewers and critics claim deserve to be ridiculed because of their heritage and lifestyle. As one blogger explained in 2010:

> Jersey Shore not only exposes, but encourages racism towards Italian-Americans through the slang words, "guido" and "guidette." The word "guido" and its new, feminine counterpart are . . . uneducated vernacular . . . dating as far back as the early 1920s . . . frequently as a demeaning term to describe lower-class Italians in America. It was a racial slur that hurt feelings and segregated people from another, and should still be viewed as such.[xl]

The terminology employed by many viewers of modern reality television—from racial slurs like "guido" and "guidette" to misogynistic slurs like "bitch," "whore," "slut," etc.—act as a means of divorcing the show's "stars" from its viewers' sense of empathy, based on ethnicity, race, or gender. Panem's Hunger Games, by denoting its tributes by district identity and visually conforming to district stereotyping in their ceremony costumes, does the same.

MSNBC quotes Todd Boyd, critical-studies professor at the University of Southern California's School of Cinema-Television, as saying, "We know all these shows are edited and manipulated to create images that look real and sort of exist in real time. But really what we have is a construction . . . The whole enterprise of reality television relies on stereotypes. It relies on common stock, easily identifiable images."[xli] Often, those stereotypes and stock images are what attract audiences in the first place. Reality TV producer Naomi Bulochnikov, the brains behind *Paris Hilton's My New BFF* and the unseen *Bridge & Tunnel*, says of the subjects of her shows—and most other lifestyle reality television—something implicit in Effie Trinket's assessment of the District 12 tributes as "ill-mannered" and boorish: "You tune in because you hate them. You stay tuned because you start falling in love with them."[xlii]

Reality shows focus at least in part on creating a sympathetic bond between the audience and show participants. But that bond, and the empathy it suggests, has distinct limitations. About.com columnist Austin Cline suggests our enjoyment of reality shows is a national case of Schadenfreude, the German word used to describe joy in seeing another's pain. "If you laugh at someone slipping on the ice, that's Schadenfreude. If you take pleasure in the downfall of a company you dislike, that is also Schadenfreude. The latter example is certainly understandable, but I don't think that's what we're seeing here. After all, we don't know the people on reality shows."[xliii]

That last line is the key: we don't *really* know the people on reality shows. Or at least we do not respond to them in the same way we do people we know in real life. One explanation that's been given for this effect is that when we, as the audience, feel as though we're watching a story—something that is encouraged by the heavily produced and even scripted "real" events on reality shows—we treat its players like fictional characters. Although we understand on one level that they are "real people," the emotional engagement is different.

This seems to be the case for television producers as well as the audience. According to Los Angeles lawyer Barry B. Langberg, who represents several reality TV show stars:

> Comments from various reality TV producers often fail to demonstrate much sympathy or concern with what their subjects experience—what we are seeing is a great callousness towards other human beings who are treated as means towards achieving financial and commercial success, regardless of the consequences for them. Injuries, humiliation, suffering, and higher insurance rates are all just the "cost of doing business" and a requirement for being edgier.[xliv]

Given the immense empathy that many fictional characters inspire, and always have inspired, in their audiences—just think of our own connections to Katniss, Peeta, Gale, and the rest of the world of Panem!—the theory that this disconnect stems only from fictionalization seems oversimplified. Instead, I'd argue that "reality TV Schadenfreude," on which both the contemporary United States and the futuristic world of Panem rely, is predicated on a combination of elements: fictionalizing people, sensationalizing events, and the presentation of both as "reality" or "fact" when, in actuality, they are heavily manipulated to present a particular narrative.

Entertainment as Social Control

There is considerable danger in allowing reality TV to become a major source of public information, as the Hunger Games so skillfully shows. Those stereotypes and that sense of Schadenfreude on the part of the privileged audience become the socioeconomic and sociopolitical norm. Class hierarchies are reinforced. And when such sources of public information are used to maintain privileged sociopolitical ideals, they can be an effective method of social control.

Because Panem's districts are all so isolated, the only representation anyone has of people outside their district, people who are not "them," is through the horror of the Hunger Games. (Katniss says she had never met anyone from a district other than District 12 prior to being reaped, and it seems to have been the same for the rest of the district, outside of glimpses of past victors on tours.) And what the Hunger Games shows seems to be very predictable. District 1, District 2, and District 4 are bloodthirsty, nouveau riche Capitol lackeys; District 3 and District 6 are weaklings and unlikely to survive; District 11 and District 12 are capable of neither winning nor comporting themselves to the Capitol's standards of etiquette. These kinds of negative generalizations are a common problem with stereotype-driven reality TV. As succinctly summed up by one anonymous blogger from Staten Island (speaking of the cancellation of MTV's *Bridge & Tunnel*): "Thank Jesus that your children don't have to grow up in a world where these people represent their hometown."[xlv]

Most district and Capitol citizens only see people who are "the Other" at their very worst: when they are killing, maiming, and dying. Peeta's assertion that he "wants to die as himself and not become a piece in their Games" gains another level of salience when you consider that he is representing not only himself, and not only District 12, but his class. He is most likely one of only a very few merchant-class tributes ever sent to the Games. Unlike Katniss, who is focused only on surviving ("I just can't afford to think that way," she claims), he understands the negative image that most of the audience will automatically have of him because of his district and wants to represent himself, his family, District 12, and the merchant class as positively as he can.

However, despite its immense flaws when it comes to representation, reality TV can be a major force for positive political and cultural change. In some authoritarian countries, reality television voting has been the first time many citizens have voted in any free and fair widescale elections. In addition, reality shows have the power to expose viewers to new situations, including ones that are taboo in certain orthodox cultures; for instance, *Star Academy Arab World*, which began airing in 2003, shows male and female contestants living together.[xlvi] In 2004, journalist Matt Labash wrote that "the best hope of little Americas developing in the Middle East could be Arab-produced reality TV." He went on to describe how:

> In China, after the finale of the 2005 season of *Super Girl* (the local version of *American Idol*) drew an audience of around 400 million people, and 8 million text message votes, the state-run English-language newspaper *Beijing Today* ran the front-page headline "Is *Super Girl* a Force for Democracy?"[xlvii]

If reality TV provides disenfranchised citizens with a voice in any way, that can be counted as a "good." Still, we should not forget that what even these "benevolent" reality shows give their audiences, in our world as in Panem, is shaped by what the media producers and Gamemakers want those audiences to see. Although Caesar can spin every interview positively and stylists like Cinna and Portia can help every tribute look their best—or their worst, as Katniss notes with grim solemnity in her recollections of previous District 12 tributes "stripped naked and covered in coal dust"[THG66]—the editors, Gamemakers, and President Snow ultimately have almost total control over how any particular tribute is perceived by the audience . . . at least until Katniss' stunt with the nightlock berries at the end of the Seventy-fourth Games, which is a part of what makes that act of Katniss and Peeta's so revolutionary.

What makes a tribute appear powerful in the opening ceremonies can be used against them in the arena itself, as with Katniss, the Girl On Fire, and the fireballs. Although Katniss may succeed at refusing to cry and Peeta can refuse to live and die as anyone other than himself, the Gamemakers and government—Panem's "big media"—can use their footage of the tributes to create almost any narrative they choose. Think, for example, of the lie the Capitol tells about District 13, pairing old footage with new threats to say the district has been decimated, when it has not.

Plutarch and Snow both have the means to create media that serves their unique political agendas, most notably seen in the Airtime Assault in *Mockingjay*, and today's media moguls do the same:

> [T]he coverage was a reminder of what we in the new media world should keep in mind: what a news organization with deep pockets can do, even now in this age of diminishment for Big Media. Top editors, once they've persuaded the financial people, can order a broad, strategic deployment of journalistic resources.[xlviii]

"Reputable" media sources that are free to report as they wish—of which Panem has none—often employ the same form of manipulation. In doing so, they can suffer from the same stereotyping and pandering to the most privileged audience members for which reality TV is denigrated. *Time* magazine, for example, frequently "tones down" its covers and lead stories for the US audience; on December 5, 2011, while the rest of the world (Europe, Asia, and South Pacific markets) saw cover images and headlines depicting rioters in the Egypt revolutions, the American audience was assured that "Anxiety is Good for You."[xlix] A few weeks earlier, on November 21, while *Time*'s cover in European and South Pacific markets derided hugely corrupt Italian prime minister Berlusconi and the Asian market debated whether the Indian or Chinese economic system would emerge as the world's most powerful in the 2010s, the US market was treated to a larger jingoistic cover story about the power and underappreciated valor of American soldiers returning from the American-led invasion of Afghanistan and simply waved a cheerful "Ciao, Berlusconi!" as a soft subtitle.[1]

This narrow focus on US events over international interests helps to maintain and promote a jingoistic view of the world: US events are the most important; US attitudes are the most valid; US viewpoints on other nations, or minorities within our own nation, are the most correct. This promotion of national stereotypes helps extend and reinforce them.

Panem's system of information dispersal seems to work similarly, through limiting the information its residents receive; the Capitol controls all the news sources and means of communication. But even Katniss, who has been severely and strategically undereducated, can sense that something is afoot when it comes to what she's been told about the state of the world:

> I know there must be more than they're telling us, an actual account of what happened during the rebellion. But I don't spend much time thinking about it. Whatever the truth is, I don't see how it will help me get food on the table.[THG42]

Like Katniss, the oppressed citizens of Panem are too busy trying to survive to spend much time thinking about politics or media, and that's a big factor in the Capitol's ability to keep the districts under its thumb. The distraction the Games present—either as entertainment or as threat—and the mutual mistrust they sow between the districts takes care of the rest.

Gender Roles and Sexuality in Panem

From Katniss' otherwise-concerned first-person narrative (at least until we read Finnick Odair's confession of being tortured as a trafficked child slave in *Mockingjay*), it seems that the nation of Panem is sexless. Because Katniss does not take an interest in sex, or gender, one could come away from the Hunger Games trilogy believing that, at least for the purposes of this story, they are not especially crucial to the narrative. But although sex and gender are not a major part of the main plot of the Hunger Games, they play a role in the series that ranks second in importance only to race, class, and socioeconomic/ethnic privilege.

The Katniss-Peeta-Gale "Love" Triangle

The obvious exception, at least outwardly, to the aromantic tone of the series is the "love triangle" between Katniss,

Peeta, and Gale. It's important to address this up front because, though sex and gender may play a pivotal role in the trilogy and in Panem, that role has nothing to do with the Katniss-Peeta-Gale story—which is not really a "love" triangle at all.

The most frequent understanding of the Katniss-Peeta-Gale love triangle is purely allegorical. Katniss, at the precipice of inevitable war and experiencing her first true chance to make affecting choices, must choose between Peeta, representing noble intentions, and Gale, representing revenge. At the time of *The Hunger Games*' writing, the United States was three years into the war in Iraq and just learning that Iraq did not in fact possess weapons of mass destruction.[li] Justification for warfare was a hot topic both in the media and among US citizens.

Although it could be argued that the "love triangle" is both an allegory and a true narrative love triangle, that is still not quite true. For the story to have been a real love triangle, Katniss would need to be in love with both Peeta and Gale, or at least romantically or sexually involved with both men. She isn't. Katniss feels a sense of duty towards both men; she seems to view possible romantic entanglement with both or either not as exciting or desirable but instead as a reciprocal obligation (if they love her and provide her with help, she must love them and provide them with help). There's no real evidence that she feels romantically inclined towards both (or either) man with any constancy, at least until after the rebellion has ended.

After all, one of Katniss' most-quoted (and most kickass) lines in the series is, "I really can't think about kissing when I've got a rebellion to incite"!

Gender Roles and Reversals

The place we must look instead, in examining sex and gender in Panem, is at the way the series' characters themselves utilize and are affected by sex and gender.

Before we really get into gender roles and gendered expectations in Panem, though, I do want to stop and clarify: as far as any analysis of the text shows, Suzanne Collins wrote Panem as confined within the same limiting gender binary we see in our world. When I say "female," I mean "cisgender and self-identifying (or identified by Katniss as) female/feminine," and when I say "male," I mean "cisgender and self-identifying (or identified by Katniss as) male/masculine."[2] This is in no way intended to discount or discourage any reader experience or interaction with the text in terms of identification with (or of) characters of nonbinary gender role placement.

It seems, in many ways, like women and men alike serve in roles of power in the Hunger Games trilogy. Coin is equally revered, in her role as leader of District 13, as Snow is as president of the Capitol; Clove is as fierce a fighter as Cato, and none of the sponsors or other tributes appear to view her as lesser (or less deadly) because of her sex.

Perhaps Panem, for all its dystopian horror, is one of those typical sci-fi futureverses where gender discrimination has been overthrown!

Or not.

Although neither sex appears to claim preferential treatment over the other, there are definitely stereotypes and prejudices still in play—and unfortunately, perhaps in part because she is our point of view character, we see those exhibited the most by Katniss herself. (This is true at the outset of the story, at least; a part of her personal narrative journey is overcoming them!)

> I've been right not to cry. The station is swarming with reporters with their insectlike cameras trained directly on my face. But I've had a lot of practice at wiping my face clean of emotions and I do this now. I catch a glimpse of myself on the

---

[2] "Cisgender" is an identifying terminology, coming into use in the twenty-first century as a replacement for the diminutive classification "gender normative." It is an oppositional term to "transgender," and it denotes the social designation of individuals whose born physical sex at birth matches their socially assigned gender identity and gender expression. It is considered preferential to "gender normative" because it denotes only the idea of "a gender-diversified experience" instead of an abnormal gender diversification.

television screen on the wall that's airing my arrival live and feel gratified that I appear almost bored.

Peeta Mellark, on the other hand, has obviously been crying and interestingly enough does not seem to be trying to cover it up. I immediately wonder if this will be his strategy in the Games. To appear weak.[THG41]

We *could* theorize that, given how far in the future the trilogy takes place, gender roles themselves have flipped—that Katniss' attitude (strength shown in a lack of emotionality) would be emblematic of a Panem female, and her view of Peeta (emotional, manipulative, and weak) typical of a Panem male. In this scene, Katniss is female but aligns herself with both behaviors and a mindset that is closer to what we would call "masculine," and disparages a character who she views as showing behaviors that we would call more "feminine." So it's tempting to interpret Panem's views on sex and gender based on Katniss' very biased narration—to say, "Katniss is strong, and Peeta is weak. Therefore, in Panem girls are strong, and boys are weak. Wow, Panem is so evolved!" The number of female heads-of-household in Panem—Mrs. Everdeen (or Katniss), Mrs. Hawthorne, Greasy Sae—and women in positions of power—Mags as mentor, Commander Paylor in District 8, President Coin in District 13—would support this idea. But if Panem is examined as a complete society, it's clear that there are as many, if not more, cultural expectations imposed on individuals due to their sex and gender in Panem as there are in the world we live in.

Gender is a construct not created within the individual but by society. Katniss' personality and views reflect just a small part of the society she lives in. In fact, she seems designed, as a character, to be diametrically opposed to Panem society, given her responsibility in sparking and bringing about the rebellion. Because how is "society" better exemplified in Panem than through the Hunger Games themselves, from the interviews to the Games strategies of different tributes?

When Katniss volunteers herself into the Games, she takes extraordinary pains not to present herself as emotional, equating the display of sadness with the appearance of weakness. It could be argued that, as a hunter, Katniss understands the importance of maintaining a façade of calm in the face of fear, but she doesn't phrase her aversion to projection in terms of hunting: she treats tears as if they would be a source of shame.

> "Prim, let go," I say harshly, because this is upsetting me and I don't want to cry. When they televise the replay of the reapings tonight, everyone will make note of my tears, and I'll be marked as an easy target. A weakling. I will give no one that satisfaction.[THG23]

And:

> Crying is not an option. There will be more cameras at the train station.[THG34]

When she reaches the Capitol, one of the primary functions of the prep team, Cinna, Effie, and Haymitch's coaching, and Caesar's guidance through her interview is to remake Katniss into the Capitol's ideal image of femininity: she giggles, she twirls, she wears sequins and has flames painted onto her manicured fingernails. She needs to seem likeable—and likeable, for a girl in Panem, is apparently appearing softer and more personable than Katniss is naturally. (The same is true for Glimmer, whom Katniss immediately pegs on sight as marketing herself to be "sexy" and who will be a sponsor-favorite tribute.) Katniss' training score of eleven (the highest score) is as seductive a selling point with sponsors as it is because it is a counterpoint to her ability to fit succinctly into the female gender role that Capitol sponsors favor. Although Katniss is not privy to the entirety of Peeta's strategizing with Haymitch, she does understand, at a primal level, the importance of being seen as District 12's *female* tribute, despite seeing Peeta as constitutionally weaker than she is. "And there I am, blushing and confused, made . . . desirable by Peeta's confession . . . and by all accounts, unforgettable."[THG49]

Coloring Katniss' understanding of how femininity and masculinity play in the Hunger Games is her memory of Johanna:

> I immediately wonder if this will be his strategy in the Games. To appear weak and frightened, to reassure the other tributes that he is no competition at all . . . this worked very well for a girl, Johanna Mason, from District 7 a few years back . . . [N]o one bothered about her until there were only a handful of contestants left. It turned out she could kill viciously.[THG41]

The main area of discussion on the internet and in academia about gender roles in the Hunger Games is the subversion within the Katniss/Peeta pairing. Katniss and Peeta are, essentially, each playing the gender role that would usually be assumed by the other in Western culture. Katniss is the sole provider for her family; she hunts, she fishes, she's terrible with emotions. She—frankly—has a very negative view of women (such as Mrs. Mellark, her mother, Venia, and Octavia, especially at the outset of the trilogy; it improves somewhat as the books continue). Peeta bakes, nurtures Haymitch (by cleaning him up after his drinking binge on the train), nurses a lifelong schoolyard infatuation, and is emotionally self-aware. Perhaps most radically, Peeta Mellark is a *man* who navigates his world through *words*, where Katniss is a *woman* who navigates her world through *action*. Still, the character who most deftly illustrates Collins' ability to contrast and foil both characters' and readers' expectations of traditional gender roles (both in our current culture and in Panem) is Johanna Mason.

Johanna knows gender roles and how to play them for effect more concretely than anyone in the series or in most YA literature as a whole. Johanna is a lumberjack, which is a stereotypically male profession. During her first Hunger Games, Katniss tells us, Johanna deliberately played the role of "a helpless girl" to throw off her opponents. However, when we meet her during the Quarter Quell, and for the duration of *Mockingjay*, Johanna's self-presentation aligns with one that is more stereotypically masculine. She eschews hygiene and personal appearance and does not allow anyone to form opinions of her based on her looks; she expresses her sexuality "like a man," stripping down just to get out of her clothes and catcalling and wolf-whistling Finnick and Gale, whom she deems "gorgeous." That doesn't mean she is no longer interested in the effect of gendered expectations or no longer willing to employ them for her own ends: she uses sudden gender-role trope reversal—fawning over Katniss' fashion, most notably—to disarm Katniss and keep her confused about Johanna's intentions towards her, which is an essential part of making sure Katniss is kept in the dark about the Quell plot.

Equally compelling as Katniss and Peeta's role reversal, but less chronicled, is the one between Johanna and Finnick Odair. Whereas Johanna is written as "masculine," Finnick is written as "feminine." He is described as beautiful and sensual; even Katniss remarks on his appearance and manner with some breathlessness. He is also described as a romantic (both in persona, for the cameras, as when he helps to perpetuate the Quell lie about Katniss' pregnancy, and in truth, when he talks about Annie) and emotional; he spends the majority of the first half of *Mockingjay* crying, which serves as a counterpoint to Katniss' catatonic stoicism and, later, Johanna's rage and bitterness. Whereas the most important events in Johanna's story line, or at least pertaining to her role in Katniss' narrative, are acts of violence (notably the climax of *Catching Fire* when Johanna cuts the tracker from Katniss' arm in the Quarter Quell), Finnick's story comes to its zenith when he weds Annie—a plot device that is more stereotypically used for female character arcs in Western literature.

In spite of being written with oppositional gender traits, however, Johanna is still described by Katniss as undeniably female and Finnick as something of the epitome of male in Katniss' eyes ("Finnick's such an amazing male specimen"[CF275]). This shows another subtle way that, by *Catching Fire*, Katniss has already begun to break with her own previous prejudices—and shows her distinct differences from Panem's ideology. Katniss does not underestimate Johanna for her femaleness, as she may have a year previously. Finnick's presentation as a Capitol mannequin does not deter Katniss from seeing him as a powerful competitor, or masculine, though just a year before Katniss saw Peeta's finer clothes and traditionally feminine profession as signs of weakness.

Panem's cultural perception of males as inherently dominant and masculine and females as submissive and feminine determines the way Katniss, Peeta, Johanna, and Finnick are "publicized" by the Gamemakers and stylists and received by Panem-at-large. But the contrast between their nonconforming gender traits and the other tributes' cultural and manufactured expectations works in each character's favor in the arena—if only because it causes their personal strategies to seem wildly unpredictable (especially in Johanna's and Katniss' cases). Unfortunately, although Katniss and the people in her life may show tremendous depth, Panem itself is no different from modern-day America in terms of wanting its women to be Girls and its men to be Men—especially on TV.

Finnick Odair and Sexual Exploitation

Of course, in the Capitol, the audience's expectations extend beyond the television set and into "real" life. Victors of the Games no longer belong to themselves; as victors, they have responsibilities, from mentoring future tributes to maintaining their personae from the Games for the enjoyment of their audience, often with tragic and highly exploitative consequences. There are repercussions to the way tributes present themselves in the arena to survive, as first illustrated by Katniss and Peeta's forced "wedding." As victors, Katniss and Peeta are expected to allow the Capitol audience into their lives as long as the viewers want to be there. The show they put on in the arena stops being for their own benefit, and instead starts being used for the benefit of the Capitol.

There is no better example of this than Finnick Odair. As Panem's biggest star, Finnick is arguably the single most tragic story in the Hunger Games franchise and the place where the darker aspects of gender, sexuality, and exploitation most clearly intersect.

The mainstream media, when covering the Hunger Games, most frequently refers to Finnick as a "sexy playboy," which is both inaccurate to his character and deeply insulting, given the scope of his character arc and the tragedy-ridden history of his real-world counterparts. In a similarly incorrect fashion, parts of fandom commonly call Finnick Odair a prostitute. It is more accurate to describe Finnick as a trafficked child or a slave.

Victims of human trafficking are not permitted to leave upon arrival at their destination. They are held against their will through acts of coercion and forced to work or provide services to the trafficker or others. The work or services may include anything from bonded or forced labor to commercialized sexual exploitation.[li] The arrangement may be structured as a work contract but with no or low payment or on terms that are highly exploitative. Sometimes the arrangement is structured as debt bondage, with the victim not being permitted or able to pay off the debt (the most common form of enslavement in our world today).[lii]

In *Mockingjay*, Finnick describes his experiences for the camera, for broadcast across Panem:

> "President Snow used to . . . sell me . . . my body, that is," Finnick begins in a flat, removed tone. "I wasn't the only one. If a victor is considered desirable, the president gives them as a reward or allows people to buy them for an exorbitant amount of money. If you refuse, he kills someone you love. So you do it."[M170]

In popular fandom theory, Finnick is trapped into his slavery by claims for reparation by his sponsors in the Hunger Games—as suggested by the mention of his trident being among the most expensive gifts a tribute has ever received in the arena, coupled with the canon knowledge from Finnick's broadcast from District 13 that favored tributes are coerced into sexual slavery in the Capitol—and by President Snow's threats against Annie and Mags. Given that Johanna tells Katniss that "Mags was half [Finnick's] family,"[CF328] it can be inferred from the text that, in at least this instance, Snow and his government made good on the threats of violence used to coerce victors into bonded sex labor.

It can be inferred that even Haymitch and Johanna were punished for refusing service to Snow and the Capitol. Johanna states that "there's no one left [she] love[s]," while Haymitch lost "his mother, his little brother, and his girl" just after his Games. (Though the reason Haymitch gives Katniss for his family's deaths is his "stunt" with the force field, he also says that Snow used him as "the example. The person to hold up to the young Finnicks and Johannas and Cashmeres. Of what could happen to a victor who caused problems."[M172-173]) Given Snow's fairly overt threats to Katniss' family, including the Hawthornes, if she does not comply with his plan for her—including her and Peeta's forced, televised marriage and all that entails—it is a popular interpretation. However, because Finnick is the only canonically confirmed survivor of the system, only his characterization serves here as the basis for discussing exploitation in Panem under this system.

Listening to Finnick's revelations in *Mockingjay*, Katniss is stunned, and her understanding of Finnick and his reputation changes completely: "That explains it, then. Finnick's parade of lovers in the Capitol. They were never real."[M170] Given Finnick's reputation for flirtatiousness and perceived promiscuity—which he presumably uses as a coping mechanism, and to protect Annie and Mags—neither Katniss nor the reader have reason to guess that he is anything other than the image he presents until his reveal in *Mockingjay*. When she discovers she was wrong, Katniss feels immediately shocked and guilty for believing ill of Finnick's sexual past (an effective chastisement for victim-shaming).

That Katniss overlooks this possibility is especially indicative of two things—Panem's traditional gender expectations vis-à-vis males and sex, and the extent to which victors, especially Finnick, have been marketed by the Capitol as hedonistic sexual beings. It is especially telling given that Katniss shows previously that she has an understanding of indentured bondage: she remarks in *Catching Fire* that Head Peacekeeper Cray is unpopular in District 12 because he is a frequent customer of girls and women driven to prostitution by the institutional disparity of the Seam:

> "Cray would have been disliked, anyway, because of the uniform he wore, but it was his habit of luring starving young women into his bed for money that made him an object of loathing in the district . . . Had I been older when my father died, I might have been among them."[CF114]

In terms of exploitation, Panem is a deeply corrupt country. The sexual violence of human trafficking is proof of that . . . but so are the Games' opening ceremonies. Is it really any wonder that a country that revels in seeing tributes under the age of eighteen paraded around the streets of the Capitol wearing nothing but a smattering of coal dust would also not be averse to buying a sixteen-year-old (or fourteen-year-old, like new victor Finnick) for sex?

It seems from the text that this sexually objectifying attitude is pervasive and commonplace—even in the districts, given Katniss' matter-of-fact tone when discussing Cray. That Katniss remarks with surprise that Cinna does not touch her nude body on their first consultation before the Seventy-fourth Games illustrates how clearly she had expected to be abused or assaulted by the Capitol's citizens, and further comments on the lack of physical privacy in Panem, for district residents if not necessarily for the people of the Capitol. Yet Katniss still did not guess the truth about how Finnick (and, likely, other victors) were treated; she sees Finnick more as a denizen of the Capitol than as a person, a man from District 4—a victim, exploited like her.

Exploitation, Fashion, and Appearance

Finnick's story is the most overt example of exploitation that takes place in the Capitol, but it's not the only one. Victors' bodies are sold as a luxury good in Panem, in a way that is not so far from how celebrities' appearances are "sold" today, to sell magazines and to sell goods like fast food, cosmetic products, and cars. It's a practice that contributes to a fundamental set of beliefs about the human body vis-à-vis marketability or salability:

> The human body is now a product . . . so we buy and sell ourselves, constantly remake our bodies, blindly believing we are "improving" them. This commercial exploitation of the body has become a norm; once normalized in a society, it's taken for granted.[liv]

The Hunger Games are a fundamental part of the Capitol's economy, and one of the major currencies of Capitol society is beauty. There's a reason stylists play such a large role in the Games; the people of the Capitol identify with, and root harder for (and therefore, pay more to sponsor), attractive tributes than unattractive, district-identifiable ones. Katniss and Peeta succeed in large part because Cinna and Portia have altered their appearance in a way that strikes a chord with the Games' viewers.

In the Capitol, the way standards of attractiveness are determined is deeply, narcissistically self-referential: tributes are styled and transformed to resemble their Capitol audience, but once they win, the victors become celebrities on whom the members of that Capitol audience model themselves. It creates a cycle of dissatisfaction in which Capitol citizens must strive (and buy) to attain a standard of beauty that is fundamentally incompatible with a Capitol lifestyle. The result is a widespread cultural dissatisfaction with the body that one can assume fuels the Capitol's economy the same way our own bodily dissatisfaction does ours.

At a party in the Capitol in *Catching Fire*, Peeta very nearly drinks from an emetic cocktail. Although many past Western cultures thought being fat was ideal because it demonstrated affluence, Panem clearly views thinness as ideal. Why? Quite possibly because their idols, the victors, have never gotten enough food to become fat. This element of Capitol culture mirrors our own contemporary US culture far more than the Roman culture suggested by the gladiatorial customs, government system, and Capitolite characters' names. At Capitol parties, socially acceptable bulimia is used not only to stay thin but also to binge more consistently on the food taken away from those who are forced to take out tesserae in the districts—like Katniss herself.

This dual exploitation of the body—both self-inflicted, of those within the Capitol, to achieve social norms, and government-enforced, of the socioeconomically disenfranchised outside—is perhaps the most salient image of how far-reaching the exploitation in Panem may be. Victors—many of whom are sold—are modeled on people who themselves are modeled on other victors . . . who were in the Hunger Games because they had to take out tesserae, because the food stores produced in their districts were sent instead to the Capitol . . . where people make themselves vomit simply to be able to eat more food at parties for victors.

The Capitol obsession with body modification is a further method of illustrating the Capitol's preoccupation with "attractiveness" and the importance placed on adhering to its beauty standards. Octavia, Tigris, and Cinna are all examples. Cinna "concedes to Capitol vanity" with only his gold eyeliner ("applied with a light hand"); Octavia dyes her entire body a shade of pale pea-green and, in *Mockingjay*, does not know how to behave or present herself in a society that doesn't agree that such a cosmetic procedure is "beautiful." Although both Cinna and Octavia fall within an "acceptable" range according to Capitol mores, Tigris does not. She has stepped over an arbitrary line delineating acceptable and not acceptable modification. She had her face stretched and tattooed with black and gold tiger stripes, and her nose flattened until it barely exists, forming a short snout. She also has surgically implanted whiskers—"longer than anyone else's in the Capitol"—as well as what Katniss describes as tawny eyes and a tiger's tail. She additionally acts much like a tiger, in the sense that she moves similar to a cat, moves her tail when she is angered, eats only raw meat, and growls. She speaks with a gravelly voice that sounds similar to a cat's purr.

Tigris demonstrates a less-discussed side of the Capitol's beauty-as-currency culture: the societal rejection of those who participate at extreme levels in this same culture of self-modification and body dysmorphia. Katniss arrives in the Capitol and is deemed "filthy" and "almost human" (by Flavius). Her natural body—a darker-skinned district body, specifically, untouched by the Capitol's expensive beauty processes and subject to Capitol bigotry—is so far from acceptable, in the eyes of the Capitol, as to be less than human. But someone like Tigris, who has gone out of her way to transform herself beyond the human, is deemed "too altered" to be desirable or marketable. (In the end, Tigris is fired from her job as a Games stylist because of her appearance.)

Although even in Panem one can "go too far," image marketing is a Capitol pastime of such prestige that it even influences the districts—especially on reaping day, when the need to impress the Capitol citizens is high. When Prim tells Katniss she looks beautiful in her mother's dress and braided hair on reaping day, Katniss tells us, "I look nothing like myself." For Katniss, not looking like herself leads to discomfort and something of a loss of sense of self—later, when she is allowed to wear her hair in her mother's signature braid as part of her official costume, she regains confidence and is comforted—but in the Capitol, not looking like oneself is a source of pride, social currency, and confidence.

The Capitol trend of dyeing the skin various nonhuman colors—Octavia's green being the most prominent example—also suggests further commentary on the race issues explored throughout the Hunger Games series. The citizens of the Capitol choose to dye their skin different colors as a sign of wealth while suppressing the liberty, safety, and equality of district citizens whose skin is naturally of "color." The fleeting scene in *Mockingjay* when Posy expresses affection for Octavia by stating "I think you'd be pretty in any color"[M63] is a strong statement about one of the major outcomes of the Second Rebellion: a Panem less divided along color lines. Young Posy's understanding of beauty as separate from skin color is a poignant illustration of hopes for Panem's future.

The Real Catwoman

Although Tigris is meant to show the absolute far edge of Capitol vanity, veering into the grotesque, she may not be a work of pure fiction. Given the time frame in which Collins was writing the series—presumably circa 2006–2008—it is likely that Tigris is based on a very real person, socialite Jocelyn Wildenstein.

Wildenstein spent more than $4 million on several silicone injections to her lips, cheek, and chin, along with a face-lift and eye reconstruction, in order to appear more "feline," much like Tigris. Also like Tigris with her tigerlike nose, Wildenstein's eyes were pulled up and back, giving them a more feline shape. She was known in the press in 2006–2010 as "The Real Catwoman" and "The Lion Queen," and in 2004 she was named "the world's scariest celebrity" on the British tabloid the *Daily Mail*'s website.

The Conspicuous Exclusion of Sexual and Gender Diversity

Some fans and civil rights bloggers have criticized the Hunger Games for its lack of open LGBTQAIP[3] characters. However, as Katniss' narration is so sexually naïve as to not even recognize her own sexuality, one could argue that Katniss just glossed over or did not recognize non-heteronormative sexualities in other characters. Also, Panem appears to

---

[3]Lesbian, Gay, Bisexual, Trans*(transgender, transsexual, transvestite)/Third Gender, Queer, Asexual/Agendered, Intersex, Pansexual

be a world without religious dogma or scripture, so our ideas of "sin," "vice," and "virtue" may not apply; it's a question whether non-heteronormative sexuality would be an issue at all in Panem. Troublingly, the only confirmed canonical examples of genderqueer/non-heteronormative sexual expression in Panem are Finnick's male clients. Are readers meant to infer that being gay is something that is only okay in the bad, bad Capitol?

There's certainly a variety of behavior discussed in the series. In May 2011, one eloquent essayist, Katybeth B., phrased her understanding of gender and sexuality in Panem as "a lot more fluid than in our society."[lv] From Finnick's list of "secrets" shared in *Mockingjay*, Capitol sexuality seems to follow very few of the mores of the contemporary United States. And contrary to the presentation of the tributes as either distinctly feminine-female or masculine-male, the Capitol citizens' aesthetic performance is not confined by contemporary gender standards. Flavius and Caesar Flickerman wear flamboyant makeup, Octavia and Tigris present as xenoqueer (nonhuman/humanoid/other-species), and Cressida shaves her head bald as a stylistic choice that, in our culture, is more commonly associated with the masculine. This gender presentation fluidity "combined with the hedonistic lifestyle of the Capitol, would suggest that everything from homosexuality (or casual homosexual behavior, at least, if not in a life choice sense) to androgyny to transvestitism is probably . . . commonplace."[lvi]

However, the presentation of non-heteronormative sexualities within the Hunger Games series is confined to the residents of the Capitol, who are, of course, meant to be seen largely as villains. This is problematic not only in the dichotomy it creates between the districts' and the Capitol's ways of life, but also in what the story, as a product of our culture, suggests about sexuality in our culture. Is the series really trying to say that any lifestyle outside of the heteronormative is as grotesque, exorbitantly performative, and immoral as the Capitol is meant to be seen?

That these forms of presentation are not found in the districts (or at least not District 12 per Katniss' description), but only in the

Capitol, suggests that in Panem, lifestyles outside of the normative—whether in terms of sex and gender, or unrelated aspects of appearance—are seen as valid only for those of significant socioeconomic stature. It's okay for Octavia to have colored skin, for example, because she bought it; it is not okay, in contrast, for Rue to have the dark brown skin because she was born with it. Trying to compare the two, in Panem, would likely be no more effective than comparing the behavior of intoxicated Capitol citizens at a party to Haymitch's drunkenness in the districts.

The Capitol, then, as Katybeth Mannix continues:

> definitely allows for a lot more freedom in terms of sexuality and genderqueerness than in our society, but in terms of [the acceptability of that behavior beyond the richest Capitol citizens]—and actual freedom in terms of queerness that doesn't adhere to traditional gender and/or aesthetic standards—I'm not sure there's much positive going on [in Panem]. Then again, there's not a ton of positive things going on there in our society at the moment in terms of the general media and public perception ("it's okay to be gay" isn't the same as "it's okay to be gay as long as you're a flaming drama queen who loves musical theatre and shopping or the butchiest butch on the softball team to ever wear flannel and a buzz cut)[lvii]

Just as with race and class, Panem's representation of sex and gender is both a product of its own national standards (while unique to each individual Panem citizen) and highly reflective of our world's—in an accurate, and unappealing, way. Panem's culture, like our own, casts sex and gender alongside race and class as quantifiable commodities to be used, traded, and sold for pleasure, pain, and profit. The validity of these sales are determined by social rank and aesthetic presentation, with outliers seen as repulsive or unworthy.

In the end, maybe Katniss is lucky to have been reaped into the Quarter Quell rather than have to complete the Capitol sham of her forced marriage to Peeta on national television, and have to engage in all that may well have entailed.

Subtextual Sexuality

One possible antidote to this problematic implication is the canonical—or at least demi-canonical—implication of a prior, consensual, fond relationship between Finnick and Cinna that some fans point to as evidence of positive homosexuality (or pansexuality) in Panem.

Katniss doesn't describe the characteristics of either man in great detail—she doesn't for most people—but she does say that both men have bronze or light brown hair and green eyes. Given that people of the same district tend to look like one another (based on the two apparently homogenous populations in District 12), this similarity could indicate that they are both from District 4.

In the lead-up to the Quarter Quell, Cinna made gold jewelry pieces to match or mirror Katniss' gold mockingjay pin, in order to subtly indicate ideological alliance for Katniss, Peeta, Haymitch—and, some readers argue, Finnick. (The gold bracelet Finnick wears into the arena resembles one Katniss had seen Haymitch wear; Katniss assumes it is the same bracelet, and Haymitch gave it to Finnick in order to signal to Katniss that the District 4 victor could be trusted [though she does initially consider that Finnick may have stolen it to trick her], but we don't necessarily know that's the case.) None of the other rebels in the Quell—Johanna, Beetee, Wiress, the morphlings, Blight, Chaff, Seeder, Cecelia, and Woof—had gold symbols to wear into the arena, which means that Cinna only made them for his actual clients . . . *and Finnick*. Even for a stylist, a handcrafted gold bracelet is a very intimate gift.

Before the Quell, during the interviews, Finnick reads a poem for "his one true love in the Capitol." This could have been intended as a tactic to appeal to sponsors, leaving his "love" unnamed so that all his past lovers in the audience could believe the poem was about them. But, as with Peeta's confession of loving Katniss the year before, it could also have been based on truth. Annie wasn't kidnapped by the Capitol until after the Quell, around the time that District 12 was being firebombed (which is why Finnick wanted so badly to go "get her in Four" on the hovercraft), so it couldn't have been her the poem was meant for. And he read it on the same night that Cinna debuted the dress that would spell his death, which Finnick knew he would do, since they'd already collaborated and Finnick had been given the bracelet.

Other than with Annie, Finnick probably didn't have much, if any, safe, sane, and consensual sex once he became a victor, and likely would have had a pretty skewed idea of love. A kind, nurturing, healthy relationship prior to the one with Annie is likely the only way that someone as abused and tortured as Finnick could really learn how to have the kind of kind, nurturing, healthy relationship we see between him and Annie in *Mockingjay*; many fans therefore assume there had to be a prior lover we didn't see.

Given how few truly kind, compassionate characters there are in the Hunger Games, especially around Finnick's age, and how few characters are ascribed color symbolism similar to his (something that is used so frequently in the series to show relationships between characters, as in the case of Rue and Thresh, Prim and the merchants, or Katniss and the Seam)—both men are represented by gold and green—the most likely candidate for that lover is Cinna.

District 4

Some of the most memorable and important characters in the Hunger Games—Finnick, Annie, and Mags—come from District 4, and that alone would make it worthy of a closer look. But District 4 is also uniquely important in the overall arc of the Hunger Games series. It's our (the readers') window to a richer understanding of Panem: through Katniss' interactions with the people who come from District 4 and their foreign (to her) customs, we receive several key details that reveal just how separate and isolated the disparate district cultures of Panem are.

District 4 Culture

We readers never "see" District 4, despite Katniss and Peeta stopping there on the Victory Tour. Its location is confirmed by Suzanne Collins to be "west," but that's the only concrete detail we are given. The "encroaching seas" mean that "west" would be something different for Panem than it is for us; the west coast of Katniss' world is required to be further east than California. Based on the likely changes to the oceanic borders and the characterization of the District 4 tributes and victors, District 4 most likely includes land in what is now Mexico.

The most suggestive clue that District 4's location is in the former site of Mexico is the way that Katniss characterizes Mags, the oldest living victor of the Hunger Games and Katniss' ally in the Quarter Quell. Mags was alive before the First Rebellion, if Katniss' estimate of her age as eighty-two is correct, and her speech is described as not only garbled but needing to be "translated" by Finnick. This could point to a stroke or some other medical issue that resulted in impaired speech (which Finnick would possess greater familiarity with, given his friendship with Mags), but Mags could also be unintelligible to Katniss because she is speaking another language: Spanish. In the Panem we see in the Hunger Games, everyone speaks the same language (possibly due to Capitol mandate or socially forced assimilation, compounded by the possible end of immigration). Katniss seems to have no idea that there ever were other languages, so her not recognizing Mags as speaking one is not so far-fetched.

Additionally, Mags' name could be a shortened form or derivation of either Margarita or Magdalena, both common Spanish names (the root of which means "pearl," which makes sense given District 4's relationship with the ocean).

If indeed District 4 is located on the former site of Mexico, then that may have implications not only for the content of District 4's culture but also for how much that culture differs from the other districts'. Due to their enforced separation, in particular since the First Rebellion, each district has developed its own specialty-specific culture. But most of the districts are in what is today the United States, and so (even without disregarding the importance of regional cultural variations), their origins would have been in US culture; District 4's would not. Because of the potentially unique perspective of District 4's citizens, as a result of the district's non-US location, District 4's tributes may be particularly suited to challenge Katniss' isolated Seam worldview and help her consider the validity of other lifestyles than her own.

Because the surviving District 4 victors become such prominent characters in *Catching Fire and Mockingjay*, we learn more about their culture than we do about most of the other districts', just from the ways they behave that are unfamiliar to Katniss' District 12 sensibilities.

The infamous (and fangirl-favorite) scene when Finnick gives Peeta CPR in *Catching Fire* is perhaps the most significant instance of culture shock that Katniss experiences:

> I'm stopped by the sight of Finnick kissing Peeta. And it's so bizarre, even for Finnick, that I stay my hand. No, he's not kissing him. He's got Peeta's nose blocked off but his mouth tilted open, and he's blowing air into his lungs. I can see this, I can actually see Peeta's chest rising and falling. Then Finnick unzips the top of Peeta's jumpsuit and begins to pump the spot over his heart with the heels of his hands. Now that I've gotten through my shock, I understand what he's trying to do.
>
> Once in a blue moon, I've seen my mother try something similar, but not often. If your heart fails in District 12, it's unlikely your family could get you to my mother in time, anyway . . . But Finnick's world is different. Whatever he's doing, he's done it before.[CF280-281]

Katniss marvels that each district seems to have not only their own strengths for the Games but their own way of life, predicated on where they live and what they must do to survive at home as well as in the arena.

Although Katniss had a cultural awakening earlier in the novel, in District 11—where she becomes aware that the Capitol and its Peacekeepers treat the districts differently (District 11 has barbed wire guard fences, stricter Peacekeepers, and harsher penalties than anything Katniss has seen in District 12)—this moment during the Quell is poignant for its innocence . . . and for its illustration of the Capitol's mistake in government. Rather than one unhappy populace, the Capitol has surrounded itself with "twelve" (thirteen) individual, insular—and angry—

nation-states that, once they find a way to bridge the divisions the Capitol enforces, *can only complement each other*, their individual strengths compensating for the others' weaknesses.

Katniss' increasing confidence in Finnick and Mags over the course of the Quarter Quell shows her growing trust in and openness to alliance with a culture other than the Seam's—something that, previously, as her rejection of potential allies from other districts (aside from Rue) and her initial refusal to ally with Peeta demonstrates, she had been at first totally unwilling and later, at best reluctant, to consider.

The CPR scene, and the expanded understanding it gives Katniss of the nuances and validity of other ethnicities and cultures, is a turning point in the series. It even happens almost exactly at the central apex of the trilogy's structure: in the middle third of the middle third of Collins' three-volume, three-act series. The fact that Katniss becomes able to see past their superficial differences and deeper cultural and ethnic differences—from District 4's reputation as a Career district to even, potentially, a foreign language—to their similarities is a monumental step for Katniss, and an important element of the eventual defeat of the Capitol.

Finnick and Annie

District 4 is easily the most popular district in fandom. Though this may be in part because of the role its victors play in Katniss', and our, dawning awareness of the greater world of Panem, it's also due admittedly to the fact that Finnick is, according to Katniss, "an amazing physical specimen"[CF275]—and the tragic timelessness of Finnick and Annie's romance.

Finnick and Annie's love story is a massive influence on Hunger Games fandom, second only to the fanaticism that Katniss and Peeta's relationship inspires. Yet Annie speaks only five lines in canon. She and Finnick are married (and alive) for less than a quarter of *Mockingjay*. What makes their story resonate so deeply?

One explanation is in the romanticism and, of course, tragedy of their tale. For the Quarter Quell, Katniss and Peeta's reaping is understood as being planned by Snow. Given that Annie was initially the female victor chosen during the District 4 reaping, which would have pitted her and Finnick against each other in the arena had Mags not volunteered in her place (and ostensibly against Panem's favorite love story, Katniss and Peeta), it is likely that her reaping was also planned. Their struggle against the Capitol, Annie's capture, torture, and subsequent rescue, their marriage and pregnancy, and Finnick's death during the rebellion give the Hunger Games novels—and their audience—the kind of star-crossed, sweeping romance that Katniss and Peeta fake for the Capitol audience.

But although fans are easily and understandably enamored with Finnick and Annie's tale, there's more to their story than the brave hero and his poor, mad girl waiting for him.

Many readers think of Annie only in terms of her impact on Finnick's story. Unlike Katniss and Johanna, she closely resembles the typical Western definition of "feminine," with outwardly passive behavior, the appearance of dependence on a male figure, and a personal narrative that includes both wedding/marriage and a pregnancy. But that doesn't make Annie any less strong a female character. She won an impossible, deadly Hunger Games (one that may have been designed to leave Panem without a victor at all, since the earthquake that broke the dam was carefully calculated by the Gamemakers), withstood torture, and continues to uphold Finnick's and her own beliefs, even after the Capitol takes Finnick from her.

Let's take a look at what we know about this only slightly developed, very mysterious character:

Annie was raised in a Career district. This would have had a large impact on how she ended up in the arena, whether or not she was a Career herself: either she volunteered or, for some reason, no one volunteered for her. The former suggests that she was neurotypical before the Games; the latter may suggest that her "madness" (as Katniss calls it) is a long-standing neuroatypicality. The latter also suggests that her reaping may have been arranged as a warning to Finnick, either for straying or threatening to break away from his indentured servitude in the Capitol.

Annie saw her district partner/ally decapitated and watched all of the other tributes drown while treading water for days. Her fellow district tribute's decapitation is the impetus to which Johanna and Peeta attribute her "going mad" when they relate the story to Katniss. (It is important for a fair and accurate analysis of Annie's character to note that this is never confirmed or stated by Annie, Mags, or Finnick; the "madness" that Katniss saw in Annie would be relative to Katniss' prior experience, which is more in the realm of depression and/or Down's syndrome [in Greasy Sae's granddaughter] than in seeing or understanding any other presentational disorders. Katniss may label Annie as "mad" only because she has no other words to describe Annie's state of being—and neither, it seems, does Panem as a whole.) But watching all of the other tributes drown—seeing water turned against her as a weapon—had to have been especially traumatic for someone from District 4, where the ocean is the main source of life and livelihood even in its danger.[4]

Annie is aware of her significant other's abuse as a trafficked slave.

Annie survived losing her natural family. Johanna tells Katniss that Annie, Finnick, and Mags are each other's only family by the time of the events in *Catching Fire*. This would imply that either before or after Annie's victory in the Games, her family died. If they died before

---

[4]Side note: In fandom, it is widely believed that the location of the arena moves from Hunger Games to Hunger Games, in part because Katniss doesn't know where the arena/s are located and in part because they are each so different. Using just one location and redesigning it from scratch seems like a waste of resources, when the Capitol has access to all the many and varied locations they could want. If the arenas are all close to the Capitol, which they seem to be given the single day's travel Katniss describes from the training center during the two she is in, then, geographically, the dam that broke during the Seventieth Games very well could have been the Hoover Dam.

her victory, it may have involved significant childhood trauma that could explain much of her "madness." If they died after her victory, it could be further evidence that her reaping was planned in order to punish Finnick for some transgression, and that she was not intended to survive.

Annie is reaped a second time for the Quarter Quell. This, as noted previously, was likely no coincidence. If District 4 is indeed a Career district, then it would stand to reason that there were far more than three victors in their Quell reaping ball—and yet Finnick and Annie, a pair of lovers the Capitol doubtless knew about from their eavesdropping bugs and close monitoring of Finnick, were chosen. Had Mags not volunteered, this would have jeopardized the execution of the Quell plot, because given the choice between saving Annie and saving Peeta or Katniss, it's difficult to believe Finnick wouldn't choose Annie. Additionally, having a second set of lovers in the Quell would have split sponsor focus from Katniss and Peeta and made their survival more difficult.

Annie loses the only two people she has in the world to the Quell. She knows they will probably both die, and indeed watches Mags die on television.

Annie is kidnapped and tortured by the Capitol for rebel information. People forget that Annie was there, too, right alongside Peeta and Johanna and Enobaria. And that when she was delivered to District 13, *she was naked.* The others weren't. She's the significant other of Finnick Odair, and whoever was detaining them in the Capitol kept Annie naked. The implications of that, considering what we learn about Finnick's abuse, are one of the most frightening aspects of *Mockingjay.*

Annie loses many of the people she knows, and her connections to Finnick's life, to the purge of victors, and then loses Finnick, too.

Despite all this, and despite Katniss' (wholly unprofessional and uneducated) assessment of "madness," after the retrieval of the captured victors from the Capitol, Annie is the most stable refugee. Although the majority of the Hunger Games series characters seem to fall apart during *Mockingjay* (due to illness, trauma, death, or a combination of any of the three), Annie grows and flourishes. Johanna and Peeta are deeply traumatized—obviously—after their torture, but Annie is strong. She holds herself together, and, one could argue, does so because she knows that Finnick needs her to. *She* takes care of *him* there. And even after losing Finnick, Annie still upholds her moral ideals and votes against a Capitol Hunger Games, even though, arguably, she is the one there who has lost the most.

Annie Cresta is not just a poor, mad girl back home. She is not this little pitiable creature who exists to make Finnick more tragic. She has her own story. We are told less of it than we are of Finnick's, but that doesn't make it smaller. Annie *is* the war widow, but she's also a prisoner of war, a child gladiator, a veteran. People forget that Annie is a victor. Whether she won with or without violence, she still survived, and survival is an impressive, impressive battle story unto itself.

People give Johanna, whose original Games were also glossed over, much more credit as a soldier than they do Annie. People remember Johanna's toughness because "there's no one left that she loved,"[CF259] but in the end, Annie has no one, either. And Annie has to go forward alone to have and raise a baby in a totally broken, third-world country, in a district that used to *train its children to be killers*. That is the world Annie grew up in, and we know that, despite this, she understood that it was wrong, and still had the idealism and optimism to refuse to let it happen again.

When Finnick was in the Quarter Quell, being tortured by the Capitol, Annie was the poor, mad girl back home. But when Annie was naked in a cell in the Capitol, being tortured for information she didn't have, Finnick was the poor, mad boy back "home" in District 13.

They're equals. And that's what makes their story one of the most compelling parts of the Hunger Games trilogy.

Trauma, Disability, and Cultural Context

Finnick and Annie both—along with Mags—are also amazing examples of strong characters with special needs.

Mags' and Annie's conditions are, in contrast, likely more physiological than psychological. The explanation for Mags' slurred speech, limp, and sunken, slack face is most likely what Katniss suggests in the text—that she's had a stroke[CF232]—but Annie's are more complicated. Many fans ascribe Annie's "mad" behavior solely to Post-Traumatic Stress Disorder, but compared to Katniss and Johanna, who are more clear-cut cases of PTSD, Annie's behavior more closely resembles the stims and echolalia of an autism spectrum disorder than PTSD alone.

I asked Dr. Elizabeth Soehngen to take a look at Annie's display behaviors and character background (what little we know of it). She suggested the following possible explanations for Annie's outward characteristics:

- An autism spectrum disorder, pre-existing the Games, which most typifies her visible behaviors such as hand-flapping, rocking, and covering her ears.
- Schizophrenia #1, manifesting around the time of her Games but not caused by them, since schizotypal disorders often manifest towards the end of puberty (around the age that Annie was likely reaped [likely seventeen or eighteen]). Schizophrenia would best account for Annie's atypical speech and listening patterns and reliance on Finnick's voice.
- PTSD, caused by the Games.
- Brain damage by drowning asphyxia, caused by the Games.

She goes on to explain that PTSD alone actually explains the fewest of her display behaviors:

PTSD is often considered an anxiety disorder like OCD. Both disorders feature intrusive thoughts or feelings of fear that seriously disrupt normal life, and both have been shown to respond well to desensitization treatments. Patients will usually report that they know their fears are excessive or unfounded, and the compulsions that characterize OCD are often recognized as disruptive or even absurd. Anxiety disorders are typically considered to be a disruption of the sympathetic nervous system (the "fight-or-flight" response) caused or exacerbated by certain illogical thoughts or beliefs, a position supported by their favorable response to cognitive therapy paired with relaxation techniques.[lviii]

Although Annie is sometimes triggered by mentions or visuals of traumatic events, her thoughts do not appear to manifest or dwell on memories of her own trauma, as they would if she were suffering from post-traumatic stress. (At one point, Katniss infers that Annie is "lost in a daze of happiness"[M240] when she loses her concentration on conversations around her.)

PTSD and anxiety disorders are often treatable with time and therapy, but the other possible explanations for Annie's condition are not.[lix] If Annie has a trauma disorder brought on by her experience in the Hunger Games, then not only is she no more "mad" than any other victor, but her condition could improve with as much success as anyone else's. However, if her condition is genetic, something she was born with, then it is more difficult to measure the effect that the Hunger Games really had on her psyche. Given that her symptoms don't clearly align with PTSD and anxiety disorders, it seems more likely that Annie's condition predates the Hunger Games.

To demonstrate the breadth of potential explanations for Annie's "madness" and the disparate natures of those explanations, Dr. Soehngen also made this helpful Venn diagram:

DISTRICT 4

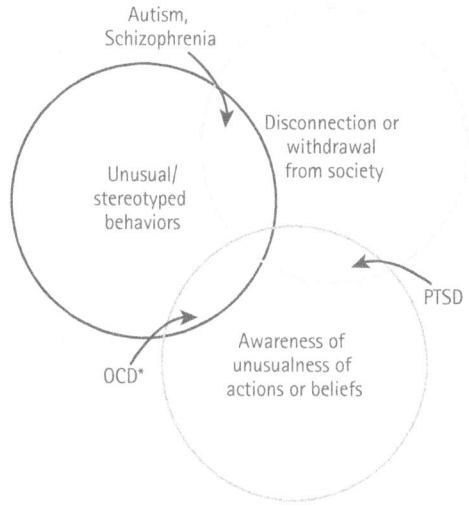

```
            Autism,
          Schizophrenia
                │
                ▼
                        Disconnection or
                         withdrawal
   Unusual/               from society
  stereotyped
   behaviors

                                    PTSD
      OCD*          Awareness of
                   unusualness of
                   actions or beliefs
```

*You could also put OCD in the very middle, although in the case of OCD, withdrawal tends to be a side effect of the sufferer's behavior and not a symptom of the disorder itself.

If we look at these characters' disabilities in terms of District 4's location in present-day Mexico, the potential cultural retention of Mexican attitudes vis-à-vis mental health suggests some interesting conclusions about how both Annie's and Mags' appear to others in District 4 and in Panem as a whole, as well as how others receive them. (Given her age, Mags in particular seems most likely to carry on traditions or values that we would recognize as Mexican.) According to research psychologists at the University of Buffalo:

> In the Mexican culture, there is no clear separation of physical and mental illnesses. It is believed that there must be a balance between the individual and environment, otherwise one may get a disease. . . . Shame may be associated with genetic defects. Physical disability is usually more accepted than mental disabilities.
>
> In general, disability in the Mexican culture is viewed as . . . punishment for something one has done. Physical disability is more accepted than a mental disability, probably

because . . . in general, a physical disability is viewed as "normal."[lx]

Given that Mags' disability is most likely the result of a stroke, her situation may have been considered more acceptable within District 4 culture. She would have been able to retain her visibility as a Games mentor and her access to other victors because her status would have been understood as a natural aspect of aging. (Finnick's insistence on carrying her as much as physically possible in the Quarter Quell may even be another example of the retention of Mexican cultural values regarding familial elders.[lxi])

In contrast, Annie's mental disability may have been treated much the same way in District 4 as Katniss privately regards it in her narrative: as "madness," something strange and vaguely frightening . . . or, at the least, out of the ordinary and to be watched carefully. It is also possible that although Katniss cannot name or attribute Annie's symptoms or display behaviors to a recognizable disorder or disability within her own District 12 culture, District 4's culture, in contrast, may have retained a traditional Mexican cultural label like "the evil eye"[lxii] or "shock"[lxiii] for her state. Despite Annie's condition being as natural as Mags' and, of course, equally as affected by genetics as by her time in the Hunger Games, we can assume that Mags was more likely to be accepted in both District 4 and Panem as a whole because her afflictions were more familiar and more easily understood. (And the fact that Finnick was able to understand Annie's temperament and nurture a relationship with her despite that extra hurdle may speak to a larger breadth of interpersonal experience. Because he had so much contact with people of other districts and cultures, he may have developed a higher cultural sensitivity than most of Panem's citizens.)

What Finnick, Mags, and Annie's conditions provide, in the context of the Hunger Games, is the same thing District 4 does overall: a greater sense of awareness of Panem and the impact of the Games than Katniss or District 12 alone can give us. All three victors help communicate the breadth of trauma the Games are responsible for; Finnick and Annie's stories in particular give us a window into the depth of the Capitol and Snow's depravity, coercion, and abuse. And the cultural differences help us understand, even before the rebellion, not just the diversity of Panem but also the potential Panem holds, once united, to change things for the better.

10

Mythology and Music in Panem

The Hunger Games wears its Roman allusions on its sleeve, from the name Panem (Latin for *bread*, from the phrase *panem et circenses* or "bread and circuses") and the Roman gladiatorial system discussed previously to the names of its Capitol citizens, which allude to figures in Roman history, particularly those included in Shakespeare's interpretation of Julius Caesar. However, although the majority of the allusions in the trilogy hail from the history of Rome, other historical and cultural practices make significant contributions to Panem's narrative mythos. Greek mythology and American folktale and oral tradition play a role in the Hunger Games series as well.

Greek Mythology

One of the most enduring—or at least most famous—Greek myths is the story of Theseus slaying the Minotaur.

In one version of the tale, King Minos of Crete, having waged and won a war against the Athenians, demands as victor that, every seven or nine years (depending on the version of the myth), seven Athenian boys and seven Athenian girls were to be sent to his palace, as tribute, to be devoured by the Minotaur.

. . . Sound familiar?

Theseus, like Katniss—and the Careers—volunteers himself to take the place of one of the youths in order to enter the labyrinth and slay the minotaur, and thereby ends the reign of tyranny. In fact, Suzanne Collins told *School Library Journal* in 2010, just before *Mockingjay*'s release, that "Theseus and the Minotaur is the classical setup for where *The Hunger Games* begins, you know, with the tale of Minos in Crete . . . as an eight-year-old, [I was] horrified that Crete was so cruel . . . in her own way, Katniss is a futuristic Theseus."[lxiv]

Theseus is one of the "founder demigods," one whose stories are tied into *synoikismos* or the founding or renovation of cities—in Theseus' case, Athens—and the monsters he fights in various myths are, like the struggles Katniss faces, most closely identified with social order (and religion, although religion doesn't exist in Panem). Like Theseus with Athens, Katniss helped to forge a new Panem, and also fits Theseus' moniker, "the great reformer." Theseus and the *synoikismos* of Athens are represented in myth as his "journey of labors," felling monsters and beasts—just as Katniss and other tributes-cum-victors like Beetee, Finnick, Haymitch, and Johanna help unify their nation through taking down political monsters, like Snow and Finnick's abusers, and battling literal monsters in the form of mutts in both arenas and during the Second Rebellion.

Theseus is not the only Greek figure that Katniss evokes. Our bow-and-arrow expert could also be seen as a modern take on the goddess Artemis, the hunter, who immortalizes her beloved dead with constellations (as Katniss memorializes Rue with flowers). The "virgin goddess," Artemis was said to have sworn off men and romance in favor of the hunt—just as "pure"[CF216] Katniss has "better things to worry about than kissing!" Artemis was also known as the "Phaesporia," or the light-bringer, and the bird goddess; Katniss plays a messianic role in Panem, bringing intellectual enlightenment to the Capitol audience and judicial enlightenment to the districts, as the Mockingjay. Artemis also had a kinship with Pan, the god of the forests and wild things, just as Katniss has an extraordinary connection to nature and finds refuge in the wild. If Katniss is an allusion to Artemis, then Gale could play the role of Orion, Artemis' hunting companion and soul mate, who was later either killed or exiled, depending on the version of the myth, and who Artemis cast into the stars in her grief. (This role could also go to Rue, again in the case of her memorialization with flowers.)

The story of Finnick Odair also finds a reflection in Greek myth. Finnick's arc in the Hunger Games series almost perfectly mirrors Odysseus' journey over the course of the *Illiad* and *Odyssey*: he is victorious in battle (the Games) but is not allowed to return home (District 4) to his wife; he has to escape the alleged paradise of the Island of the Lotus Eaters (the Capitol) and is threatened by the Laistrygones and evil witch–queen Circe (Snow); he is forced to endure and must escape the sexual perversions of the Sirens (Capitol citizens, his sex slavery); he has to make his way home between the monsters of Scylla and Charybdis (his choice between slavery and torture in the Capitol or the death of Annie, Mags, and his family if he fails to comply with Snow's wishes); and he goes to Hades and back to find his wife again (the Quarter Quell and the retrieval of Annie from the Capitol). Further evidence of Finnick's connection to the *Iliad* and *Odyssey* is his chosen talent of poetry.

Finnick himself, however, most notably mirrors the myth of Ganymede, the water-bearer. Spotted by Zeus for his beauty, just as Finnick was immediately a favorite for his looks during his first Games, Ganymede is kidnapped (often called "the rape of Ganymede") and given immortality on Olympus. There, he is doomed to bear water or nectar to the gods until they tire of him and find another boy more beautiful, just as Finnick is sentenced to serve his Capitol "admirers"/ sexual abusers.

Finnick can also be tied to other, similar stories of kidnap, capture, or loss, including the tale of Persephone, who must spend her winters in the underworld with Hades, as his bride, while spending her summers happily at home with her mother. Finnick must similarly divide his time between the Capitol, under Snow, and in District 4's temperate, subtropical, summerlike climate, happily with Annie and Mags. Seen in this way, President Snow represents the figure of Hades; the Capitol his home, the underworld; and its citizens the soulless ghosts that inhabit the underworld's Fields of Asphodel.

Like another figure of Greek myth, Orpheus, Finnick is a poet and a romantic. As described in a classic anthology of Greek myths, "The major stories about [Orpheus] are centered on his ability to charm all living things and . . . his attempt to retrieve his wife, Eurydice, from the underworld; and his death at the hands of those who could not hear his divine music."[lxv] Similarly, Finnick was famous for his charm throughout Panem and used his voice and words to bring his future wife, Annie, back, not only from her flashbacks in *Mockingjay* but from her torture cell in the Capitol.

There's one more character who especially parallels a character from Greek myth: Haymitch, who is reminiscent of other modern takes on Dionysus—most notably *Percy Jackson and the Olympians*' Mr. D, a modern variation of Dionysus himself in the modern age—where the god is depicted as a crass alcoholic with untold cleverness. Dionysus bears the epithet *Eleutherios* ("the liberator") for helping free people from their normal selves (usually with wine)—a title that could be given to Haymitch, as well, for his role in the rebellion.

American Folk Music

Music plays a crucial role in each of the novels in the Hunger Games series, as well as in our understanding of its characters and their relationship to Panem. In the first book, Katniss and Rue communicate, and communicate their alliance, through music—Rue's four-note song—and Rue's last request is for Katniss to sing to her, illustrating the importance of music to the series: it is both soothing and stirring, a way to communicate both camaraderie and rebellion. Mockingjays, who can imitate any song and any voice, are a hallmark motif of the series, and in the final book of the series, as Katniss sings to soothe Pollux, the mockingjays join her in a "freaky"[Mjl26] chorus of the song Katniss learned from her father, "The Hanging Tree," once again illustrating the power of music to at once both calm others and rouse them to anger.

"The Hanging Tree" is a lament of lost love, about a man who works in the orchards and loves a crop-working woman. He watches out for her every day, but one day she doesn't come; he discovers that she has been hanged from one of his orchard's trees. The song is most often construed by readers as a social comment on lynching in Panem, as it is very similar lyrically and thematically to the 1939 Billie Holiday song "Strange Fruit," which uses the imagery of orchard trees to comment on lynching. However, during the Second Rebellion, "The Hanging Tree" also serves a purpose similar to the one served by songs such as "Follow the Drinking Gourd" in the antebellum plantation society in the same geographical area: as a covert sign of noncompliance and cultural identity.

Across much of the Hunger Games, both in District 12 and District 11 as well as during the Second Rebellion, the emotional resonance of music appears intended to be evocative of "slave songs" or "Songs of Freedom." According to Allana Gillam-Wright, a journalist and historian of Canadian black history, these songs were "seemingly innocent . . . [but] more than simple hymns of endurance and a belief in a better afterlife. As sung by slaves and their descendants, the spirituals allowed the slaves to communicate secret messages and information to each other."[lxvi] Although the traditional slave spirituals such as "Follow the Drinking Gourd" and "The Gospel Train's A-Comin'" commonly communicated literal directions towards stops on the Underground Railroad, the songs in the Hunger Games are more referential of personal narratives—perhaps, given that interdistrict communication in Panem is not possible through letters, digital communiqués, or speech, songs gave district citizens a way to share their stories about the Capitol's cruelty.

Darling Nelly Gray

Katniss ruminates on the factual basis for "The Hanging Tree" in *Mockingjay*, when she explains the history of lynching in District 12 and theorizes that the song's history made her mother consider the song dangerous. Was "The Hanging Tree" based, in the world of the Hunger Games, on a true story?

A lesser-known slave spiritual in our world, "Darling Nelly Gray," was based on a true story about lost love:

> the story of two young lovers whose romance ended when Nelly was sold and taken to a plantation far away from that of her young man, Ned.
>
> The two had planned to escape together to Canada and then to Owen Sound. Ned and Nelly lived on plantations close to each other. Due to the plantation owners' practice of keeping slaves segregated, they met through an intermediary, an old Scottish professor. The professor was to help Ned escape to Canada, with a small amount of money and food. Ned was to find work, make enough money—$200—to send to the professor, who would purchase Nelly's freedom and send her on to Canada to be with Ned.
>
> However, on the night before the plan went into action, Nelly disappeared. Upon some careful enquiring, Ned discovered a stranger had visited the plantation, leading one empty horse. He looked over the selection of slaves, made Nelly his choice, and paid a substantial amount of money for her purchase. As no one recognized him, it was believed he was from a fair distance away and tracing Nelly's whereabouts would be impossible. To complicate matters, slaves were known by their owners' names, not their own, i.e., Jim Thompon's Joe, So and So's Maggie, and so on. Nelly would have a new name in her new home.
>
> To express his and Ned's sadness, the professor composed a little verse, and then added a melody. Sung sorrowfully by his glee club, it soon became very popular and he eventually added

more lyrics to create a full-blown song. The sheet music was soon for sale on newsstands, and, not long after, was sung, whistled, and hummed in every state.

The song even had a role in politics: many historians believe it "was a major force in shaping public opinion on the issue of slavery, leading to the election of Abraham Lincoln as President of the United States in 1860."[lxvii]

"The Hanging Tree" holds personal significance for Katniss because of its connection to her father. But the reaction Katniss remembers her mother having upon hearing her husband and daughter singing it—panic—suggests that the song held other, more dangerous meanings as well. Given that Mr. Everdeen also spoke openly about the unfairness of the Capitol's Games–tesserae system, it's possible to infer that the song is in some way connected to the rebellion, and serves a political purpose not unlike that of "Darling Nelly Gray." (Mr. Everdeen's potential connections to the rebellion are further explored in chapter twelve.)

* * *

Suzanne Collins has succeeded, with Panem, in creating a nation that is wholly its own, but by building this new, futuristic world around familiar heroes, morals, and tales from our own world, she has made Panem also unmistakably the product of its Western heritage and the millennia of tradition that came before it—and therefore more accessible and resonant for a contemporary audience.

This technique, in which pieces of our world are used to make Panem feel at the same time both familiar and new, is never more clearly in play than in the district we have seen the most of, after Katniss' own: District 11.

District 11

District 11 is one of the few places in Panem that we see firsthand through the Hunger Games novels. Although Katniss relates and infers information about District 4 and we see the ruins of a war-torn District 8 and the Nut in District 2, *Catching Fire* brings us directly into the main square of District 11, where we see the populace of the district, its layout and aesthetics, and its relationship to the Capitol (through its reaction to the Victory Tour and the Peacekeepers' reactions to the District 11 protesters). The amount of time that the novels spend in District 11, compounded by the importance of the roles played by citizens of District 11—Rue, Thresh, Chaff, and Seeder, as well as the protesters in the Victory Tour riot—makes it clear that District 11 is vitally important to the Hunger Games trilogy and Panem itself.

Our first pieces of information about District 11 come from Rue, in the conversations she and Katniss have in the arena. Rue describes her home district as "strict," a place with enforced public whippings, constant hard work for all citizens—including children—and harsh punishments by the Peacekeepers. But even her descriptions did not prepare Katniss for her first glimpse of the district itself, during the Victory Tour:

> Rue did give me the impression that the rules in District 11 were more harshly enforced. But I never imagined something like this.
> Now the crops begin, stretched out as far as the eye can see. Men, women, and children wearing straw hats to keep off the sun straighten up, turn our way . . . small communities of shacks—by comparison the houses in the Seam are upscale—spring up here and there, but they're all deserted. Every hand must be needed for the harvest.[CF55]

District 11 reads as a direct slavery allegory. They seem to be alone among the districts in not having a merchant class: instead, their only light-skinned citizens seem to be the Peacekeepers (who are all white in District 12, and so also, we infer, in Panem at large) who rule from guard towers and are quick to fire their weapons. Many times larger than District 12, District 11 is located in the Deep South, with its Justice Building in what seems to be the ruins of either Atlanta, Georgia, or New Orleans, Louisiana; Katniss describes a crumbling arena that might be the Georgia Dome or the Superdome. District 11 specializes in agriculture, the growing of cereal crops and orchard produce, and given the particular focus on fruit orchards, it's more likely that District 11 is intended to be Georgia, the Peach State.

Another subtle clue to District 11's potential antebellum ties and southern location is something Katniss says about how the district is described in Panem's education system:

> In school they refer to it as a large district, that's all. No actual figures on the population.[CF55]

From 1787–1865, slaves in the United States—located primarily in the South—were counted as only three-fifths of a person each in census counts; further, "slaves were enumerated on all federal census records, 1790–1860, but not by name. From the 1870 census, the researcher should proceed backwards to the 1860 and 1850 separate slave schedules that list, under the name of the owner, each slave by sex, specific age, and color only; no slave names are given."[lxvii] However, detailed personal records were kept by slaveowners of the number and condition of their slaves because they were legally considered their property. Although the Capitol clearly keeps track of District 11's population between the ages of twelve and eighteen, at least, for the reaping, the lack of population counts for District 11 in Panem—according to Katniss, at least—implies that District 11 operates similarly. This lack of population figures may indicate that the Capitol views District 11's citizens as an expendable resource: it is the largest district, with the most people, and the Peacekeepers there do not seem shy about killing them for rule infractions. The citizens of District 11 may be seen by the Capitol as their property, to be used and disposed of as needed, even more so than the rest of the districts.

Other District 11 allusions to slavery are more overt: every day, for twelve hours at no pay, the people work the fields to send food off to the Capitol. They are allowed only meager rations of what they harvest, and Katniss surmises that its citizens begin work at a much younger age than in District 12; certainly Rue, at twelve, already has a position of some responsibility in the fields as the human dinner bell. (Her job is one that would have made her well known, or even well loved, to the viewers back in her home district, though clearly not so beloved that anyone was willing to volunteer in her place. It was also a job that ends up working to her advantage in the Games by giving her an inimitable skill, which would have been a by-product unexpected by the Capitol akin to Katniss' starvation in District 12 teaching her to forage and hunt. The poor conditions of the districts helped to train tributes for survival in the arena.)

Then, of course, there are also the visual racial markers these characters are assigned by Katniss as she encounters them—markers that feel familiar to us as racial identifiers in ways that the Seam's visual markers are not but still ambiguous enough to leave the dominant District 11 race/ethnicity open to our interpretation:

> And most hauntingly, a twelve-year-old girl from District 11. She has dark brown skin and eyes, but other than that, she's very like Prim in size and demeanor.[THG45]

Like the unclear, mixed racial background of the Seam one district over, the specialty class of District 11 is described ambiguously. "Dark hair and dark skin" could indicate Latin American, Native American, South Asian, or East Indian/Pakistani descent just as easily as African American heritage. However, given the parallels between the district and the antebellum South, it seems likely that they are intended to be of African or African Caribbean descent. Regardless of the depth of skin tone or equivalent contemporary ethnicity, it is clear from the text that District 11 citizens have the darkest skin in Panem, and their tributes' lack of support from Capitol sponsors—as well as the brutal nature of the Peacekeepers' treatment and an institutional poverty even greater than that of the Seam—imply that District 11 is considered Other to a degree that the districts that include white-skinned merchant classes are not.

Culturally, District 11 presents both a subtle and, at times, overt amalgamation of details of the African American experience that have been appropriated and transformed into a recognizable, if fairly stereotype-reliant identity, not unlike the Native American allusions we see in Katniss. In other words, the series plays on traditional Western stereotypes of the African American experience so that readers will more clearly understand the role that District 11 and its citizens play in Panem. Peeta noted that the signature bread from this district was a crescent-moon-shaped roll dotted with seeds. These may be intended to resemble benne (or sesame) seeds, which are believed to have been brought to America by West African slaves and are used in customs representative of good luck or good fortune in the Deep South, particularly among the descendants of freed slaves in North Carolina. Rue's burial in flowers and music may be an allusion to New Orleans–style funerary customs, which include the use of flowers and bright colors, as a celebration of life over death, as well as music. The orchards, again, are reminiscent of Georgia, while the grain fields "stretched as far as the eye can see"[CF55] suggest Virginia.[lxix]

Perhaps the clearest connection between District 11 and African American cultural history is in the oppression perpetrated on District 11's citizens by the Capitol and Peacekeepers, especially the violent response to their peaceful protest during Katniss and Peeta's Victory Tour. The themes here in District 11 echo Dr. Martin Luther King, Jr.'s "I Have a Dream" speech, especially in how, another few centuries later in Panem, very little has changed:

> One hundred years later, the Negro still is not free. One hundred years later, the life of the Negro is still sadly crippled by the manacles of segregation and the chains of discrimination. One hundred years later, the Negro lives on a lonely island of poverty in the midst of a vast ocean of material prosperity. One hundred years later, the Negro is still languishing in the corners of American society and finds himself an exile in his own land.[lxx]

Although the Victory Tour riot might be the first thing that comes to mind when one thinks of a show of Capitol violence against innocents in District 11, Rue relates an anecdote to Katniss during their time in the Seventy-fourth Games that exemplifies the horrific conditions under which District 11's citizens lived. The moment is so fleeting that many fans forget it entirely. However, this may well be the incident that gives Katniss "the impression" that life in District 11 is harsher than in District 12: the calculated execution of Martin, a handicapped child, by the Peacekeepers, after he mistakenly attempted to keep a piece of Capitol property.

> "These aren't for sun, they're for darkness," exclaims Rue. "Sometimes, when we harvest through the night, they'll pass out a few pairs . . . one time, this boy Martin, he tried to keep his pair. Hid it in his pants. They killed him on the spot."

> "They killed a boy for taking these?" I say.
> "Yes, and everyone knew he was no danger. Martin wasn't right in the head. I mean, he still acted like a three-year-old. He just wanted the glasses to play with," says Rue.
> Hearing this makes me feel like District 12 is some sort of safe haven . . . I can't imagine the Peacekeepers murdering a simpleminded child.^{THG204-205}

In District 12, Capitol-led violent atrocities (Gale's whipping, the crackdown on the Hob that effectively accounted for forced starvation of many Seam families) start only after the rumblings of the Second Rebellion begin; in District 11, obeisance to the Capitol and Peacekeepers is a much more immediate matter of life and death, given that not only starvation but beatings and executions are already common occurrences. It is no wonder that District 11 is one of the first to overthrow the Capitol and take control of its own resources during the Second Rebellion in *Mockingjay*. Martin Luther King, Jr.'s statement on the nature of freedom and racial equality seems an apropos description of the civil unrest that led to the Victory Tour uprising:

> We can never be satisfied as long as the Negro is the victim of the unspeakable horrors of police brutality.[lxxi]

It's a quote that further demonstrates the rights leader's appropriateness as likely inspiration for giving the name "Martin" to the symbol of injustices done to District 11.

Race and racial cooperation appears many times in the Hunger Games, from Katniss and Peeta to Haymitch and Maysilee, Mr. Everdeen and Mrs. Everdeen, and Katniss and Cinna. But the key moment of cooperation across racial lines, the moment that most visibly rocked Panem itself, was that of Katniss and Rue. Katniss herself memorializes this relationship, as well as her gratitude for and "life debt" to Thresh, on the Victory Tour for the Seventy-fourth Games, and it is what leads to the violent riot that signifies the official start of the Second Rebellion in the districts, despite prior protests in Districts 8 and 4. This presents a marked contrast to the initial stages of battle in District 2, where skin is presumably lighter (extrapolating from the Capitol's heavy preference for District 2 tributes and the fair skin of the District 2–bred Peacekeepers). In District 2, the battle begins with gunfire, but in District 11, it begins with a salute to fallen tributes and a silent, peaceful demonstration of thanks to Katniss and Peeta.

This kind of response—reacting to nonviolent protest with violent action—is a familiar pattern from the history of race relations in the United States. Just one example is the tragic real-world events in Birmingham in 1963, when city Commissioner of Public Safety Theophilus "Bull" Connor ordered violent police action against peaceful demonstrators—including children—protesting against segregated schooling. Connor ordered the use of attack dogs and water cannons, eventually inciting mass riots against the Birmingham police that led President John F. Kennedy to send 3,000 troops to Birmingham to restore order—an act that is echoed in the Capitol's decision to respond to the District 11 riots by sending more Peacekeepers, and more strict/violent officers, not only to District 11 but to all noncompliant districts.

Despite Katniss' claims early in *The Hunger Games* that District 11 tributes were usually weak and unprepared for the Games, Thresh and Rue—and the following year, Chaff—made it to the Games' final eight. District 11, likewise, had more living victors than District 12—at least by a margin of one. (The only District 11 victors we meet are Chaff and Seeder, but Katniss does inform the readers in *The Hunger Games* that District 12 has won the Games the fewest number of times; there were only two District 12 victors prior to Katniss/Peeta's win.) And District 11 was immediately ready and able to wrest control of their resources, land, and means of transport and export from the Capitol when given the opportunity.

Katniss acknowledges on the Victory Tour that she and Peeta could not have won their Hunger Games had Thresh not exhibited extraordinary integrity in sparing her life, integrity in his refusal to join the Careers, and immense power in drawing Cato away from their cave for three entire days of filming, inadvertently—or advertently—giving Peeta time to recuperate somewhat from his wounds. (That "missing" span of three days between Cato and Thresh battling out in the rain is one of the most compelling and mysterious in the entire Hunger Games series: *What could have been so gruesome and intense that the Capitol had no further call for blood for three whole days?* Because after all, while the Katniss/Peeta romance was thrilling, the Capitol audience relishes the Hunger Games for its displays of gruesome violence. It is likely that, given Cato's character, that is what they were given.)

Chaff, despite being a minor character in the series, displays a similar balance of physical power, rebelliousness, and integrity. Despite the resources available to victors, he doesn't appear to become subject to any material vice—unlike even his close friend Haymitch—and as a visible sign of rejection of Capitol ideals, refused a prosthetic hand after he lost his in his own original Games. He also remains alive in the Quell until its very last chaotic moments, and was only killed by Brutus during the catastrophic error that was meant to be the collecting of both Chaff and Peeta onto the hovercraft with the other rebel victors. His actions in the Quell were similar to both Rue's and Thresh's: he avoided confrontation, but not out of a lack of ability to fight. (Rue hid in the trees and calculated careful strategy with Katniss; Thresh hid in the fields and avoided contact with other tributes until he needed something from the feast and confrontation became necessary.) Chaff, like the tributes he mentored in the previous Games, seemed to have adopted "if they can't catch me, they can't kill me" as his mantra—an apropos parallel to the mindset of escaped slaves and freedmen using the Underground Railroad.

Thresh's behavior in sparing Katniss' life, along with Seeder's empathy in *Catching Fire* and the closeness that Chaff shares with Haymitch, suggest that District 11's culture (like the Seam's) is very communal, and deeply values teamwork and interpersonal support—almost the direct opposite of the values of the Career districts and the Capitol, which are egoistic. The fact Thresh dies battling Cato and his probable mentor, Chaff, dies battling another District 2 Career (and possibly even Cato's mentor), Brutus, provides a continuity of characterization between the two districts.

Finally, although the Hunger Games films are neither necessary to an analysis of the novels' text nor applicable to the analysis in this book, they do provide one final real-world look at the prejudice faced by—and, in the future version of our world depicted by the Hunger Games, perhaps leading to the systemic oppression of—District 11. On the film's release, pockets of deep-seated racism erupted against actress Amandla Stenberg, who played Rue in the film, and actor Dayo Okeniyi, who portrayed Thresh. Despite the novels' clear description of their "dark brown" skin and the overt parallels to historical events involving slavery, racism, and the 1960s civil rights movement, some users of the social media network Twitter spoke out in language not at all different from what could be expected in the antebellum South, the turbulent Birmingham of the 1960s, or Panem's Capitol: "when I found out rue was black her death wasn't as sad [*sic*]."[lxxii]

12

The Architects of the Rebellion

The Hunger Games' Second Rebellion is like any other tumultuous political uprising in history: its origins are messy, unclear, and traceable to any number of singular sparks that could have caused the fire to spread. The question of who actually instigated the rebellion—who planted the first seeds of the plan—has been a hot topic of debate in the fandom. From Haymitch and his known contact with the victors of other sympathetic districts to Mr. Everdeen and the possibility that his death was a Capitol assassination to Madge and her knowledge of the significance that Maysilee's pin would have held for Haymitch, several different characters have garnered staunch supporters as lead architect of the Second Rebellion.

Each of the following characters played some kind of role in the Second Rebellion; the question is how much of that role was premeditated and backed from the start by rebellious intention. Who is the man or woman most responsible for the rebellion? And were his or her actions intentional?

Haymitch Abernathy

We know Haymitch Abernathy played a significant role in the design of Katniss and Peeta's strategy in the arena during the Seventy-fourth Hunger Games, particularly in strategizing with Peeta and Katniss individually in the ways they were most receptive to—Peeta by talking things out, Katniss through an unspoken system of reciprocity—and, we assume, through unseen actions in his role as mentor in the Capitol. When he's sober—and perhaps even when he's not—he has a sharp mind and a knack for advance planning; his victory in his Games was the result not of brute strength but of remarkable mental acuity and forethought. He's likely *capable* of engineering something like the Second Rebellion. But did he?

Haymitch has something that few others in Panem did—a persona that could be adapted to keep him below the radar in both Capitol and district locations. Haymitch Abernathy, the drunk victor of District 12, had the advantage of being noticed when he wanted—such as making a mockery of the reaping ceremony of the Seventy-fourth Games with a well-timed and well-executed fall—and unnoticed when he didn't . . . say, in the bars and clubs where, as we learned in *Mockingjay*, fellow rebel Finnick Odair gathered intelligence. Despite living in District 12, he is required to take yearly trips to the Capitol to mentor his tributes, which would have put him in regular contact with the other mentoring victors.

Throughout the Seventy-fourth Games, Katniss is aware that Haymitch has some sort of plan, which is communicated to her through an unspoken system of deed and reward via sponsorship gifts. However, she does not find out, or even suspect, until afterwards that he had been operating based on a fully fleshed-out strategy. Haymitch's plan encompassed both what Cinna tells Katniss, to be herself and to speak honestly as if to a friend, and compensated for Katniss' personal annoyance with Effie, Peeta, and the majority of the people they were to encounter in the lead-up to the Games. The nuance of this strategy suggests that Haymitch may have coordinated with Cinna and Portia beyond color schemes and polite hellos, something Katniss takes for granted at this point because of her distaste for her mentor.

Some readers believe that, to understand Katniss so well, Haymitch had to have had knowledge of Katniss' personality and abilities in advance of the Games themselves, and went into the Games intending not only to make her a victor but also a symbol that Panem could rally behind. Such advance knowledge could have been indirect and unintentional—both Katniss and Haymitch were from the Seam, a close-knit community—but it is also possible that, as the only living victor of District 12, he kept a close eye on the poorest children of reaping age in the district for knowledge of exactly this type. Katniss would have been particularly easy to track given her movements in the Hob, where Haymitch spent much of his time drinking.

Haymitch's intimacy with the Quarter Quell plot and his covert, continued communication with the victors of rebellion-sympathetic districts in the lead-up to the Seventy-fifth Games also suggest that, at least until his withdrawal in District 13, Haymitch was a heavy hitter in the planning and execution of the uprisings, if not one of the original architects. His ability to navigate the District 11 Justice Hall quickly suggests that he had been there multiple times (despite Katniss, at least, having no evidence of him leaving District 12 other than once a year for the Games), and may foreshadow the network of hidden tunnels that the rebels make use of during *Mockingjay*. Whether alongside other victors or in a sphere of his own, Haymitch had extended contact in advance of the Quarter Quell with at least Plutarch Heavensbee, Cressida, and President Coin in the strategizing for war; during *Mockingjay*, he continues to serve as a conduit between the conspirators and Katniss, who does not trust them but finds that, after they comfort each other about Peeta's capture, she does trust Haymitch. Both represent supreme votes of confidence in his ability to lead others, and his importance to the cause.

Plutarch Heavensbee, Seneca Crane

The role of Head Gamemaker is clearly an influential one. The Head Gamemaker has control of not just the events that occur within the arena (including, through scores, each tribute's chance of obtaining sponsors) but the way those events are produced and seen by viewers. There is no bigger or better platform in all of Panem. As well, a person who ascends to Head Gamemaker status must necessarily be skilled in planning; he or she must coordinate and oversee the construction of the arena, as well as the "story" of the Games themselves. Could either of our Head Gamemakers, Seneca Crane or Plutarch Heavensbee, be the lead architect of the rebellion?

The evidence for Seneca Crane planning the Second Rebellion lies mostly in the revolutionary outcome of the Seventy-fourth Hunger Games. The level of clout he had in the Capitol and his role in the creation of the Games' obstacles themselves would have allowed him access to the arenas and the ability to engineer the outcome of the Games to the rebels' best advantage. The rule change at the end of the Seventy-fourth Games, rebellious enough on its own that it directly led to Crane's assassination by Snow, suggests that it may not have been as innocent, as much for entertainment reasons, as it otherwise might seem. The film version of *The Hunger Games* suggests Crane was put to death solely for allowing the Capitol to be susceptible to manipulation—and by a teenage girl, no less—and therefore fallible. Although this does not necessarily imply rebellious intention, it does not refute the idea, either; the choice of nightlock berries, Katniss' tool of rebellion, as the method of execution might even suggest such rebellious intent. And there is no clear indication either way in the books, where

Crane's death is unseen. We know he was killed for what happened during the Seventy-fourth Games, and nothing more.

However, Plutarch Heavensbee was also a Gamemaker or part of the gamemaking team under Crane during the Seventy-fourth Games (he references being in the judging room when Katniss shot an arrow into the apple in the feast pig's mouth), in addition to becoming Head Gamemaker for the Seventy-fifth (a role, it's implied, that was not in much demand after Crane's death), and the evidence for his part in engineering the Second Rebellion is much stronger.

Certainly, by the Capitol party that kicked off Katniss and Peeta's Victory Tour in *Catching Fire*, there is a true "revolutionary cell" that has been formed right under Snow's nose, and it is clear that Plutarch holds a position of power within it. At this party, he shows Katniss the mockingjay image on his pocketwatch: a clue, Katniss finds out later, to the design of the Quell arena, as well as a covert symbol that he is on the rebels' side. The rebels in the arena suffered, but ideal tools for all of the pieces to their plan—from Beetee's cylinder of wire for the Quell plot's electrified target (and the lightning storm portion of the arena itself to power it) to Finnick's personal trident—did make their way into the Cornucopias.

In *Mockingjay*, his involvement in ending the Hunger Games from within the system is even more evident. He is one of the leaders of the base in District 13 and is tapped for a high position in the government of New Panem. The fact that he brought with him to District 13 some of his original team from the Capitol—Cressida, Castor, and Pollux—further serves to illustrate the depth of his involvement in the rebellion as a whole.

Mags

There's another kind of access that would be of use to a potential architect of the rebellion: privileged information about the world, or at least Panem, before the current sociopolitical regime. The complete isolation of Panem from both a "rest of the world" (if there is such a thing in Panem's time) and historical record (beyond general geography, such as Katniss' reference to District 12 being located in "Appalachia"[THG41]) lends itself to the almost illogical organization of Panem as a nation under the Games system and Snow: economists would argue Panem would be a nation on the brink of collapse even without revolutionary leanings. The Capitol simply does not know how to beget loyalty in Panem's citizens, or how to most successfully organize the country's communications, transport, or production—which is part of why the first objective of the rebels was to organize work stoppages and strikes. The Capitol's weakness would be easiest to recognize and perhaps even best exploited by someone who had seen a world before it was dictated by the Capitol, and there is one person we meet during the course of the Hunger Games with both that knowledge and the personal motivation to use it.

Mags is the oldest living victor; she was alive, though very young, during the First Rebellion, and her potential authority in the rebellion is mostly a matter of circumstantial evidence, along with sheer longevity. If we assume that she does in fact speak Spanish, it would give her the ability to speak her mind without being understood by the Capitol. That and her age and breadth of experience working as a liaison between the districts and the Capitol—as well as the apparent level of authority she held over other victors, particularly Finnick, who was a naturally charismatic leader himself—have led to speculation that Mags may have had a long-running role in at least uniting the victors of each district as they became mentors, if not in the strategic planning of the Quell plot or the early stages of the rebellion itself.

Unfortunately, one of the narrative consequences of Mags' death in the Quarter Quell is that we never see her interact on the page with other rebellion leaders like Haymitch, Plutarch, or Coin, and cannot see what her relationship to them is like in terms of leadership, cooperation, or alliance. However, given the smallest glimpse that we do see—her insistence that the skill she demonstrates for the Gamemakers will be "napping"—we can guess that if she did lead, she did so with humanity and humor, and garnered respect for her wisdom by being genuine in her actions.

Mr. Everdeen

> My father could have made good money selling [his bows and arrows], but if the officials found out he would have been publicly executed for inciting a rebellion.[THG5]

Could Katniss have come by her involvement in the rebellion naturally—through her father? Though Mr. Everdeen's potential role in the rebellion is necessarily limited, given his death several years before the Seventy-fourth Games, the text does imply that his sympathies, at least, lay with the rebel cause.

A popular theory within the Hunger Games fan community (though one minimally substantiated through the novels' text) is that the mine collapse that killed Katniss' and Gale's fathers was a calculated political assassination—an attempt to quash a rising mutiny. Given that both men were roughly the same age as Haymitch, another popularly theorized architect of the Second Rebellion, some have theorized that there was a "rebel cell" in District 12, and that Haymitch, Mr. Everdeen, Mr. Hawthorne, and others killed in the mine collapse may well have been emulating the fabled rebels who utilized the mockingjays to send messages between districts. Although Katniss offers only minor indications of her father's politics—likely because, given that she was so young when he died, she didn't fully notice or absorb them—we do get a few intriguing nuggets of information.

Although the song "The Hanging Tree" holds personal significance for Katniss, because of its connection to memories of her father, her mother's reaction upon hearing her husband and daughter singing it—panic—suggests that it may have been tied to outlawed, or at least frowned-upon, attitudes and/or behaviors. Given that Mr. Everdeen also spoke openly to Katniss about injustice and the unfairness of the Capitol's

Games–tesserae system—potentially in the forest where he also taught her to hunt: as we learn in *Catching Fire*, the Capitol has bugs of some sort there, and there is no telling how long they have been in place—it's possible to infer that the song is connected to rebellion in Panem.

And of course, Katniss' initial thoughts on mockingjays tie her father and rebellion explicitly:

> A mockingjay. They're funny birds and something of a slap in the face to the Capitol . . . The rebels fed the Capitol endless lies, and the joke was on it . . . My father was particularly fond of mockingjays.[THG42-43]

Madge Undersee

> Madge walks straight to me. She is not weepy or evasive, instead there's an urgency about her tone that surprises me. "They let you wear one thing from your district into the arena. One thing to remind you of home. Will you wear this?" She holds out the circular gold pin that was on her dress earlier. I hadn't paid much attention to it before, but now I see it's a small bird in flight.
> "Your pin?" I say. Wearing a token from my district is about the last thing on my mind.
> "Here, I'll put it on your dress, all right?" Madge doesn't wait for an answer, just leans in and fixes the bird to my dress. "Promise you'll wear it into the arena, Katniss?" she asks. "Promise?"
> "Yes," I say.[THG38]

Madge Undersee clearly plays a key role in the course of the Second Rebellion. She is the one who puts the mockingjay pin in Katniss' hand and makes her promise to wear it into the arena, therefore inspiring the chief symbol of the rebellion. She does so with a surprising amount of intensity, which raises the question: Why? Is it just because of who the pin used to belong to, her mother's fallen twin sister, another District 12 tribute? Or is there some other, more seditious motivation at work?

THE ARCHITECTS OF THE REBELLION

The most important thing to remember about the mockingjay pin is that it first belonged to Maysilee, Mrs. Undersee's sister and Madge's aunt—and Haymitch's district ally in the Fiftieth Hunger Games. A tribute had already worn that pin into the arena, and she died wearing it.

Madge would have known the significance, to Haymitch if nothing else, of giving Katniss the pin that her aunt had worn. Haymitch would have recognized that pin. Whether Katniss was aware of it or not, that pin on a District 12 tribute would have reminded Haymitch of Maysilee and the circumstances of her death—that she had died after leaving her alliance with Haymitch. Perhaps Madge only meant to rouse Haymitch out of his drunken stupor, to give Katniss the mentoring she needed to have a fighting chance at surviving. But perhaps it was also a message: that the strategy Haymitch and Maysilee had attempted, in their short-lived alliance, could be used here. (Though we have no direct evidence Madge knew about Peeta's crush, it seems like it was a pretty poorly kept secret—except, of course, from Katniss.)

Perhaps, too, the mockingjay pin meant something more, and not only to Madge. The mockingjay pin sees two tours into the arena—both times that District 12 managed a victory. The pin represents survival—both literally, in that it presumably inspired both Haymitch's strategy of cooperation and Cinna's designs, and figuratively, in that the mockingjays are throughout the Hunger Games a symbol for the will to survive against all odds (pun intended). The pin represents the Capitol's failure to understand the ability of its oppressed people to survive, just as it did with the jabberjays it released into the wild to die. Giving Katniss that mockingjay pin made a likely intentional anti-Capitol, anti-Games, pro-teamwork statement. And as one of the few people in District 12 who, as the mayor's daughter, we can assume would ever be in a position to meet people from other districts—to meet people, too, from the Capitol—Madge could have known that others would recognize it, too.[5]

---

[5] In this single interaction, the course of the Seventy-fourth Hunger Games has been subtly spelled out: the mockingjay pin attracts notice; notice begets favor, especially in terms of life-saving monetary or goods transfer—and money leads to berries.

The mockingjay pin itself finds its origin in a social class that, as was argued earlier, can be seen as specifically designed to oppress Katniss' own social class, and yet is owned by and identified with Katniss and used in overthrowing that oppressive system. Similarly, Madge doesn't conform to the ideals of the Capitol and her Capitol-appointed father, and some fans suggest that she could have used her wealth and position and privilege to help take that system down.

Katniss always describes Madge's behavior as unusual, given her father's position and her membership in the merchant class:

> [W]e go to the back door of the mayor's house to sell half the strawberries, knowing he has a particular fondness for them and can afford our price. The mayor's daughter, Madge, opens the door. She's in my year at school. Being the mayor's daughter, you'd expect her to be a snob, but she's all right. She just keeps to herself. Like me.[THG12]

Katniss even says that Madge's white dress on reaping day isn't typical for her—that Madge usually wore the same plain clothes as anyone else in the district, a further deviation from what would be expected, given her Capitol-sponsored lifestyle. Fandom has twisted Madge into a strawberry-swilling, lace-dress-wearing Capitolite Lite, but the way Madge is described, she seems much more interested in playing down her father's authority and her family's wealth than luxuriating in them.

Katniss also notes that:

> Since neither of us really has a group of friends, we seem to end up together a lot at school. Eating lunch, sitting next to each other at assemblies, partnering for sports activities. We rarely talk, which suits us both just fine. [THG12]

If Madge had been coming to school with full feasts for lunch while Katniss was starving to death, it seems doubtful Katniss would have been friends with her at all.

In *Catching Fire*, Madge breaks the law by bringing Gale the morphling that her addict mother depended on. Whether you ship[6] Madge and Gale or not (as many online Hunger Games fans do), this act shows a stronger respect for true justice and for humane treatment than for Capitol law.

This sense of compassion could have come from many places, but one option is her privileged access, as the mayor's daughter, to the Capitol and to past victors. Because Madge had more access than the majority of district citizens to Capitol media—her father's newspapers, for example—and likely met Hunger Games victors year after year on the Victory Tour and saw their humanity and their suffering, her belief in justice and humanity could be rooted in knowledge that the Capitol is wrong. Some believe such knowledge may have driven her, or her family, to use her position to help rebellion conspirators communicate with each other across districts to forge plans.

Cinna

Cinna is perhaps the most natural candidate for lead architect of the Second Rebellion. Without him, there is no fire, there is no mockingjay, there is no rebellion—at least as we know it. He is the one who tells Katniss and Peeta to hold hands during the chariot scene, creating the idea of their partnership for the Games' audience. He designs the "wedding" dress that cements Katniss as the mockingjay, at the cost of his own life, demonstrating his commitment to the cause. He is instrumental in creating the necessary conditions for Katniss' survival and the eventual defeat of the Capitol. The real question is whether the latter was intentional right from the start.

One reason many believe Cinna may be a chief architect of the rebellion is his historical namesake: Cinna Cornelius, an infamous

---

[6]"To ship" is a fandom term for "to believe in, promote, or condone a romantic relationship between."

conspirator against Julius Caesar. While other characters share names with the historical men who took down Caesar, Cinna is named after the man Shakespeare immortalized as, literally, "Cinna the Conspirator."

We know that by the time Katniss returns to the Capitol for the Seventy-fourth Hunger Games victory party, Capitol citizens have begun wearing the mockingjay symbol as a fashion statement. By initially introducing this symbol into Capitol culture—or, perhaps more accurately, Capitol pop culture—by making sure Katniss wore it into the arena, and, later, by reinforcing it through her transformed wedding dress, Cinna made sure that the image of the mockingjay became synonymous with Katniss and, therefore, emblematic of her cause.

In some ways, the Hunger Games' Cinna is as Machiavellian as Snow or Coin, though unlike Snow and Coin, his morals are pure despite his murky ethics. He used Katniss as a game piece, made her a symbol—but when it really mattered, he gave her a choice (even after his own death): Did she want to put on battle armor and "decide to be the Mockingjay on [her] own,"[M43] or let others lead the charge in the war? Cinna set up the board for her to become the rebellion's symbol, but of all of the adults who use Katniss for their own ends (Snow, Coin, Haymitch, Plutarch), he is the only one who gives her the choice to be used—and, I think, would have allowed her to say no.

Although Cinna may not have been the lead architect of the rebellion, he is irreplaceable in his importance in the rebellion and to the Hunger Games as a series—and, as we'll see, inscrutable enough that considering his role in the rebellion raises as many questions as it answers.

13

Truly, My Name Is Cinna

Cinna is a deeply enigmatic character, and one of the most tragic tales in a series full of tragic tales. Unlike many of the other Capitol characters, his last name is not revealed. And the full motives behind his actions remain unclear.

Who was Cinna to the rebellion? Where did he come from? Was he driven initially by devotion to his art versus devotion to his cause? How much, precisely, does Panem owe him for its freedom?

Cinna the Outsider

Cinna presents himself differently, both in personal style and in demeanor, than the rest of the Capitol, even his own prep team. He dresses simply, all in black, and his face is unpainted save for gold eyeliner "applied with a light hand,"[THG63] in stark contrast to the heavy, caked makeup of

Caesar Flickerman or the full-body modifications of Octavia or Tigris. Katniss notes that Cinna's voice even lacks the Capitol accent.

Cinna is clearly marked—or marks himself—as an outsider to Capitol culture and ideology, despite his proficiency with Capitol style. And through his interactions with Katniss, as well as his sacrifice for the cause of rebellion, it appears that his true sympathies lie with Panem's districts. All of which raises the question: Is Cinna from the Capitol at all?

There are almost as many theories as to Cinna's origin as there are fans of the Hunger Games. Here are some of the most popular and salient.

The Capitol

The evidence for Cinna being originally born and raised in the Capitol stems mainly from a straightforward read of the text: if Cinna lives in the Capitol and works in the Capitol and it is not specifically stated that this was not always the case, it can be assumed that he has always been a Capitol citizen. His visibility in major Capitol media, through the popularity of his fashion, suggests he is somewhat influential in the propaganda machine of Capitol politics as well, indicating the absence of any reason for Snow or the other political leaders of Panem to doubt that he holds with Capitol ideals (which they very well might, if he were originally from one of the districts). Cinna also works in a highly skilled artisan profession, which may only be possible to attain in Panem in the Capitol (although, by the same token, we are never directly told that is the case).

District 4

The belief that Cinna was born, and perhaps raised, in District 4 stems from the same source as the evidence that Cinna and Finnick have a relationship—whether romantic or platonic—prior to the run-up to the Quarter Quell (see chapter eight).

At least in District 12, people from the same districts or socioeconomic classes resemble each other: the merchants of District 12 share blonde hair and pale eyes and the residents of the Seam share olive skin, gray eyes, and straight black hair. It's not unreasonable to extrapolate that this is the case in other districts, too. Cinna and Finnick are described using similar physical descriptors: light brown hair and green eyes. Katniss describes relatively few characters in the series in any physical detail at all, so—like with Prim and Peeta—this attention to detail may be meant to convey a deeper narrative meaning.

There are three differences in accent or speech pattern that Katniss notes in the series: the Capitol "affectation," Mags' "garbled" speech that requires "translation," and Cinna's lack of distinct accent. This is solid evidence that Cinna is not from the Capitol, at minimum. Some readers suggest that calling attention to Cinna's lack of a Capitol accent, without an accompanying note specifying that his speech sounds the same as Katniss', is meant to suggest traces of a District 4 accent. However, this particular inference does not seem very credible.

District 1

District 1's specialty is luxury goods, which has led some to suggest that Cinna may have been raised in District 1 and recruited by the Capitol for his high skill level. In *Catching Fire*, Cinna demonstrates proficiency in working with one of District 1's proprietary goods, gold (it seems unlikely he would have left making the gold tokens for Peeta, Haymitch, and [possibly] Finnick to someone else).

District 8

The evidence that Cinna hails from District 8 comes from a similar place as the belief that he is from District 1: the district's specialty, textiles. Given that Cinna works with fabrics and textiles in the Capitol, it's possible that he may have been recruited from District 8 to work as a designer for the Games because he showed extraordinary skill.

District 8 is the first district in which a true violent revolt occurs during the Second Rebellion, perhaps suggesting that its citizens are most sensitive to Capitol injustice and most prepared to fight for their freedom, the way Cinna is sensitive to the plight of the tributes and is prepared to die for his belief in Panem's emancipation. District 8 is also where the mockingjay crackers—a symbol of rebel sympathies shown to Katniss by District 8 refugees passing through District 12 on their way to District 13—originate. As Cinna is also heavily tied to the mockingjay's use as a rebel symbol at all, it may suggest commonality between Cinna and the District 8 populace.

District 12

The best evidence for Cinna hailing from District 12 is the simplest: he requested to style District 12's tributes in his first Games as a lead stylist. Why would he, as a Capitol man, choose the least prestigious district? A personal connection to the district is more plausible than a personal connection to Katniss, Peeta, or Haymitch.

But there are other suggestions in Katniss' narrative, however small, that Cinna may have had a presence in her home district during the time between Haymitch's Games and her own—though they require a little more reading between the lines than most of the other district origin theories.

Katniss, as a rule, does not describe much that does not specifically pertain to her survival. One example that online Hunger Games fandom tends to remark on most is that Katniss describes food in copious detail but does not offer any description of most of her fellow tributes in the Seventy-fourth Games. Likewise, she does not remark much on her everyday clothing or the clothing of others. She does, however, spend a lot of time describing the clothing Cinna creates for her—which, in a way, also helps keep her alive.

Before she arrives in the Capitol, we are meant to understand that clothing does not matter to her. But she describes her reaping dress in the same level of detail that she devotes to Cinna's designs:

> To my surprise, my mother has laid out one of her own lovely dresses for me. A soft blue thing with matching shoes.
> "Are you sure?" I ask . . . [T]his is something special. Her clothes from her past are very precious to her . . .

"You look beautiful," says Prim in a hushed voice. "And nothing like myself," I say.^{THG15}

Later, while she is waiting for the train to take her to the Capitol, Katniss makes reference to another lush fabric:

> I know velvet because my mother has a dress with a collar made of the stuff. When I sit on the couch, I can't help running my fingers over the fabric repeatedly. It helps to calm me as I try to prepare for the next hour.^{THG34}

These other descriptions of fabrics certainly could be coincidence or instances intended to foreshadow the importance of fashion generally later on. But given that Cinna's creations are the only articles of clothing she describes anywhere else, it could also suggest that these items from Mrs. Everdeen's merchant past, too, were Cinna's handiwork—especially when paired with Cinna's inexplicable attachment to District 12.

If Cinna is indeed meant to be read as being an outsider in the Capitol, then the portrayal of him gains a secondary level of mystery when we consider that, in working for the Games, in residing in the Capitol, he has made himself into an outsider to the districts as well: yet another enigmatic facet of Cinna's character. Katniss trusts him and comes to see him as a surrogate father figure and source of comfort, but Gale's reaction to her camaraderie with Cinna is negative and he refuses a gift of Cinna's gloves because they are "from the Capitol."^{CF94} It's hard to believe many other rebels would feel much differently. In short: Cinna played a leading role in the revolution that freed a people from whom he can be read as wholly separate.

Cinna the Artist

Cinna is an employee of the Capitol, and a vital part of the Games that oppress Panem's citizenry. But he uses his position and his skills in a way that suggests his work is more than just a job or a way to gain higher standing in the Capitol. What he creates is *art*. His focus is never on fame, though we can assume he experienced plenty of it after the Seventy-fourth Games. Instead, he expresses, through his actions as much as through his understated clothing, that his art is what should be looked at and judged and discussed, not his person. Cinna is literally the opposite of flamboyant; his art is what stands out and gets noticed, not the man in the background. That speaks volumes about who he is and what his goals are, especially in a city like the Capitol.

Cinna is the consummate artist, and an undeniably powerful one. Through his work with Katniss' Games costumes, which couple the long-standing Western symbolism of birds of peace and birds of war with the Eastern tradition of fire as a form of protest (both of which seem to resonate with Panem the same way as they do with us), he achieves something very, very few people ever do: the successful utilization of his art as a method of social change, not just commentary. His art not only encapsulates and expresses his ideas but actually communicates them to people of different mindsets and encourages them to think and consider a viewpoint different from their own. And as a result, minds are changed. A country is changed.

Cinna uses the visibility of the Hunger Games as a form of political expression, a tradition that has existed since the days of Rome itself, when satirical theater was the primary mode of artistic political commentary. There are so many artists who work hard to gain the world's attention, but then, once they have it, don't really know what they want to say. That's certainly not the case with Cinna. He adeptly uses Katniss' wedding gown debut in the Quarter Quell opening ceremonies not only to invoke the fire imagery citizens of Panem (districts and Capitol alike) would recall from her previous Games but also the mockingjay imagery that had since come to be associated with her, and with her rebellion. In doing so, he manages to embed that imagery into the public mindset so flawlessly and strongly that viewers begin to sympathize with his message—that Katniss, like the mockingjay, is unprecedented and will survive despite the Capitol's wishes—before they even realize their minds are changing.

Cinna the Conspirator

By the same token, his artful use of that imagery to bend others ideologically to his will can also be read as deeply manipulative. The result of that manipulation was undeniably positive—an end to the Capitol's reign, and a chance for a free Panem to do better by its citizens—but that does not change the fact that, because of it, we cannot view Cinna purely as an artist (or at least not one whose primary motivation is to create art!).

This duality is also reflected in the probable origins of Cinna's name. As with many other names in the Hunger Games (see the Lexicon), "Cinna" has a direct connection to the story of Caesar. Historically, there were two Cinnas of note involved in Caesar's death: Cinna the Conspirator, and Cinna the Poet.

The first Cinna was a conspirator against Caesar, who played a key role in enlisting Brutus to the assassins' cause. In 78 BC, Cinna allied himself with Roman statesman Lepidus in an attempt to overthrow the Roman constitution of dictator Sulla. As a result, he was exiled. Before he left Rome, he sought out the support of Julius Caesar for the rebellion, which was not forthcoming, though it was Caesar who later recalled Cinna from exile to use him in the Roman Senate against Caesar's senatorial opposition. On the day of Caesar's funeral, the Roman populace was in such rage at Cinna for his role in Caesar's death that a group of citizens murdered Helvius Cinna, tribune of the plebs, because they mistook him for Cinna the Conspirator. When the murder of the tribune took place, the other Cinna was walking in Caesar's funeral procession.

Helvius Cinna is better known as Cinna the Poet, thanks to William Shakespeare and the Roman historian Plutarch. Most historians at the time only recorded that this Cinna was a representative of the people, but Plutarch preserved the information that he was also a poet. Shakespeare adopted Plutarch's version of Cinna's death in his *Julius Caesar*, with the black humor through which he often expressed his distrust of the crowd:

> III.iii.—
> CINNA.   Truly, my name is Cinna.
> FIRST CITIZEN.   Tear him to pieces, he's a conspirator.
> CINNA.   I am Cinna the poet, I am Cinna the poet.
> FOURTH CITIZEN.   Tear him for his bad verses, tear him for his bad verses.
> CINNA.   I am not Cinna the conspirator.
> FOURTH CITIZEN.   It is no matter, his name's Cinna. Pluck but his name out of his heart, and turn him going.

So Cinna shares his name with one of history's most infamous conspirators . . . and also the innocent man who was killed in his place. Like Helvius Cinna, the Hunger Games' Cinna is both a representative of the people and a poet. But he is a conspirator, too.

We know that Cinna is ambushed and beaten at the outset of the Quarter Quell, in full view of Katniss, Peeta, and his fellow conspirators, after they have been locked onto their plates. We know that he was not killed that day but was instead tortured for information on Katniss' whereabouts and the plans of the rebels. We know that unlike Portia's death and that of Peeta's prep team, his end was private and solitary—and that his prep team was not being held with him.

But we do not know what Cinna knew, what his final acts were, or what his final moments were like. What happened to him in his final interrogation? Was he able to help Peeta, Johanna, Enobaria, and Annie survive? Did he share information? Did he mislead the Capitol? Or did he remain silent in protest, leaving the Girl On Fire as his legacy?

14

District 13 and the Capitol: Two Sides of the Same "Coin"

In one important way, the Capitol and District 13 are diametrically opposed. There is no place more visible in Panem than the Capitol: literally visible, in the fences and white-helmeted Peacekeepers in the districts, and ideologically visible in the districts' isolation, propagandist education, and strict socioeconomic caste system. And there is perhaps no place less visible than District 13: until the end of *Catching Fire*, neither we nor most of Panem even know it exists; it is, literally and figuratively, underground.

In another way, however, the two can be seen as two sides of the same coin. They may be on opposite sides of the Second Rebellion but, as Katniss realizes during the course of *Mockingjay*, they are not so different when it comes to political goals.

The Capitol and District 13, and their leaders, have both strong similarities and obvious differences. And by comparing one with the other, we come to understand each of them better.

History and Philosophy

The details we receive about the history of Panem are limited. We know that, seventy-five years ago, there was something called the First Rebellion, in which the districts, led by District 13, attempted to overthrow the Capitol and were defeated and punished by the inception of the Games–tesserae system . . . except for District 13, with whom the Capitol struck a secret accord, agreeing to let them live in secrecy as long as they did not disrupt the Capitol's rule of the twelve remaining districts.

The word "rebellion" suggests that the First Rebellion was a response to a pre-existing economic or political stranglehold on the districts, but there may have been another reason for the attempted revolution—some sort of institutional oppression or attempts at segregation, for example. We know that as a result of that First Rebellion, District 13 was allowed to secede from the nation of Panem under terms of absolute secrecy—and that the rest of the populace were intentionally misinformed that District 13 had been annihilated. We know that, for the past seventy-five years, the idea of District 13's destruction has been leveraged as a threat against the remaining twelve districts . . . and that, for the past seventy-five years, despite knowledge of the Hunger Games, the Games–tesserae political system, socioeconomic genocide, class struggle, and the poverty epidemic, District 13 did nothing. (It could be argued that, after nearly a century, they did start the Second Rebellion to help liberate the remaining districts from Capitol rule. But there is equal validity to the argument that their involvement came at the behest of the conspirators who lived in the districts—or Capitol, in the case of Plutarch—and did not grow out of their own altruistic intentions. Although communication between District 13 and select outsiders would have been necessary to put together rebellion plans, there is no direct textual evidence that it was something District 13 sought out—or even really welcomed, as Gale relates to Katniss that the District 12 survivors were regarded with deep suspicion and derision by those who dwelled in District 13.)

The parallel between the Capitol, which perpetrates evils against the populace, and District 13, which turns a blind eye and allows the evils to continue, raises the essential question that takes *Mockingjay* from dystopian sci-fi to philosphical treatise: Who is more to blame for atrocities, those who enact them, or those who stand by when they could have prevented them? As writer and Holocaust survivor Primo Levi put it:

> Monsters exist, but they are too few in numbers to be truly dangerous. More dangerous are the functionaries ready to believe and act without asking questions.[lxxiii]

District 13 is certainly not innocent. And having its leader spearhead the rebellion effort changes this from a story about the good, noble rebel force that throws off oppression to take down the corrupt government to a story about two opposing leaders grappling for power . . . with the only truly innocent party, the populace, caught in the middle.

Katniss reacts negatively to the excess of the Capitol. She is aggressive towards the Gamemakers, disdainful of her prep team, and disgusted by the partygoers at the victory party after the Seventy-fourth Games. But she reacts negatively to the bleak, regimented lifestyle of District 13, as well. Katniss derides the schedule she, like everyone else in District 13, is required to print on her arm, and refuses to adhere to it; she mocks the titles given to parts of the day—replacing "Reflection" with "Cat Adoration," for example—and the system of promotions and demotions given to the "Soldiers" under Coin.

Politically, both the Capitol and District 13 are unique mixes of capitalism and socialism: Panem under the Capitol can produce immense quantities of goods, but you must pay penance to the state to receive them; District 13 cannot produce goods, but they are your right as a functioning citizen.

These differing views on rights and privileges are reflected in the histories of the Capitol and District 13 as independent/ruling states. The Capitol came about because of the government's desire for total control. Its current leader's reign began through deception and murder, with the poison he used to eliminate his competition, just as the Capitol government operates by "poisoning" Panem from its heart outward by eliminating the citizens who don't fit the vision of Capitol lifestyle, children in outlying districts first.

District 13, in contrast, began with the ideal of freedom from oppression and persecution. However, seventy-five years later, District 13's citizens have as little freedom as those in the other twelve districts or in the Capitol. Arguably, they have even less, given that they are only allowed outside for specific, set hours of the day and reprieves like Katniss' hunting trips back in District 12 are not possible. We are never told the circumstances of Coin's ascent to power, but her method of ruling in District 13—and plan for taking retribution on the Capitol citizens if she becomes the supreme leader—is not ideologically different from Snow's. Despite outwardly involving a cabinet of advisors and votes on measures (like the proposed Capitol Hunger Games after Snow's death), Coin intends a unilateral rule. She certainly seems to have one in District 13; she doles out rewards and punishments according to her own personal whims rather than qualifications (such as when she demotes Gale when Katniss storms out of a battle meeting in Coin's office and he tries to go after her).

Although District 13's political system and ideals were born of a direct opposition to the Capitol, over the seventy-five years between their inception and Katniss' introduction to them in *Mockingjay*, they have become just as harsh, vindictive, and Machiavellian, with the same disregard for human life as anything other than political fodder. Both the Capitol and District 13 have governments predicated on little more than the continuous reinforcement of their own power, and both have their presidents to blame: Snow in the Capitol, and Coin in District 13.

Parallels Between the Capitol and District 13

Mockingjay provides parallels not only between District 13 and the Capitol but also between key characters associated with them. Although we don't see any of these pairs of character foils interact with each other directly—in some cases, one member of the pair does not appear in *Mockingjay* at all—the roles that they play in the story or in Katniss' life are equivalent, and comparing the two provides a richer understanding of "gray area" in the Second Rebellion.

Cinna and Boggs

Capitol stylist Cinna and District 13 soldier Boggs are both men that Katniss comes to trust despite their position and status in hostile governments. Both also die for the same cause and are taken down (though in Cinna's case, not yet killed) within view of Katniss, whom they are protecting and serving. However, while Cinna contributes to the cause of the rebellion through art, Boggs does so through skillful tactical warfare.

Cinna and Boggs represent two different approaches to revolution: Is it better to change people's minds, like Cinna, or to change their actions forcibly, like Boggs? The narrative implies that both are necessary. And each man's death for the revolution—or in service to Katniss, given that both were killed due to their positions in protecting her—reflects the work he did in life. Cinna's death is long, slow, difficult, and unseen, mirroring the process of ideological revolutionary change, while Boggs' death is gruesome, violent, and highly visible, a representation of revolution through brute force.

Caesar Flickerman and Cressida

Both television presenter Caesar and television producer Cressida are influential figures in Panem's media, and both arguably (see chapter eight) have the best interests—regardless of their official side in the rebellion—of the district tributes at heart. Their methods, however, are different: Caesar works in front of the cameras as an agent of the Capitol, attempting to help the tributes make themselves look and sound more pleasing to potential sponsors. Cressida, in contrast, works behind the scenes, physically cutting and editing the footage of the Seventy-fifth Games, in *Catching Fire*, and the war, in *Mockingjay*, to better communicate a pro-district message.

Both Caesar and Cressida manipulate the media in the tributes' favor. But Cressida manipulates the media with the aim of a greater societal good—the end of the Hunger Games and of the Capitol's reign—while Caesar's manipulation is on behalf of single individuals, to humanize them and thereby increase their chances of surviving. Cressida works to change the system for the better; Caesar works to improve the individual fates of those the system oppresses. Caesar focuses on the humanity of individuals and Cressida focuses on the inhumanity of actions.

In Caesar and Cressida's respective manipulations, we see how easily media can be used for good or for evil, and how fine the line between the two really is.

The Avoxes and Katniss' Prep Team

Both the Avoxes and Katniss' prep team serve the role of innocent prisoners of war. The Avoxes we see during the Hunger Games series appear to come from the districts. They are effectively imprisoned in the Capitol, physically tortured (by having their tongues removed), and degraded to the point that they become "less than human" (something their lack of speech emphasizes). The Capitol claims the Avoxes are being punished for treason, but they can also be seen as prisoners of the Capitol's long-term, large-scale class war. Unfortunately, but poignantly, the equivalent happens to Katniss' prep team after District 13 ransacks the Capitol torture chambers to free Peeta, Annie, Johanna, and Enobaria. They're imprisoned, beaten, and subjected to starvation and water deprivation for a different brand of treason: stealing a slice of bread.

Although Katniss herself in earlier books refers to the prep team in nonhuman terms—as "a flock of colorful birds"[THG62]—seeing them treated in a manner so similar to the Avoxes is an epiphany for her in terms of her opinion about District 13. She realizes that it and the Capitol are not so different; that abuse happens as often and as savagely in District 13 as it did in District 12 and elsewhere under the Capitol's purview.

Presidents Snow and Coin

The most obvious and important set of parallel characters in *Mockingjay*, of course, is President Snow and President Coin. The two are presented as obvious literary foils, from physical character details (like their opposing genders) to symbolic or abstract ones (like their preferred methods of control, Snow's preference being for blackmail and poison, Coin's for humiliation and bombs). Both Snow and Coin are effective leaders because of their tyrannical style of unilateral rule, and both are feared by their citizens enough that they are able to rule more through threat, supported by select negative actions, than through negative action itself. As a result, both lead mainly through charisma and speechmaking.

The biggest question about District 13, and a major topic of debate within fandom, is whether a new government helmed by Coin would have been freer than Snow's. Katniss certainly doesn't think so, as she foregoes her opportunity to kill Snow—her main objective during the war—and instead assassinates Coin.

The actions of both Snow and Coin, from Snow's "fixing" of the Quarter Quell reaping to Coin's plan to reinstate a version of the Hunger Games with tributes specially chosen from the old government officials' children (including Snow's granddaughter), are comparable to real-life dictators who seized power through forceful means. Snow's threats against District 13 in *Mockingjay* perhaps most recall French dictator Maximilien Robespierre's guillotine-heavy Reign of Terror. Snow tries to force the hand of the rebels by threatening innocent lives in District 13, aligning the whole district with the rebel movement instead of targeting only the soldiers themselves; Robespierre used similar fear tactics to try to control the population; he declared terror as a legal policy in September 1793:

> It is time that equality bore its scythe above all heads. It is time to horrify all the conspirators. So legislators, place Terror on the order of the day! Let us be in revolution, because everywhere counter-revolution is being woven by our enemies. The blade of the law should hover over all the guilty.[lxxiv]

By declaring everyone guilty, the policy encouraged citizens to report those involved in treason; the innocent, it was believed, would report the guilty to save themselves, and the guilty would turn themselves in to spare the innocent.

At the same time, Coin's determination to rule through terror, even after deposing a tyrant, mirrors the actions of Robespierre's own Jacobin party after the French Revolution. According to one French Revolution history text:

> If virtue be the spring of a popular government in times of peace, the spring of that government during a revolution is virtue combined with terror . . . Terror is only justice prompt, severe and inflexible; it is then an emanation of virtue . . . The government in a revolution is the despotism of liberty against tyranny.[lxxv]

Coin, and her style of rule, represent the despotism of liberty: either Panem is bound under Snow or it is bound under Coin, but in neither case are the citizens allowed to escape the idea of violent reparations for their ancestors' wrongs.

Katniss' choice at the end of *Mockingjay*—to vote "yes" for a Capitol Hunger Games—is, and should be, shocking to the reader, given what she's gone through in the arena, districts, and war herself. However, it is also the signifier that Katniss understands, finally, that there is gray area in life. Although Snow was a vehemently horrible man, he was not pure evil; he was a product of the Capitol environment as much as Katniss was a product of the Seam. And although Coin may possess a more populist ideology, she is not "a greater good," given that she was willing to sacrifice, abuse, and murder others to gain power for herself and to promote her own political ideals. Katniss chooses to use what she has learned from Peeta and Cinna—manipulation—to remain close enough to Coin to assassinate her and effectively end the cycle of violence in Panem—at least for a few generations.

Katniss' choice to rid Panem of Coin instead of Snow reveals that she has gained an understanding that violence is a cycle and that—as evidenced by the Treaty of Treason that had taken Katniss' home, sister, and youth—requiring the deaths of innocents as recompense for the deaths of innocents would never give Panem the peaceful future that she had hoped the end of the Hunger Games would bring. Once Katniss decides not to kill Snow, her focus shifts—from revenge against Snow to the full emancipation of Panem from tyranny.

15

Accountability for Acts of War in the Hunger Games

Although *Mockingjay* is easily the least popular of the three Hunger Games series novels, it is not due to any lack of intrigue, excitement, romance, world-building, or character development. Most commonly, this is attributed to the final novel's lack of continued delineation between "good characters" like Gale and Peeta and "bad characters" such as President Snow. *Mockingjay* hinges on providing no good guys, bad guys, or morally satisfying conclusions to Panem's—or Katniss'—story.

This is implicit from very early in the book, when Katniss first arrives in District 13 and learns that, rather than being a small, struggling, ragtag commune, District 13 is a thriving, strict, structured society. The Capitol's citizens are ignorant of the horror of the Games; the citizens of District 13 know, understand, and purposely ignore the horror of the Games, so long as their lives are not affected. This similarity between ignorant compliance and willful

175

negligence, and what that means for ethics and morality in our world, are *Mockingjay*'s central focus.

The question of District 13's culpability in the Hunger Games is a vital part of *Mockingjay* as capstone of the Hunger Games series. But there are two other issues that encapsulate the debate regarding accountability in the Hunger Games series as a whole: the Career culture of Districts 1, 2, and 4, and the death of Prim Everdeen.

Career Culture

The idea of nebulous morality and shared responsibility for violent acts is brought to the fore in *Mockingjay*, but it's been a part of the Hunger Games series from the beginning. Although questions of war take center stage towards the end of the trilogy, *The Hunger Games* places the Careers at its heart: Are Cato, Clove, Marvel, and Glimmer child monsters or victims in their own right?

In the Seventy-Fourth Hunger Games, Katniss describes Cato, a Career from District 2, as "monstrous." She details how fellow District 2 Career Clove taunts Katniss with details about Rue's death as she prepares to kill her, and the circumstances of Rue's death paint District 1 Career Marvel as a bad guy for killing her. In *Catching Fire*, we learn that Enobaria, a District 2 victor from some years past, won her Games by biting out an opponent's throat and has since had her teeth sharpened into symbolic trophies and very real weapons. The characterization of the Careers in both novels is limited, but it clearly casts them as smaller-scale villains, often without giving them an opportunity for redemption before their deaths.

But there is plenty to suggest that, rather than monsters, the Careers are meant to be seen as victims of the Games–tesserae system as much as, or more than, the other tributes. Cato dies after the wolf-mutts attack him at the Cornucopia, following a drawn-out, torturous process that ends only when Katniss mercy-kills him in an act of humanity; Enobaria is taken hostage with the other victors after the Quell plot is bungled, and Katniss insists that she be rescued along with Annie, Peeta, and Johanna. Both examples suggest Katniss recognizes their shared victimhood, even if the other tribute does not. The movie's interpretation of Cato's death even shows him having an overt epiphany about the true evil of the Games and closes his character arc with a redemptive assisted suicide, though in the novels, there is no indication of such.

Are Cato and Clove psychopaths, acting roles for the camera, or the product of their district's insular Career culture, raised not to appreciate the gravity of death?

Katniss and Gale have a conversation early on in *The Hunger Games* that shows how little separates her from the Careers:

> "Katniss, it's just hunting. You're the best hunter I know," says Gale.
> "It's not just hunting. They're armed. They think," I say.
> "So do you. And you've had more practice. Real practice," he says. "You know how to kill."...
> The awful thing is that if I can forget they're people, it will be no different at all.[THG40]

The inclusion of this realization so early on suggests that we, as readers, are meant to use it as a framework for understanding the actions of the tributes in the Games—not as some unknowable evil but as something frighteningly close to what we, too, could imagine doing to survive.

But that empathetic understanding, it's implied, should not be used as an excuse: forgetting that the other tributes are people is still something "awful." Because Katniss is the heroine, we forgive her for killing Marvel and brush off her blasé acceptance of Foxface's death; because Cato, Clove, Glimmer, Marvel, Brutus, and their kin are the narrative's villains, we are prepared and—in some cases—glad when they die. But there are tributes whose names we never learn: the District 3 boy at the Cornucopia, those lost during the bloodbath at the start of every Hunger Games, the morphlings. We view their deaths as spectators, unconcerned with their personal stories or outcomes; in a way, we forget they're people, the same way Katniss is afraid of doing.

Part of this reader detachment likely stems from growing up in a media culture where death on-screen is commonplace and expected. However, the deaths of the nameless characters are particularly forgettable for just that reason—they're nameless. By removing such a central human characteristic, they are made less human than Katniss, Peeta, Rue, Finnick. Even the "villain" characters are more relatable—and more favored in fandom—than the nameless "good" characters.

There are other significant parallels between Katniss, who is "good," and the Careers, who are "bad." When Katniss enters her arena, she is able to hunt with a bow ("a rarity,"[THG5] as she describes it, in the districts), throw knives, forage, identify plants and animals, and swim. Peeta was a wrestler, used to pain from the hot ovens of the bakery and his mother's abuse, and could dead-lift probably any tribute other than Thresh, and was a master manipulator, a skill he would have cultivated to protect himself from his mother's moods. What makes Katniss and Peeta any different from those who Katniss deems Careers? Did Katniss and Peeta survive to the end because they were, essentially, Careers from District 12?

Katniss describes the Careers as being well-trained tributes who volunteered for their positions in the arena. But Katniss was well trained . . . and she also volunteered.

> The other kids make way immediately allowing me a straight path to the stage . . . With one sweep of my arm, I push her behind me.
> "I volunteer!" I gasp. "I volunteer as tribute!" . . .
> District 12 hasn't had a volunteer in decades and the protocol has become rusty. The rule is that once a tribute's name has been pulled from the ball, another eligible boy . . . or girl . . . can step forward to take his or her place.[THG22]

As Katniss tells us, this is not uncommon in some places in Panem:

> In some districts, in which winning the reaping is such a great honor, people are eager to risk their lives, the volunteering is complicated. But in District 12, where the word *tribute* is pretty much synonymous with the word *corpse*, volunteers are all but extinct.[THG22]

Here's how Katniss describes the District 2 and District 12 reapings:

> A monstrous boy who lunges forward to volunteer from District 2 . . . Last of all, they show District 12. Prim being called, me running forward to volunteer. You can't miss the desperation in my voice.[THG45]

There is very little difference between Katniss "running forward to volunteer" and Cato lunging forward to volunteer. The major difference—the only difference—is motivation. Both Katniss and Cato desperately volunteered out of their own personal sense of what is right; however, Katniss' driving motivation was survival and familial duty while Cato's was the desire to serve district and country.

The key difference between the Careers and the other tributes is cultural attitude. The District1/District 2/District 4 Career culture is wholly different from survival; in the Career districts, it was the idea of jingoistic and socioeconomic glory that drove future tributes more than survival or duty. (The Peacekeepers, especially given that they are trained in District 2, may be a direct comment on the danger of glorifying violence in the service of nationalism; the people called "Peacekeepers" in Panem are likely citizens who grew up as Careers, trained to kill.) For the Careers, to be a tribute in the Hunger Games is a high distinction and an honor bestowed by the Capitol.

Of course, Katniss, too, received a Capitol honor, hers prior to her reaping, and equally as meaningless as the "honor" of becoming a tribute: a medal of distinction for her father's death.

> The girl who five years ago stood huddled with her mother and sister, as he presented her, the oldest child, with a medal of valor. A medal for her father, vaporized in the mines.[THG22]

This cultural difference between Career districts and other districts—that of the value of nationalism—also seems to be exacerbated by an institutional element: that Careers are allowed to train openly, while those in the other districts are not.

> My father could have made good money selling [his bows and arrows], but if the officials found out he would have been publicly executed for inciting a rebellion.[THG5]

Given the racial graduation of the districts and the status of the Peacekeepers as unanimously former District 2 citizens, however, it may not be official edict that allows the Careers to train and the other districts' citizens to be punished: it may come down to socioeconomic and geo-ethnic bigotry on the parts of the Peacekeepers and/or local mayors.

Regardless of reason, the result is a balance between district oppression and Capitol nationalism in the wealthier districts that makes Careers equal parts victim and perpetrator. Their attitude about the Hunger Games—their ruthlessness and bloodthirstiness—is the biggest difference between the Career tributes and the tributes who become their victims. And we can criticize the system that shaped that ruthlessness without absolving the individual tributes of their responsibility for it.

The Death of Prim Everdeen

This leads to what is perhaps the most heated, divisive question in the Hunger Games series:

Who killed Prim Everdeen?

Although there are no definitive answers—the "culprit" behind Prim's death is never clearly revealed—different stances on the part of various groups of fans, and where they place the blame, play into differing ideas about morality in war as a whole. Who is to blame when it comes to the atrocities of war? The weapons' makers or the ones responsible for deploying them? The people who drove the necessity for war to begin with?

The most contentious claim, and probably the most widely supported, is the idea that Gale is responsible for Prim's death, ostensibly because he had a hand in designing the bomb that caused it. It's his role in Prim's death that puts the final nail in the coffin of his hopes for a romantic future with Katniss. If the second round of parachute explosions was intentional, and not the result of accidental delay—and if it was the rebels, and not the Capitol, that dropped the parachutes in the first place—then the weapon Katniss saw Gale work on in District 13, one that plays on human sympathy, does suggest a certain amount of culpability in Prim's death. However, if Gale is to be blamed because of his role in creating the weapon, then Beetee must be blamed, too, because he is the one responsible for the bomb's technology. And if those who create war technology are primarily at fault for the deaths their technology causes, then it likewise stands to reason that the Gamemakers are primarily at fault for the deaths of all tributes in the arena—something most Hunger Games fans do not agree with, instead placing the blame largely on Snow or the Games–tesserae system itself.

Why, then, not blame Presidents Snow and Coin for Prim's death? Certainly, many do. Snow is generally considered as the person most "at fault" for the horror of the Hunger Games because he was in a position to stop them and instead chose not only to continue them but also condone, if not request, increasing levels of inhumanity and manipulation within them (such as the mockingjays trained to sound like loved ones in pain for the Quarter Quell). Similarly, then, Snow is also arguably at the root of the Second Rebellion, given that the rebellion is against him and his government. Katniss, certainly, believes at first that Snow is most at fault for Prim's death—both ideologically, as the representative of the government that made the rebellion necessary, and directly, as the person who ordered the parachute bombs dropped. But Snow claims that the latter, at least, is not true—that he had no reason to kill Capitol children or order the second round of detonations—and convinces Katniss that it was Coin who deployed the bombs that killed Prim, in order to make the Capitol government appear even more sadistic and destroy the Capitol citizens' loyalty.

If Coin did, indeed, know that a second round of detonations would take place and still chose to send Prim onto the battlefield, then she is the most logical "culprit" behind the killing. Even if she did not intend to put Prim in particular into the line of fire, the fault for Prim's death still appears to lie with her. However, the Gamemaker argument remains in play here, as well: Why would Coin be more at fault for creating or approving the battle plan than the person who actually detonated the weapon? Does that mean that Seneca Crane—or Plutarch—would be more at fault for Rue's death than Marvel, who physically killed her?

Snow also implies that the mastermind behind the double round of explosions—which were conveniently televised live across the Capitol, horrifying the public and "instantly snapp[ing] whatever frail allegiance"[M357] they still felt towards Snow's government—may have been Plutarch. As Snow points out to Katniss: "It's that sort of thinking you look for in a Head Gamemaker, isn't it?"[M357] There are those who believe that Coin must have been at fault because she is the one who would have most benefitted from Prim's death had it not led to her own at Katniss' hand. But Plutarch stood to benefit as much from the end of the war as Coin did: Plutarch, alone of the known Hunger Games characters and perhaps alone out of Panem, would have found financial gain in the creation of a free market Panem, by capitalizing on the loss of the Hunger Games and the personal connections he forged during the rebellion with Panem's celebrities: Katniss herself and Peeta, among others. Prim's death, in Plutarch's eyes, may have just added drama to Katniss' narrative. The deaths of those Capitol children, and of the brave rebel medics who went to tend to them, certainly added drama to the conclusion of the war. Should Plutarch's financial gain be considered a lesser motive than Coin's political motivation in causing, or excusing, Prim's death?

Or, of course, perhaps Katniss, the Mockingjay, the emblem of the war and the rallying point of its battles—including the battle in which Prim died—is to blame for Prim's death. It's an argument that ignores the idea of actual, physical culpability: Katniss did not drop the bomb that killed Prim nor did she build it or chart its course. But if Katniss had never volunteered in Prim's place—if she had not performed her feint with the berries, had not become the Girl On Fire or the Mockingjay—then Prim would not have been in the Capitol on the day she died. The rebellion may still have happened, but Prim Everdeen likely would not have been a part of it.

With each possible explanation for Prim's death come further possibilities and doubts: If Katniss is to blame, then would not Cinna be as well for turning her into a symbol? If Cinna is to blame for creating the symbols that made Katniss a revolutionary icon, then does it not circle back to Snow being at fault for propagating the Hunger Games that made her a star in the first place? Or does it all go back to the First Rebellion, before Katniss and Prim's grandparents were even born: Was Prim, as an innocent victim of war, always marked for death in a society like Panem? (Narratively, the answer is *yes*: the Hunger Games series begins, really, with Prim's reaping and ends with her death—Prim suffers a predictable, unnecessary death caused by the Hunger Games after all.)

By never revealing the actual source of the bomb, by never revealing who ordered it dropped or whether it was one that Gale or Beetee designed and built, Collins creates a resonant microcosm of war itself: *Who killed Prim Everdeen?* can only be answered insofar as *Who causes war?* can. There is no one distinct point of origin, no single individual responsible, for the Second Rebellion or Prim's death—or for similar suffering in our own world.

Final Notes

Capitol Viewers and the New Panem

The nebulous conclusion of the Hunger Games series is a fitting illustration of what makes the series as a whole so remarkable within the Young Adult genre: rather than leading its readers to a set, cut-and-dried moral, the series treats revolution and war with the same ambiguity that they have in life, with none of its characters fully culpable or fully innocent and no conclusions fully satisfying.

Other popular YA and Middle Grade series of great depth and nuance—Percy Jackson and the Olympians, Harry Potter, A Series of Unfortunate Events—tend to divide their characters' worlds and the characters who populate them into good versus evil. And at the opening of the series, the Hunger Games' characters, too, seem to be clearly divided between "good" and "bad" in the comfortable and expected dichotomy. The people of the Seam are good; the people of the Capitol are bad. But over the course of the series, as Katniss' experience with the world grows far beyond the fences of District 12, her beliefs shift, her mind opens, and her—and our—understanding of Panem becomes richer.

The Hunger Games begins to chip away at its own veneer of a morally simplistic, easily delineated Panem right away: from Madge's quiet rejection of her wealthy upbringing to Peeta's abuse at the hands of his mother, the graduated loss of the privileged veneer of the merchants' side of District 12 is our first inkling that perhaps there is *more* going on in Panem than just the Hunger Games. And the pages that follow are full of one destroyed preconception after another, from the revelation that winning the Hunger Games may be an even worse fate than losing to the realization that, in backing the rebellion, President Coin may not have the best interests of Panem's citizens in mind at all.

A common reaction from Hunger Games fans is that they feel "shell-shocked" after turning the final page of *Mockingjay*, as ill at ease with the end of the Second Rebellion and the Hunger Games as Katniss professes to be at the end, as she watches her children dance on a graveyard. Although a number of readers dislike the openness of the ending, it is a fitting close to the Hunger Games series: we are left with more loose ends than answers. How did Annie care for herself and Finnick's baby? Where did Johanna go? How in the world did Katniss and Peeta get far enough past their experiences in the Games and the war to decide to have children? Did Plutarch really start airing *Panem Idol*?

The biggest question, though, and one that affects all of the rest, is, *What happened to Panem?*

How did District 12 become a center of medicine production—and if not from coal, once the District 12 mines were closed, where did the rest of Panem get its power? What did District 6 do if not manufacture medicine? Did its skilled workers migrate to District 12? Or did districts become responsible for producing more of their goods locally, returning to a system more akin to the one North America knew before the world wars? How did all of the various district cultures intermingle in the years after the war?

Was Plutarch's cryptic prediction, that Panem was only enjoying a brief cease-fire between periods of violence, correct?

The beauty of the questions with which the series leaves us is that, through fandom—through interpretation and reinterpretation, through careful, loving extrapolation—these questions never need to go unanswered. There can be thousands of answers, shaped by different readers' unique experiences and perspectives on the world, just as the canonical Panem is shaped by Suzanne Collins through Katniss'. And through that unique transformative process of interaction with the text and interaction with others who love the Hunger Games, we discover

FINAL NOTES

that the question of "what happened to Panem" after the rebellion is, in effect, the same question with which the series began, lingering still after turning the final page: *How could the Hunger Games ever become accepted; how could our North America fall so far as to think of killing children as entertainment?*

The final question behind the Hunger Games series, one that we attempt to answer over and over again, is not *What happened to Panem?* but *What's happening to us?*

The Hunger Games Lexicon

> In late summer, I was washing up in a pond when I noticed the plants growing around me. Tall with leaves like arrowheads. Blossoms with three white petals. I knelt down in the water, my fingers digging into the soft mud, and I pulled up handfuls of the roots. Small, bluish tubers that don't look like much but boiled or baked are as good as any potato. "Katniss," I said aloud. It's the plant I was named for. And I heard my father's voice joking, "As long as you can find yourself, you'll never starve."[THG52]

Every name in the Hunger Games series plays a significant role in characterization, either revealing possibilities for untold backstory or foreshadowing the character's final fate in the series. The Capitol characters' names tend to relate to their real-world historical parallels in the ruling or fall of Imperial Rome, like Cinna, while district-born characters' names are often reminiscent of their home's specialty, like Thresh, both the strong and deadly District 11 tribute of the Seventy-fourth Games and a lethal, efficient aspect of agricultural cultivation (to *thresh* is to beat grain from its stalks; a *thresher* is a highly dangerous farming machine).

The Hunger Games series is Katniss' story. However, due to Suzanne Collins' extraordinary attention to detail and skill with historical, scientific, and literary allusion, the books also tell dozens of further, deeper stories about the Second Rebellion and fall of the Capitol. Embedded in its characters' names are personal histories, motivations for rebellion, and connections between the page and our world that make the Hunger Games grow from an enjoyable reading experience to a rich, thought-provoking analysis of the contemporary Western world.

From a fangirl's perspective, this richness makes for a more entertaining experience, as well! After all, who wouldn't be inspired by learning that Woof's name likely refers not to the sound a dog makes but the cross-threads of a loom, which ties him to his home in District 8?

This lexicon includes a look into every character name in the Hunger Games trilogy, with discussions of their possible origins, etymologies, and figurative resonance.

A Note on District Names

Names in Panem, like any names, have meaning beyond their linguistic origins. They also reflect the culture they come from, and the culture of the parents that choose them.

One interesting result of the isolation of each district and its culture in Panem—as well as the further separations we see within individual districts, between district specialty classes and merchant classes—is the variation in naming practices. Although each individual name in the series has its own potentially meaningful peculiarities, we also see similarities in the names of people who share the same district origin—and stark differences between naming practices in different districts. Those who live in the Capitol—and a few key characters from Career districts who sympathize with Capitol ideals—have names derived from Roman history; characters from the districts have names related to their districts' specialties or elements of nature. Young girls, in particular, are all named for flowers, while adult characters from the Hob have largely proprietary names that come from contemporary phrases, songs, or nursery rhymes—holdovers in Panem from our own culture, perhaps.

Names in our world work in a similar way; they follow specific cultural norms. Economist Steven D. Levitt and Stephen J. Dubner, authors of *Freakonomics*, explored the issue of names' relationship to culture on their podcast in 2005 and in two *Slate* articles that they published concurrently. They heavily cite a study done in 2004 by Levitt and a young, black Harvard colleague, Roland G. Fryer Jr., whose area of study is the role of race in economics, in which they looked at the birth certificates for every child born in California from 1961 to 2004, which afforded them information from names and races to gender, birth weight, parents' marital status, zip code, means of paying the hospital, and level of education. (The Panem equivalent of this might be district origin, tesserae taken out, and whether the child was of the specialty or merchant class.) One of the things they discovered was a stark difference in naming practices between black and white parents, a cultural difference that was only intensified by economic differences.

They suggest that the choice of a "distinctively black" name may be "a black parent's signal of solidarity with her community."[lxxv] But these connections between a culture and certain names are not just meaningful to the people who choose them and those within their community. They also affect how the names' recipients are seen by those outside the community.

We experience this sort of stereotyping in the Hunger Games series largely through Katniss, as she reacts to others' names. Nature and specialty class names seem to be familiar to her; she does not seem to find Rue's or Thresh's names strange, and her description of Prim's appearance is tied not only to Prim's namesake but to other natural imagery:

> Prim's face is fresh as a raindrop, as lovely as the primrose for which she was named.[THG3]

In contrast, she reacts to the name of the female District 1 tribute with distaste:

> Glimmer I hear someone call her—ugh, the names the people in District 1 give their children are so ridiculous.[THG182]

We can probably assume that other districts' names carry their own baggage in Panem, depending on who's judging—including the names of Seam residents like Katniss, Gale, Haymitch, and Hazelle.

Evidence from real-world studies suggests that "all [parents are] trying to signal something with a name, and an overwhelming number

A NOTE ON DISTRICT NAMES

of parents are seemingly trying to signal their own expectations of how successful they hope their children will be."[lxxvii] This may partially explain why some Career tributes, like Cato, have Roman names like Capitol citizens. The Capitol is a symbol of wealth and luxury; for a Career district resident, what could signal success more clearly than a name that is popular there?

Katniss identifies Glimmer as a representative District 1 name, despite never having been there or met anyone from District 1 in real life. We don't know whether girl names like *Cashmere* and *Glimmer* are the only kind we'd see in District 1, but we do know that there is a breadth of names among the girls in District 12, from *Katniss* (from the Seam) and *Delly* and *Madge* (from the merchant class) among the sixteen-year-olds to *Primrose* a few years later and, interestingly, another floral name—*Posy*—in the Seam after that. That level of variety would suggest that names in every district may display more variance than the names of tributes in either *The Hunger Games* or *Catching Fire* would lead us to believe. However, Glimmer *may* be a very common name among girls who volunteer as Career tributes for the Hunger Games, a source of wealth and fame in Panem (and therefore, as in all other cultures, success).

In our world, Levitt and Dubner suggest that, when it comes to what names are popular and why, "There is a clear pattern at play: Once a name catches on among high-income, highly educated parents, it starts working its way down the socioeconomic ladder. Amber, Heather, and Stephanie started out as high-end names. For every high-end baby given those names, however, another five lower-income girls received those names within ten years . . . many parents, whether they realize it or not, like the sound of names that sound 'successful.'"[lxxviii] So maybe if Haymitch had been more likeable, District 12 would have become overrun with little Haymitches or Abernathies. Maybe in the months after the Seventy-fourth Hunger Games, newborn girls were named Katniss or Sagittarias and boys were named Peeta or Ryes. In the other districts,

I'd bet that there are many Finnicks and Brutuses and yes, Cashmeres and Glosses—and Glimmers.

So yes: *Glimmer* is something of a ridiculous name, but Katniss considers it ridiculous because it is not a name anyone would have in District 12 and we, the readers, consider it ridiculous only insofar as our own culture does not use it. But in District 1, where there may even be a previous victor named Glimmer, it likely isn't a ridiculous name at all, but a name associated with predicted success in the Hunger Games.

As of this writing in 2012, the predicted most popular baby names in America for the year included names based on Roman origin (like *Flavius*, *Caesar*, *Plutarch*, and *Cinna*), as well as exotic floral names (like a certain *Primrose*) . . . and names based on the Hunger Games series itself (like *Katniss* and *Gale*)! So although Katniss might consider *Glimmer*, *Marvel*, *Cashmere*, and *Gloss* to be ridiculous names, the rest of us might need to start getting prepared to hear people calling them out on the playground in a few years.[lxxix]

Panem Names

ABERNATHY, Haymitch

Abernathy is a habitational name—one that is derived from a place or home—that means *from the mouth of the River Nethy*. It is a name of Pictish (a Scottish language) origin. One potential origin for the name may be American civil rights leader Ralph Abernathy, a close associate of Martin Luther King, Jr., who, like Haymitch, worked for improvement for the lives of the poor. The organization he ran, the Poor People's Campaign, reflected Abernathy's deep conviction that "the key to the salvation and redemption of this nation lay in its moral and humane response to the needs of its most oppressed and poverty-stricken citizens."[lxxx]

Haymitch is a proprietary name; as far as I could tell, it does not directly derive from anywhere else. Possible partial origins include *hayseed*, given that District 12 is in a historically rural area, and *Mitchell*, a Medieval English name meaning *he who is like god*. If one thinks of Haymitch as the brains behind the Second Rebellion, that *could* fit.

Haymitch is also similar to Hamish, which is the "anglicized form of a Sheumais . . . or . . . of Seumas."[lxxxi] Seumas is the Scottish form of *James*, a name that appears several times in the Bible; one biblical James is viewed as Jesus' brother. James also comes from the same Hebrew name as *Jacob*, meaning he *who supplants*. Considering the definition of supplant (to take the place or move into the position of), the name is appropriate for Haymitch, who, in a way, becomes a father figure for and protector of Katniss and Peeta, who are missing a father and a protector, respectively. His role in the Second Rebellion, also, is to help supplant the existing government of Panem.

ATALA

CAPITOL TRAINER FOR THE SEVENTY-FOURTH HUNGER GAMES

Atala has three likely possible origins:

The first is the novella *Atala*, which criticizes the idea of *the noble savage*. Atala helps the tributes learn to survive, a noble act; however, she does it because she is a part of the institution condemning them to violent death, and therefore is a savage native.

The second is *Eumaeus atala*, a species of butterfly that nests and feeds among toxic plants—something beautiful that survives on plants that kill other insects and animals. (Incidentally, the butterfly is named after the novella.)

The third is Atalanta, a champion runner and athlete in Greek mythology.

BEETEE
DISTRICT 3 TRIBUTE IN THE QUARTER QUELL

Beetee is most likely related to the District 3 specialty of electronics/technology, derived from BTU, the unit of measurement traditionally associated with energy. (On a fun but likely irrelevant note: 1 watt [of electricity, which is a component of District 3's specialty] is **3**.41214 BTU/h.)

However, another possible derivation, considering Collins' military knowledge and background, is the WWII training aircraft Vultee BT-13 Valiant or "the Bee Tee." Two variations were produced and the difference between them was in their electrical systems. Like Beetee, they were not used in active battle zones during the war but instead were involved in the training and preparation of pilots before deployment.

BLIGHT
DISTRICT 7 TRIBUTE IN THE QUARTER QUELL

The literal definition of *blight* is rapid, infectious plant death. One possible extrapolation of Blight's name can be found in Johanna's assessment of him—"He's not much, but he was home"[CF349]—and Johanna's general view of District 7, the Capitol, and its control over victors: as the source of rapid, infectious death. The Capitol is a metaphorical blight on the districts.

BOGGS
HIGH-RANKING SOLDIER IN DISTRICT 13

One possible origin for Boggs' name comes from a figure of US military history: William Robertson Boggs. This Boggs was a general in the

A NOTE ON DISTRICT NAMES

Confederate Army (unpopularly but undeniably a rebel army) during the American Civil War, playing a leadership role similar to the one District 13's Boggs plays in *Mockingjay*.

A "bog" is also a marshland; they are known in Ireland to preserve dead bodies well), perhaps foreshadowing his character's death in *Mockingjay*.

BONNIE
ESCAPEE FROM DISTRICT 8

Bonnie is a traditional English/Scottish name meaning *pretty girl*.

BRISTEL
DISTRICT 12 COAL MINER

The most likely meaning behind Bristel's name is the verb form of *bristle*: to react angrily or defensively, typically by drawing oneself up. Bristel in the Hunger Games is one of the few miners from Gale's crew who stands up for him against Cray at his whipping in *Catching Fire*. He also helps to fashion a stretcher and bring Gale back to the Everdeens' in the aftermath. In its noun form, *bristle* is a sharp instrument used to make brushes. Bristel's name denotes a rebellious nature. However, it could also be a reference to the explosive/volatile properties of coal.

BRUTUS
DISTRICT 2 TRIBUTE IN THE QUARTER QUELL

Brutus is one of the several Hunger Games names that come from those involved in the assassination of Julius Caesar. However, Brutus is a district citizen and not a Capitolite. This is markedly different from most of the other district characters in the Hunger Games—and markedly similar to another District 2 Career tribute, Cato, who is also named for a Roman figure rather than his district specialty.

In William Shakespeare's telling of Caesar's assassination, Brutus' involvement in the conspiracy is treated as dramatic irony; he is one of Caesar's closest friends (just as District 2 is the district most loyal to the

Capitol in *Mockingjay*). This could suggest that he had potential to turn against the Capitol, but because Peeta kills Brutus in the last moments of the Quarter Quell, we will never know.

Of note: The historical Brutus' father was killed by Pompey the Great in dubious circumstances after he (the father) had taken part in the rebellion of Lepidus (the same rebellion that caused the banishment of Cornelius Cinna), suggesting the possibility that Brutus' lineage could have ties to the First Rebellion, before the introduction of the Hunger Games into Panem culture. Both the historical *and* Shakespearean versions of Brutus married a Portia . . . which leads to further theories that the Hunger Games' Brutus had ties to the rebellion, despite not being a known entity to those involved in the Quell plot (although there is no canonical evidence of such).

The phrase *Sic semper tyrannis!* ("Thus, ever [or always], to tyrants!") is attributed to Brutus at Caesar's assassination.

CARDEW, Fulvia
PERSONAL ASSISTANT TO PLUTARCH HEAVENSBEE

Cardew may derive from Cornelius Cardew, an experimental composer. Cardew was a Communist and composed what he called "people's liberation music" in the 1970s. His music often drew from traditional English folk music, which he used to communicate lengthy Marxist-Maoist exhortations. Examples include "Smash the Social Contract" and "There Is Only One Lie, There Is Only One Truth."[lxxxii]

The historical Fulvia was an aristocratic Roman woman who was married to three of the most promising Roman men of her generation: Publius Clodius Pulcher, Gaius Scribonius Curio, and Mark Antony. All three husbands were supporters of Julius Caesar. Though Fulvia is more famous for her involvement in Antony's career, many scholars believe that she was politically active with all of her husbands; as Plutarch Heavensbee's assistant, the Hunger Games' Fulvia accompanies him to District 13 and into the field to create propos and plan publicity around the rebellion's battles.

CARTWRIGHT, Delly
DISTRICT 12 REFUGEE TO DISTRICT 13

A *cartwright* is someone who makes carts. Alexander Cartwright supposedly invented baseball, which is cool but not necessarily related to Delly—unless one considers that baseball is "the American pastime" and Delly is a strong exemplar of the New Panem: cooperative and willing to trust those from other districts, or even the Capitol, to work together towards a better future.

Sir Fairfax Leighton Cartwright was an author and British diplomat who became ambassador to the Austro-Hungarian Empire before World War I. His wife, Lady Cartwright, almost accidentally started an international incident between Russia and Austria at a party; Delly ameliorates a tense dinner scene between her, Peeta, and Katniss in *Mockingjay* after Peeta is hijacked.

Delly means *from a dell (valley)*, which would be appropriate, given District 12's location in the foothills of the Appalachian Mountains. But *Delly* is also a diminutive, or a nickname that often denotes small size, childishness, or affection, and there are several possible longer names from which Delly's could be derived, including *Adelaide* (of German origin, meaning *of a noble kin*) and *Cordelia* (the daughter of Shakespeare's King Lear, who was exiled for her honesty against the tyranny of the king).

However, the most interesting possibility for Delly is *Delilah*, a biblical name meaning *one who weakened*. Delilah was approached by the lords of the Philistines to discover the secret of Samson's strength in exchange for riches. Three times she asked Samson for the secret of his strength, and three times he gave her a false answer. On the fourth occasion he gave her the true reason: that he did not cut his hair in fulfillment of a vow to God. When Samson fell asleep on Delilah's knees, she called up her man to shave off the seven locks from his head, then betrayed him to his enemies.

Although one can see some parallels between Delly and Peeta's interactions in *Mockingjay* and Sampson and Delilah's story—Peeta sees Delly as a form of comfort; Delly repeatedly questions him in search of (what he sees as) the truth—Delly doesn't betray Peeta to his enemies (unless you count his perception of Katniss as an enemy).

CASHMERE
DISTRICT 1 TRIBUTE IN THE QUARTER QUELL

Cashmere is a soft wool obtained from goats. It is fine in texture, as well as strong and light, and garments made from it provide excellent insulation. Cashmere is considered a luxury material.

The word *cashmere* is a Romanization of *Kashmir*, a region of India famous for cashmere wool, saffron, silks, and other luxury goods—just like District 1.

CASTOR
CAPITOL CAMERAMAN TURNED REBEL PROPOS PRODUCER

The literal translation of *Castor* is *beaver*, but more saliently, Castor is one of the twins who became the constellation Gemini in Greek mythology; the other is Pollux. Castor was mortal while his twin was immortal, because they were sired by different fathers, and only Pollux's father was divine. When Castor died, Pollux asked Zeus to let him share his own immortality with his twin, and they were transformed into the Gemini constellation. They are the patrons of sailors (and the Hunger Games' Castor, along with Pollux and Cressida, works frequently with ocean district victor Finnick to make propos in *Mockingjay*).

Castor and Pollux are sometimes credited with accidentally starting the Trojan War, since they left Helen in Paris' charge at a party.

Of note: The mythological Castor was killed by his kin when he and Pollux were stealing cattle from their cousins' farm; the Hunger Games' Castor's name could therefore be considered foreshadowing for his death by friendly fire from the District 13 rebels.

CATO
DISTRICT 2 TRIBUTE IN THE SEVENTY-FOURTH HUNGER GAMES

Cato is a historical Roman figure who is featured in Shakespeare's *Julius Caesar*. Interestingly, in both history and the Shakespeare play, Cato committed suicide, though historically, Cato did so two years before the assassination of Caesar rather than in the immediate lead-up (perhaps we are to assume the gap between Cato's death and Snow's death to be significant?). Because the Hunger Games' Cato begs Katniss for a mercy kill, this naming choice could suggest we should equate his death with suicide.

The historical Cato was a figurehead of the anti-Caesar platform. This could be an intentional juxtaposition with the Hunger Games' Cato, who is from the district most loyal to the Capitol.

CECELIA
DISTRICT 8 TRIBUTE IN THE QUARTER QUELL

Cecelia is a Latin name meaning *blind*.

A very similar patrician name, *Caecilia*, was shared by all the women of a plebeian Roman family known as the Caecilii Metellii. They traced their lineage (mythologically) to Vulcan (Hephaestus, in Greek culture), who gave their family life through a single *spark*. The Hunger Games' Cecelia was a victor with many children and much to lose under the existing Panem government; it's easy to extrapolate from this that she joined the rebellion of the Girl On Fire to give her family a better chance at life.

Caecilia is also the genus name of amphibious snakes; perhaps the Hunger Games' Cecelia name draws on the symbol of snakes as malevolent or sneaky.

CHAFF
DISTRICT 11 MENTOR AND TRIBUTE IN THE QUARTER QUELL; HAYMITCH'S BEST FRIEND

Chaff's name is almost certainly derived from the District 11 specialty of farming/crop work, as *chaff* is a term for the protective casing of the seeds of cereal grain. Chaff (the grain casing, not the victor!) is inedible for humans; both chaffs denote toughness.

Etymologically, *chaff* comes from Middle English *chaf*, from Old English *ceaf*, related to Old High German *cheva* or *husk*. The character of

Chaff, in contrast—and in contrast to his friend Haymitch—is far from a husk; he seems full of life and vitality as he approaches the battle of the Third Quarter Quell.

CINNA

Cinna is a prime example of a Capitol character who owes his name to Roman imperial history as well as Shakespeare's *Julius Caesar*, as detailed in chapter thirteen. Historically, there were two major Cinnas of note involved in Caesar's death: Cornelius Cinna, Cinna the Conspirator, and Helvius Cinna, Cinna the Poet.

Cornelius Cinna was a conspirator against Caesar who played a key role in enlisting Brutus to the assassins' cause. Previous to this, however, he and Caesar were friends; Caesar called Cornelius back from exile from Rome and even granted Cinna a praetorship. The Capitol gave the Hunger Games' Cinna a similarly high position, as a Games stylist—though choosing to design for District 12 was seen by many as something like a career exile, giving him and Cornelius something else in common.

Helvius Cinna was a poet, well known enough to be included by Ovid in his list of celebrated erotic poets and writers. He was also a friend of Roman historian Plutarch—just as the Hunger Games' Cinna and Plutarch seem to have been friends . . . or at least co-conspirators.

Both Cornelius and Helvius were men of some mystery, which seems only appropriate for the namesakes of the Hunger Games' enigmatic Cinna.

CLOVE

DISTRICT 2 TRIBUTE IN THE SEVENTY-FOURTH HUNGER GAMES

The English word *clove* derives from Latin *clavus* or *nail*. As a spice, clove has some medicinal purposes; the use of a clove on a toothache is said to decrease pain.

However, *clove* is also the past tense of the verb *to cleave*, which can mean either to bind or to sever. In the Seventy-fourth Hunger Games,

Clove favors fighting with a large knife, so "to sever" is the most likely origin for her name.

COIN, Alma

Although the most obvious meaning for Coin is, well, coins—cash, money—COIN is also a US military abbreviation for *CO*unter-*IN*surgency operations. Given Collins' military background and the role that Coin plays in Panem's insurgency, this is the more likely derivation of President Coin's surname. Another related military association: military coins, which are tokens (similar to the mockingjay crackers distributed by rebels and sympathizers in Panem's District 8) that are given to members of covert organizations both to enhance morale and to prove membership when challenged.

Alma is, interestingly, Spanish for *soul*, as well as a Latin word meaning *nourishing*. However, it's more likely that President Alma Coin is named for the Battle of Alma, the first battle of the Crimean War, which was fought between the Russian Empire on one side and French, British, and Ottoman Empires and the Kingdom of Sardinia on the other from 1853 to 1856. In the Battle of Alma, the British troops abandoned their usual ordered precision and fought guerilla-style, similar to the rebellion's preferred approach.[lxxxiii]

The battle also spawned a folk song in the United Kingdom, the lyrics of which are reminiscent of the battle for the Capitol in *Mockingjay*, particularly the targeting of the Nut and Snow's mansion:

> But when the Alma came in view,
> The stoutest heart it would subdue . . .
> They were so strongly fortified
> With batteries on the mountain side . . .
> The shot and shell it fell like rain
> While we the batteries strove to gain,
> And many's hero then was slain
> Upon the heights of Alma.

Following the victory at the Battle of Alma, the name became a popular girls' name in the United Kingdom, and many survivors of the battle made a pact that each man would name his firstborn son Alma.

CRANE, Seneca

The crane may be the oldest bird on Earth; there is fossil proof that they existed more than 60 million years ago. Traditionally, the crane is a bird of omen, and in Eastern symbolism, the crane represents *unparalleled faithfulness*—which may allude to Crane's loyalty to the Capitol, despite being killed for treason.

The historical Seneca was tutor and later advisor to Emperor Nero. He was forced to commit suicide for conspiring to assassinate Nero but may have been innocent, echoing the uncertainty around the Hunger Games' Seneca Crane's hanging for his actions as Gamemaker during the Seventy-fourth Hunger Games.

It is alleged that the historical Seneca moved to Rome from Spain, which makes him, like the historical Plutarch, a high-ranking Roman official who came to the empire from outside of Rome (which suggests interesting origins for the Hunger Games' Seneca and Plutarch). His writings expose traditional themes of Stoic philosophy, including ones consistent with the philosophy of the Games in Panem: contentment is achieved through a life in accordance with duty to the state; human suffering should be accepted and has a beneficial effect. In particular, Seneca considered it important to confront one's own mortality.

CRAY

HEAD PEACEKEEPER OF DISTRICT 12

Cray's name has many possible points of origin, but the most likely is the *Cray-1*, the world's first supercomputer. It was later replaced by the *Cray-XMP*. The major function of both supercomputers was to read and decode an information request and then bring forward additional information about the query—just as Cray is in District 12 in part to keep the Capitol abreast of what is happening in the district, digging up information and bringing it forward to his superiors.

Alternately, it is possible that Cray is named for crayfish, which are freshwater crustaceans that feed on both living and dead organisms in, metaphorically, the same way that Cray is willing to "feed on" the people of District 12 by taking advantage of hungry young girls for his own pleasure.

CRESSIDA
HUNGER GAMES PRODUCER/DIRECTOR TURNED REBEL FILMOGRAPHER

Cressida was a Trojan woman who allegedly fell in love with Troilus, the youngest son of King Priam, and pledged to him her everlasting devotion. However, when she was sent to the Greeks as part of a hostage exchange, she formed a liaison with the Greek warrior Diomedes, and is consequently most often depicted by writers as "false Cressida," a paragon of female inconstancy as well as deception and betrayal. In the Hunger Games series, Cressida defects from the Capitol to District 13 and uses her knowledge of Panem's government and mass media system to help the rebellion.

In addition, there is a species of carnivorous butterfly named *Cressida cressida*, which rather fits The Hunger Games' Cressida—a Capitol butterfly outside but a government-toppling rebel inside!

CRESTA, Annie
DISTRICT 4 VICTOR WHO BECOMES FINNICK'S WIFE

Cresta most likely derives from *crest*, which is the top (or amplitude) of a wave—more symbolically, the part that rises from the sea. Given Annie's victory in the Seventieth Games—she is the only tribute not to drown; literally the only one "to rise from the water"—the surname Cresta is a fit not only for Annie's ocean-centric home district, District 4, but also her personal backstory.

Annie is a diminutive form of *Anne*, meaning *gracious, merciful*. Annie's vote against a Capitol Hunger Games in *Mockingjay*, extending mercy to the children of the Capitol, may point to this etymology as the reason the name was chosen. And the fact that Annie's name is one of the few diminutives in the Hunger Games universe is very telling, as it sets her on a younger/lower plane than the other victors. This could be indicative of the way she is used as bait for Finnick and why Mags would volunteer to take her place in the Quarter Quell. On the other hand, diminutives are commonly used to show familiarity and/or love, so that's a positive attribute to her name.

DALTON
DISTRICT 10 REFUGEE TO DISTRICT 13 WHO SPECIALIZES IN GENETIC MANIPULATION

Dalton means *from the valley town*. He may be named for Sir Howard Dalton, a British geneticist who died in 2008—approximately during the writing of *Mockingjay*, in which the Hunger Games' Dalton appears.

DARIUS
DISTRICT 12 PEACEKEEPER WHO BECOMES AN AVOX

Darius is etymologically Persian, and means *he possesses* or *rich*, *kingly*. However, the Darius of the Hunger Games most likely derives his name from the historical Roman Darius, who was a prefect of the praetorian Eastern Roman Empire. He presided during a major legal regime change but did not hold lawmaking power himself—just as Darius was a Peacekeeper in the time leading up to Panem's own regime change, and had only limited power, as best exemplified by his beating, dismissal, and ultimate denouncement as a traitor when he attempts to stymie Gale's whipping in *Catching Fire*.

DONNER, MAYSILEE
MADGE'S AUNT; DISTRICT 12 TRIBUTE IN THE FIFTIETH GAMES

Donner is a variation of *Donar*, the German name of the god Thor. In modern German, it means *thunder*.

In the United States/North America, the name is most commonly associated with the Donner Party, a group of American pioneers who set out for California in a wagon train in 1846. Delayed by a series of accidents and bad weather, and snowbound for months in the Sierra Nevadas, some of the emigrants resorted to cannibalism to survive. Maysilee Donner died shortly after deciding to split from Haymitch, with whom she had an alliance, in the Fiftieth Hunger Games; perhaps the name *Donner*, here, is intended to denote the departure from normal morality the Hunger Games represents or a break in interpersonal cooperation that leads to death.

Maysilee is a proprietary name of indeterminate origins.

EDDY
CHILD KILLED IN THE HOSPITAL FIREBOMBING OF DISTRICT 8

Eddy is a diminutive (a shortened form or nickname, but not derived from the traditional *-ie* affectionate format) form of any name beginning with *Ed-*. *Edward* means *wealthy guardian*, which is a poor match with Eddy's role in the novels: inspiring Katniss to embrace her symbolic role as the Mockingjay. *Edan*, an Irish name, is a better match; it means *a little fire*. *Edom*, a Hebrew name meaning *red*, is another possibility.

ENOBARIA
DISTRICT 2 TRIBUTE IN THE QUARTER QUELL

Enobaria is most likely a female form of *Enobarbus*, the name of a character in Shakespeare's *Antony and Cleopatra*. In the play, Enobarbus is considered a friend so loyal and so trusted by Antony that he is allowed to critique the government. In the context of the Hunger Games, this may just reflect Enobaria's origins in District 2, which is considered the most loyal of the districts. But in the play, Enobarbus frequently serves as commentator on the action. He moves about freely, seeing much that occurs among the heads of state, and uses that information to form his own conclusions, which he shares with other characters as well as the audience.[lxxxiv] Enobaria's filed teeth certainly serve as a comment on the Capitol's bloodlust and infatuation with appearance.

Enobaria is one of the delicious characters in the Hunger Games whose background must be almost entirely extrapolated from the morsel of her name and few details that Katniss discloses, given that she does not play a major role in our first-person narrator's life. Enobaria is described as a popular fixture of the Capitol and Hunger Games broadcasts and, if Enobarbus and his freedom to collect information and use it at will was, indeed, the inspiration for her name, she may well play the same role in the Capitol that Finnick does: a coerced slave who learned to trade personal favors for secrets.

EVERDEEN

When Suzanne Collins spoke with *EW's Shelf Life* just before *Mockingjay* was released in August 2010, she talked a little about the origins of Katniss' last name[lxxxv]:

> I sort of half read Thomas Hardy's *The Mayor of Casterbridge*. It was assigned in 10th grade, and I just couldn't get into it. About seven years later I rediscovered Hardy, and consumed four of his novels in a row. Katniss Everdeen owes her last name to Bathsheba Everdene, the lead character in *Far From the Madding Crowd*. The two are very different, but both struggle with knowing their hearts.

Everdeen is also an appropriate name for Katniss and her family in that it seems to be a portmanteau of *evergreen* and *Dean*.

An evergreen plant is one that has leaves in all seasons; like the Everdeens, it possesses the ability to survive and flourish despite harsh conditions. Like evergreens, which grow in the summer and are dormant in winter, Katniss and her family are renewed in the seasons between hardships. Between the Seventy-fourth Hunger Games and the Quarter Quell, Katniss begins to forgive her mother and the Everdeen women regain their closeness as a family; between Katniss' second reaping and the war on the Capitol, Prim matures and comes into her own as an apprentice to Mrs. Everdeen.

A NOTE ON DISTRICT NAMES

Evergreen plants grow well in poor soil or on disturbed ground. The shelter provided by existing evergreen plants can make it easier for younger evergreen plants to survive cold and/or drought, much like the shelter Katniss provides for Prim. Owing to the botanical meaning, the term *evergreen* can refer metaphorically to something that is continuously renewed or is self-renewing, like Katniss' resolve.

Dean means *of the valley*, which here is reflective of District 12's location in the foothills of the Appalachians. Katniss herself is also, metaphorically, like a valley between two mountains: on one side, Gale—revenge—and on the other, Peeta—forgiveness and peace.

Katniss

Katniss, as she herself explains in the books, is a starchy, aquatic root vegetable also called *sagittaria*. This name comes from the Latin *Sagittarius*, meaning *belonging to an arrow*, and refers to the shape of the leaves. In our Katniss' case, *belonging to an arrow* takes a more metaphorical meaning, one related to her proficiency with a bow and arrow. Katniss plants are found in canals, ponds, ditches, and slow rivers but are never abundant.

Given Collins' love of Greek mythology, *Katniss* might also be an intentional partial homophone of Artemis, the virgin goddess of the hunt, who was considered a bird goddess and whose traditional symbol is a bow and arrow.

Katniss' birthday is the only concrete date that we know in the series: May 8. In history, on May 8th:

- In 1450: Kentishmen revolted against King Henry VI in Jack Cade's Rebellion in London.
- In 1794: French chemist Antoine Lavoisier, who was also a tax collector with the Ferme Générale, was tried, convicted as a traitor, and guillotined all on the same day in Paris during the Reign of Terror.
- In 1919: Edward George Honey proposed the idea of a moment of silence to commemorate the WWI Armistice in

the United Kingdom in a letter to the *London Evening News*. Later, his idea was implemented in the United States as Memorial Day.
- In 1933: Mohandas Gandhi began a twenty-one-day fast in protest against British oppression in India.
- In 1941: The German Luftwaffe launched a bombing raid on Nottingham and Derby. A year later, also during WWII, the Battle of the Coral Sea ended while, elsewhere in the Pacific Theater, gunners of the Ceylon Garrison Artillery on Horsburgh Island in the Cocos Islands rebelled in the Cocos Islands Mutiny. Their mutiny was crushed and three of the soldiers were executed. Also on that day, in one of the final acts of the war in the African–European Theater, hundreds of Algerian civilians were killed by French Army soldiers in the Sétif massacre. The day also marked the end of the Prague Uprising.
- In 1973: The seventy-one-day standoff between federal authorities and the American Indian Movement members occupying the Pine Ridge Reservation at Wounded Knee, South Dakota, ended with the surrender of the militants.

Given the location of the Seam and its possible ethnic makeup, as well as the disparity between the rebels and the Capitol—and Suzanne Collins' age and the events that would have shaped her social consciousness—it is very possible that Katniss' birthday was intended to coincide with the end of Wounded Knee. However, the most likely reason that May 8th is Katniss' birthday is that May 8th is also V-E Day, which marked the end of fighting in the European Theater in WWII.

Primrose

The primrose is a small, blooming flower that closes at night. In the language of flowers, it represents three ideals: *I can't live without you*, *early youth*, and, for the evening primrose, *impermanence*, all of which are themes expressed through Prim and especially through her relationship with Katniss.

The language of flowers, also known as floriography, is a means of communication devised in the Victorian era that allowed coded messages to be sent through the arrangements of various flowers, permitting individuals to express feelings that otherwise could not be spoken—a system that would undoubtedly have been useful in Panem!

English primroses are actually one of the few endangered flower species, with sanctions imposed to prevent extinction through overpicking.

FLAVIUS
MEMBER OF KATNISS' PREP TEAM

Flavius was the family name of an imperial dynasty in Rome whose members were popular with the common people, much as Katniss grows to be fond of her whole prep team (including Flavius himself) despite the vast differences between them in culture and socioeconomic class.

In Rome, the Flavians initiated economical and cultural reforms, such as lowering taxes on the plebian class and increasing the silver content of Rome's coins, to bolster the Roman economy. A massive building program was enacted to celebrate the ascent of the Flavian dynasty, leaving multiple enduring landmarks in the city of Rome; the most spectacular of these was the Coliseum, which later housed the gladiatorial Games.

Although the Hunger Games' Flavius does not participate in the bloodshed of the Games, he, like his Roman namesakes, does help make them visually extravagant.

FLICKERMAN, Caesar

Flickerman has a few possible derivations. *The Flickerman* is the name of a somewhat obscure internet/radio docudrama about a life under the lens—an idea that would be familiar to the tributes as well as Caesar

Flickerman himself. The series' themes also resonate with those in the Hunger Games:

> The Flickerman is a ground-breaking, cross-platform drama in which the dividing line between the real and the imagined is increasingly hard to distinguish. It unfolds through radio broadcasts, audio downloads, on line movies, blog entries and multiple internet channels.[lxxxvi]

Flicker is also a term for the visible fading displayed on video screens between broadcast cycles, as well as a slang term for remote control.

The most obvious reference point for Caesar's first name is Julius Caesar, who was the figurehead of dictatorial Rome. Flickerman serves as a sort of figurehead for the Hunger Games, which serve as the epitome of the brutality of Snow's dictatorial Capitol, but given that Flickerman himself is not presented as a dictator, it's worth looking at other meanings of the name.

The original meaning of *Caesar* is unknown. The four most common derivations of the cognomen *Caesar* (a cognomen is a piece of Roman nomenclature similar to a last name) are given by the writer of the *Historia Augusta*). Two are applicable to the Hunger Games' Caesar:

> from *caesaries*, "hair", because the founder of this branch of the family was born with a full head of hair. (Julius Caesar himself was balding in later life.) This is the etymology favored by Festus . . .
> from *caesius*, an eye color variously translated today as "grey", "blue-grey", and even "blue" . . .[lxxxvii]

In Katniss' first Hunger Games, Caesar Flickerman's hair, lips, and eyes are all dyed pale blue.

FOXFACE
DISTRICT 5 TRIBUTE IN THE SEVENTY-FIFTH HUNGER GAMES

Proprietary figurative name.

The most straightforward meaning of Foxface's name is the one that inspires Katniss to name her Foxface in the first place: her face

A NOTE ON DISTRICT NAMES

looks like a fox's. As per traditional Western fable tropes, she is also "clever as a fox" or "sly as a fox."

Foxberry is another name for the lingonberry, but this is not the only connection in our culture between foxes and berries. Aesop's fable "The Fox and the Rowan Berries" also pairs the two, and is a possible origin for Foxface's name:

> The fox who longed for berries, beholds with pain
> The tempting clusters were too high to gain;
> Grieved in his heart he forced a careless smile,
> And cried, "They're sharp and hardly worth my while."[lxxxviii]

Related proverbs: "Sour, said the fox about rowan berries" (the origin of the phrase "sour grapes") and "The fox says of the mulberries when he cannot get at them; they are not good at all." Foxface, too, found that berries were not good (given that, instead of feeding her, the nightlock berries she eats poison her).

GLIMMER
DISTRICT 1 TRIBUTE IN THE SEVENTY-FOURTH HUNGER GAMES

To *glimmer* is *to shine faintly or unsteadily; to give off a subdued unsteady reflection; to appear indistinctly with a faintly luminous quality*. This name suggests the District 1 specialty of luxury goods but may also reflect both Glimmer's beauty and her early death in the Games.

GLOSS
DISTRICT 1 TRIBUTE IN THE QUARTER QUELL

In the verb form, to *gloss* is to *make attractive or acceptable by deception or superficial treatment*; the noun form means *a surface shininess or luster; a cosmetic that adds shine or luster; a superficially or deceptively attractive appearance*. Both definitions seem appropriate to the popular Career from District 1, and suggest not only District 1's luxury goods specialty but also the brutality that lies beneath the Career tributes' surface appearances. A *gloss* can also be a brief notation explaining the meaning of a word or wording in a text, suggesting perhaps that Gloss' characterization provides a brief explanation of the culture of Careers or of victors.

GREASY SAE
DISTRICT 12 RESIDENT
Proprietary name.

Interestingly, the name *Sae* is a folk derivation of *Suzanne*. Greasy Sae is there from the beginning of the series, is one of the few citizens of District 12 to escape to District 13 successfully, and is among the first to return home, following Katniss and Katniss' journey to its end. Could Greasy Sae be a subtle way for Suzanne Collins to insert herself into the story?

HAWTHORNE

The last name *Hawthorne* may refer to American writer Nathaniel Hawthorne, who often dealt with the theme of the inherent evil and sin of humanity and whose works often have moral messages. Gale's black-and-white worldview and deeply entrenched moral code are similar to those reflected in Hawthorne's works.

Hawthorne may also refer to a genus of shrubs and trees also known as *hawthorn* or *thornapple*, which has fruits with stone seeds similar to the ones in peaches and plums but also bears thorns. Like his possible namesake, then, Gale Hawthorne can provide sustenance and sweetness—if you can get through the harsh exterior first.

The giggling fangirl in me insists that I also share the traditional Scottish saying, "Ne'er cast a cloot til Mey's oot," which basically boils down to "Never take your clothes off until the hawthorn's in bloom." Gale *did* kiss all those girls on the slag heap, after all . . .

Gale

A *gale* is a very strong wind, and here, in the case of Gale Hawthorne and his revolutionary tendencies, may refer to the winds of change.

Another possible point of origin for Gale's name is Richard Nelson Gale, a British soldier who served in both WWI and WWII. He famously came away from his war experience with a distrust for weapons-heavy battle strategy—something that, of course, Gale shows expertise in, but that proves to be his undoing, as it ultimately severs his ties to Katniss.

Alternately, Gale may come from *nightingale*. Traditionally in Western literature, nightingales have represented sorrow or lament.

A nightingale appears in the Middle English debate poem "The Owl and the Nightingale." In the poem, the nightingale, who is either the antagonist or the antihero, continuously insults the owl, despite being of a lower class and appearance—key characteristics of Gale's. The poem itself offers no concrete resolution for the argument the two birds have in the poem, much as in *Mockingjay*, there is no concrete resolution to Gale and Katniss' story.

Unmated male nightingales sing most loudly at dawn—just as Gale most often hunts, with Katniss, at daybreak—as a way to mark and protect their personal territory and to attempt to attract a mate.

Hazelle

Hazelle may be derived from hazel, a genus of flowering shrubs. Unlike most other plants, hazel plants are either specifically male or specifically female. The plant has some medicinal uses; extracts from its bark and leaves are soothing and restorative, used in aftershave lotions and lotions for treating bruises and insect bites. In the same comforting vein, Hazelle is the only positive mother figure in the Hunger Games series, and one of the few adults that Katniss professes to respect.

Posy

Posy's name is not actually a flower, the way Rue and Prim's are. However, Posy's name is still aligned etymologically with those of the other young girls in the Hunger Games: *posy* is a term for a small bouquet.

Posies have existed in some form since at least medieval times, when they were carried or worn around the head or bodice to mask the unpleasant smells of the time, and are mentioned in the macabre children's rhyme "Ring Around the Rosy," which is about the mass death of the black plague. Katniss recounts that Posy suffered a very serious illness in early childhood, which could be the inspiration for her name.

The meaning of posies in the language of flowers is symbolically to create happiness wherever they go, which does indeed seem to be Posy's role as a precursor to the idea of "the new Panem" or a post-war Panem, especially in *Mockingjay*.

Rory

Rory means, literally, *the red king* in Irish Gaelic. One potential derivation for Rory's name is Rory O'Moore, an Irish activist and the principal organizer of the Irish Rebellion of 1641. After having more than 180 family members killed by English forces, Rory O'Moore became an enemy of Queen Elizabeth I of England, head of Ireland's governing body at the time; Rory himself isn't mentioned much in *Mockingjay*, but his brother spearheaded the migration from District 12 and helped to plan and execute attacks on the Capitol, which certainly ties the Hunger Games' Rory to the rebellion.

Vick

Vick may be short for *Victor*, which is really interesting, all things Panem being considered.

However, it's also possible—and perhaps more plausible—that Vick is derived from *victual*, meaning *food supplies or provisions of food*. *Victual* stems from the Latin *victus*, or *sustenance*, which would certainly have had great value in the Hawthorne family.

HEAVENSBEE, Plutarch

"Heavensbee" is a portmanteau and proprietary name. In southern vernacular, the phrase "Heavens be!" is a mild expression of surprise. But the name could also come from a line in the "Life of Pericles" (part of *Parallel Lives*), written by Heavensbee's namesake, the historical Plutarch:

A NOTE ON DISTRICT NAMES

Diopeithes introduced a bill that those who did not recognize the gods, or who taught theories of the *heavens*, *be* prosecuted.

A Greek historian, biographer, essayist, and Platonic philosopher best known for his *Parallel Lives* and *Moralia*, the historical Plutarch was born to a Greek family under the name Ploutarchos, and was renamed upon becoming a Roman citizen. This may suggest that the Hunger Games' Plutarch came from somewhere outside the Capitol and took a Capitol name to avoid suspicion as he plotted the Second Rebellion; more likely, however, it is the historical Plutarch's work, not his background, that served as the inspiration for the Hunger Games' character.

The historical Plutarch focused most of his adult life on pointing out the moral deficiencies and inadequacies of Roman officials. His best-known work is *Parallel Lives*, a series of biographies of famous Greeks and Romans, many government officials, arranged in pairs to illuminate their common moral virtues and vices. The surviving *Lives* contains twenty-three pairs, each with one Greek Life and one Roman Life, as well as four unpaired single *Lives*—including Lives of Caesar, Coriolanus, Romulus, Cato, and Brutus. Plutarch was not concerned with the accurate recording of history so much as the influence of character, good or bad, on the lives and destinies of men.

Similarly, the Hunger Games' Plutarch worked to expose (and depose, in the case of Coriolanus Snow!) corrupt officials. He did this much in the same way the historical Plutarch did: just as Plutarch was interested in preserving and telling people's stories through popular writings (i.e., the *Lives*), Plutarch Heavensbee is interested in displaying and telling people's stories through reality TV programming (the Games, his proposed singing show).

JACKSON
SHARPSHOOTER FOR DISTRICT 13 SQUAD 451

Jackson's name is most likely taken from Andrew Jackson, whose nickname was "The Sharpshooter."

LAVINIA
THE REDHEADED AVOX GIRL IN *THE HUNGER GAMES*
Lavinia means, literally, *woman of Rome*. Lavinia is a character in Virgil's *Aeneid*, the only daughter of the king.[lxxxix] The prospect of her marriage to Aeneas, which would merge the Trojans and Romans, is opposed on both sides and causes a war; the capture of Lavinia and the boy she is running away with is Katniss' first real brush with the tensions between the districts and the Capitol that later lead to war.

A Lavinia also appears in Shakespeare's *Titus Andronicus*, and she suffers the same horrific fate as the Hunger Games' Lavinia: she is captured during a "royal hunt" and violently attacked. To prevent her from being able to tell of what she endured, her tongue is cut out. Lavinia later writes the names of her attackers in the dirt using a stick held in her mouth.[xc]

LEEG 1, LEEG 2
DISTRICT 13 SOLDIERS; PART OF THE STAR SQUAD
Leeg is a contraction of the Old Dutch *lithag* (which itself stems from the Proto-Germanic *lipugaz*); in Dutch, *lithag* means "empty, hollow; listless, lethargic."

However, a more likely origin, given Leeg 1 and 2's positions as career soldiers, is *league* or *legion*, possibly from Roman Legion, a part of the Imperial army formed of elite heavy infantry and recruited exclusively from Roman citizens. A singular soldier of the Legion was called a *legionary*. Legionaries underwent especially rigorous training; discipline was the base of the army's success, and the soldiers were relentlessly and constantly trained with weapons and especially with drill.

LEEVY
DISTRICT 12 COAL MINER
The name *Leevy* is likely a derivative of *levy* but may also derive from *Leah*. A levy is a legal seizure of property to satisfy a tax debt; it's also a military term meaning to conscript troops for service, which may relate to the conscription of Seam adults to work in the mines. *Leah* means *weary*.

A NOTE ON DISTRICT NAMES

LYME
COMMANDER OF THE REBELS IN DISTRICT 2

Lyme may derive from Lyme disease, a bacterial infection spread through tick bites. Left untreated, symptoms can involve weakness or paralysis of the joints, heart, and central nervous system; Lyme's name may reflect the effect on the Capitol of the crippling blow it suffers at the battle at the Nut, under Lyme's command.

MAGS
Mags may be a nickname for *Margaret* (or *Margarita*), which means *pearl*. Madge's and potentially Effie's names also share this same root, and Peeta gives a pearl to Katniss as a symbol of his affection (and possibly in wry recollection of Effie's misguided statement during the Seventy-fourth Games that putting coal under pressure creates a pearl) in *Catching Fire* . . . making the pearl—a beautiful, rare thing hidden in an ugly, hard-to-open, hard-to-find package—one of the Hunger Games' most-used symbols, alongside fire, berries, and roses, and, of course, the mockingjay.

In traditional Western literary tropes, the pearl is used to symbolize wisdom, integrity, and spiritual guidance, an apt association given Mags' longtime role as mentor for District 4 and her steadfast calm during the Quarter Quell. In astrology and Eastern symbolism, the pearl is a lunar symbol, also representing water and women.[xci] (Also interesting to note: rural American folk wisdom states that for every pearl present on a woman's wedding day, the husband will give her a reason to cry.)

Because Mags' weapon of choice (besides napping!) is the awl, a sharp, needlelike instrument, and/or the fishhook, it is possible that Mags' name came from Goethe's poem "Margaret at her Spinning-Wheel," about a woman who sings of lost love:

> The world's wide all
> Is turned to gall.

Alas, my head
Is well-nigh crazed;
My feeble mind
Is sore amazed.

My heart is sad, . . .

I'd sink in death!

MARTIN
MURDERED CHILD FROM DISTRICT 11

Martin, derived from the Latin *Martinus*, means *son of Mars* or *servant of war*. Based on the literal meaning, Martin is an unlikely name for the murdered, disabled child that Rue once knew in District 11. However, as discussed in chapter eleven, the name Martin may have been chosen more for its historical connotation; it also belonged, most famously, to Martin Luther King, Jr., who represented and stood peaceably for the ideals that the Capitol, and their so-called Peacekeepers, has erased from the nation of Panem. Like his possible namesake, Martin was murdered for resisting oppression—Rue recounts that Martin was killed for taking a pair of glasses they were given to assist in their work, and Martin Luther King, Jr., was assassinated while on a trip to support African American sanitation workers who were striking in Memphis.

MARVEL
DISTRICT 1 TRIBUTE IN THE SEVENTY-FOURTH HUNGER GAMES

A *marvel* is something that evokes surprise, admiration, wonder, or astonishment. Marvel's name, as with Glimmer, Gloss, and Cashmere, denotes his status as a citizen of District 1 by obliquely referencing their district's specialization in luxury: the goods produced in District 1 are meant to be "marveled" at, or admired.

MASON, Johanna
DISTRICT 7 TRIBUTE IN THE QUARTER QUELL

Although *Mason* generally refers to stonelayers when derived from French, the Old English *mason* means to *make*. Considering that Johanna is from District 7 and their specialty is lumber and forestry, it's unlikely that the connection to stonemasonry is the inspiration for her last name. Given her involvement in the Quell plot and the Second Rebellion, it is more probable that her surname refers to the Freemasons, an international fraternal organization sometimes referred to as a secret society.

Freemasonry "uses the metaphors of operative stonemasons' tools and implements . . . to convey what has been described by both Masons and critics as 'a system of values and beliefs veiled in allegory and illustrated by symbols.'"[xcii] They are also dedicated to the principles of liberty, equality, and the pursuit of truth, just like Panem's rebels—like Johanna.

Another potential origin is the mathematical Mason's Rule, which deals with the transfer of equilibrium in a branch of engineering and mathematics called control theory.

Johanna is a German name, and is different from the English *Joanna* in both origin and meaning. *Joanna* means *God is gracious*. *Johanna*, however, means *God is merciful* or *God's merciful gift*—ironic, given Johanna's original Games strategy, as related by Katniss: show no mercy.

One possible inspiration for the name is Johanna Sigurðardóttir, the current prime minister of Iceland. When she was sworn in to the office on February 1, 2009, she became both Iceland's first female prime minister and the world's first openly gay head of government of the modern era. Back in the 1990s, when she lost a bid to head the party, she lifted her fist and declared, "My time will come!"—a phrase that became a popular Icelandic expression.

"Visions of Johanna" is also Bob Dylan's most critically praised song, which one critic described as "stranded between extremes—total freedom and abject slavery."[xciii]

MELLARK, Peeta

Mellark is likely a portmanteau and proprietary name. It could find its origin in *lark*, a type of songbird, which could relate to the pointed mention in *The Hunger Games* that, when Katniss sings, "all the birds stopped to listen."[THG301] In old Europe, lark tongue was considered a highly prized delicacy; certainly Peeta's speech is of high value to the rebellion. Additionally, the *Oxford English Dictionary* lists *Mell* as meaning, *to speak, talk. Of birds: to sing.* Suzanne Collins has stated that one of Peeta's intrinsic gifts is a "facility for language,"[xciv] and that speech is "how Peeta navigates his world."[xcv]

Interestingly, it should be noted that larks have traditionally been used in Western literature in several of the same ways as mockingjays are in the Hunger Games trilogy—in particular, as harbingers of change or markers of ingenuity. Western literature also uses the lark to symbolize merriment, as the lark sang hymns at the gates of heaven and announced the coming of the day. Because of the bird's boundless energy, the lark is also used as a symbol of hope, happiness, good fortune, and creativity—all things that Peeta symbolizes in the Hunger Games series!

Peeta is a homophone for *pita*, a type of bread—appropriate given that the Mellark family's vocation is baking, in which Peeta personally seems to take a genuine interest. *Peeta* is also a Dutch derivation of *Peter*, meaning *the rock*, which is a role that Peeta plays for Katniss. Despite Katniss' best efforts, she does indeed need his grounding to stay alive, sane, and—eventually—happy.

The additional homophone *pietà* is Italian for *pity* or *lamentation*, and is particularly used in a religious context; Michelangelo's favorite of his sculptures was the *Pietà*, Jesus' body cradled by Mary. It has long been legend that Michelangelo stabbed a man to achieve the knowledge necessary to sculpt the human form in its moment of death so accurately, a story that is fueled in part by a perceived stab wound in the abdomen of the Christ figure. The *Pietà* stabbing wasn't in the leg—and Michelangelo's fabled victim probably didn't frost himself in mud—but the image of Katniss cradling Peeta in the cave still works as a compelling reference to the Madonna cradling the body of Christ.

When paired with Finnick's, Peeta's name evokes the phrase "loaves and fishes," suggesting that the two help "feed" the multitude in Panem. Panem's society is a bureaucracy of welfare, where people submit their names to the Hunger Games in exchange for grain and oil;

Peeta and Finnick's roles in the Second Rebellion both literally and metaphorically feed Panem's citizens by eliminating that barrier to obtaining food and freedom.

Peeta's name also suggests a direct connection between him and Panem itself, as panem means *bread* and *pita* is a type of bread. As evidenced throughout the series, the connection between Panem and Peeta is reflexive: whatever is happening to Peeta is also happening to Panem, or vice versa. When Peeta is falling in love with Katniss during the Seventy-fourth Hunger Games, so is Panem. When Peeta speaks of the unfairness of the Quarter Quell and reaches out to the other victors for support, the rest of Panem's populace is beginning to erupt in civil unrest, supporting each other in a series of interdependent uprisings. And, most importantly, when Peeta is captured and tortured into insanity, Panem itself simultaneously dissolves into fractious, chaotic disarray. The ending of Peeta's story is the same as the ending of Panem's story: because of Katniss, both are able to attain peace and new growth.

MESSALLA
CRESSIDA'S ASSISTANT

One possible Roman origin for Messalla's name is the historical Messalla Corvinus. Corvinus was educated partly at Athens, together with Horace and the younger Cicero, which mirrors the Hunger Games' Messalla's Capitol upbringing and longtime working relationships with Cressida and Plutarch Heavensbee. In early life he became attached to republican principles—the Roman equivalent of rebel plans in the Hunger Games world—which he never abandoned, although in later life he avoided offending Caesar Augustus by not mentioning them too openly, much like the Hunger Games' Messalla. Corvinus was most famous for the phrase, "I am disgusted with power."[xcvi]

Alternately, the name Messalla could have been taken from a Roman empress named Valeria Messallina, who conspired against her husband and was executed when the plot was discovered. The only ones who mourned for Messalina were her children; the Roman Senate ordered Messalina's name removed from all public or private places and all statues of her removed.

OCTAVIA
MEMBER OF KATNISS' PREP TEAM

One of the most prominent women in Roman history, the historical Octavia was respected and admired by contemporaries for her loyalty, nobility, and humanity, and for maintaining traditional Roman feminine virtues. The Hunger Games' Octavia, too, exemplifies feminine virtues: she is described as fashionable, curvaceous, and "girlish," and as part of Cinna's prep team is hell-bent on "feminizing" Katniss (by removing "unsightly" hair, polishing her nails, etc.). Like the historical Octavia, whose "virtue was such as to excite even admiration in an age of growing licentiousness and corruption,"[xcvii] Octavia is a good person at heart, despite her Capitol upbringing.

The beauty of Rome's Octavia was believed to be greater than even that of Cleopatra. In other words, as Posy says of the Hunger Games' Octavia: she "would be pretty in any color"![M63]

ODAIR, Finnick
DISTRICT 4 TRIBUTE IN THE QUARTER QUELL

Finnick is most likely a portmanteau meant to evoke traditional Irish naming. It is most likely a combination of *fin*, for District 4's ocean-oriented fishing specialty, and *nick* or Nicholas, meaning "victory of the people."

Odair may be a play on *Adair*, a Scotch-Gaelic name meaning "happy spear" (like Finnick's trident!). It's possible that it is meant to evoke the Irish name practice of using the prefix *O'* to denote that a person is of a certain family or place, though *Dair*, the Irish name of the seventh letter of the Ogham alphabet, meaning *oak*, does not appear to relate in any way to Finnick.

Given Suzanne Collins' lifelong love of Greek and Roman mythology,[xcviii] Odair may also have been chosen because of its similarity to the name *Odysseus*; as discussed in chapter ten, Finnick's arc in the

Hunger Games series almost perfectly mirrors Odysseus' journey over the course of the *Illiad* and *Odyssey*.

PAYLOR (Commander Paylor)
REBEL LEADER OF DISTRICT 8 AND FIRST PRESIDENT OF THE NEW PANEM

One possible origin for Commander Paylor's name is Master Sergeant Irving Arthur Paylor, who was held as a prisoner of war during the Korean War. He was unaccounted for after the war and is presumed to have died or been killed while in captivity.

However, given that the Hunger Games' Paylor is a woman, it is of note that a CSM Larry Paylor is quoted in a recent official military brief as saying:

> We (leaders) don't look at gender anymore when making assignments. Our missions are too critical. [. . .] Physically, it's obvious they are women, but their professionalism and expertise in their jobs are what stands out and helped them achieve all their substantial accomplishments. They are the most proficient soldiers I have worked with in my military career.[xcvix]

POLLUX
CAPITOL CAMERAMAN TURNED REBEL PROPOS PRODUCER

The literal translation of the name *Pollux* is *much sweet wine*; in Greek mythology, he was the demigod son of Dionysius, the god of wine and pleasure. Greek myth's Pollux was the twin brother of Castor, and one-half of the constellation Gemini. (See lexicon entry on Castor.)

PORTIA
PEETA'S STYLIST IN THE SEVENTY-FOURTH HUNGER GAMES AND THE QUARTER QUELL

Portia is perhaps the most puzzling name in the Hunger Games, in terms of how it relates to her relationship to other characters. The Hunger Games' Portia serves as an assistant/partner to Cinna, but in history, the best-known Portias had ties to Cato and Brutus.

Collins may have chosen *Portia* as a name just because it was so common in Rome at the time of Caesar's assassination; *Portia* is the feminine form of the *gens* (or family) Porcii, a *nomen* (or family name) that branched into three influential Roman lineages.

The likeliest option for Portia's namesake is Portia Catonis. She was the second wife of Marcus Junius Brutus, the most famous of Julius Caesar's assassins. She is best known for her suicide: swallowing live coals. In Shakespeare's *Julius Caesar*, she appears in fictionalized form as Brutus' wife. It is a small role, but the only female role of note in the play. In the fourth act, it is reported that she died by swallowing fire. Her association with fire certainly makes her proprietary knowledge of the technology for the fire that adorned Katniss and Peeta's opening ceremonies costumes appropriate. And in a way, the Hunger Games' Portia could also be said to have died by fire—the sequence of events that ended with her death on live television began with the outfit that made Katniss the Girl On Fire.

Another plausible source origin for Portia's name is the Porcia Lex, a set of codified Roman laws that prohibited "degrading and shameful forms of punishment, such as scourging with rods or whips, and especially crucifixion."[c] The Porcia Lex also established the right of Roman citizens to appeal to the representatives of their districts and made it legal to kill any citizen plotting to become a dictator or tyrant, a law most notably used to absolve the conspirators behind the death of Julius Caesar.[ci]

The Porcia Lex also granted a Roman citizen, condemned by a magistrate to death or scourging, the right to appeal to the people—including the common people. This was a crucial addition to the law, because it meant the consuls no longer had the power to pronounce sentences in capital cases against Roman citizens without the consent of the people. The Hunger Games' Portia was an important part, through her work as stylist, of gaining similar rights for Panem's citizens against unfair laws of the Capitol.

A NOTE ON DISTRICT NAMES

PURNIA
DISTRICT 12 PEACEKEEPER

Purnia is the name of a district in India, but it may also be derived from the Roman name *Calpurnia*.

Although the name may be taken from Calpurnia Pisonis, the final wife of Julius Caesar, it is more likely that she received her name from the Lex Acilia Calpurnia, a set of codified Roman laws against legal political corruption, as Purnia is the only Peacekeeper to step forward in protest when Gale is whipped in *Catching Fire*.

RIPPER
HOB BOOTLEGGER

The name *Ripper* may be a homage to moonshine culture in the Appalachians, where moonshine is also called "fence-ripper," for the propensity of those who drink it to get drunk and fall down. In Hungary, the most alcoholic distilled fruit alcohols are (informally) referred to as *"kerítésszaggató"* in Hungarian, which literally means *fence-ripper* and also referring to a drunkard's loss of balance. Famous bootlegger Al Capone was also a member of the gang "The Brooklyn Rippers" in his childhood.

ROOBA
DISTRICT 12 BUTCHER

Rooba is an Estonian surname, which may offer some insight into the cultural origins of the people of District 12 (though it's unlikely, if Melungeon heritage is the intended model). The homophone *Ruba* is a town in Belarus.

It is possible that Rooba is a variation on the first syllables of the traditional American nursery rhyme "Rub-a-Dub-Dub," which involves a butcher, a baker, and a candlestick maker. Given that Rooba's profession is butcher and she is a part of Katniss' trade route as much as the candlestick maker (as Katniss frequently trades for paraffin)—and, obviously, the

District 12 baker!—this rhyme allusion might be a sly nod to the idea of the Hob, which is a gathering place for these types of independent craftsmen.

Further evidence that her name may be an allusion to the Hob comes from the origins of the nursery rhyme itself. As the butcher for District 12, it stands to reason that Rooba is a merchant—and therefore, should not be participating in the Hob's black market (although, technically, no one should really be participating in a black market; that's what makes it a black market). There are distinct regional variances in the rhyme between England and the United States, but the three most common versions are:

> Rub-a-dub-dub, three men in a tub. And who do you think were there? The butcher, the baker, the candlestick maker, and all jumped out of a rotten potater. It was enough to make a man stare.

> Hey, rub-a-dub, ho, rub-a-dub, three maids in a tub. And who do you think were there? The butcher, the baker, the candlestick maker, and all of them going to the fair.

> Rub-a-dub-dub, three men in a tub. And who do you think they be? The butcher, the baker the candlestick maker. Turn them out, knaves all three.[cii]

In all three cases, the "respectable tradesfolk" are caught doing something they shouldn't have been: the "rotten potater" suggests that they were cheating their customers; "the fair"—another term for a bawdy house—and "knaves all three" implies the men are at a gay bathhouse. Choosing to sell meat from dying animals at the Hob rather than from properly butchered livestock in the merchant area suggests that Rooba may be a bit of a "rotten potater" herself.

RUE

DISTRICT 11 TRIBUTE IN THE SEVENTY-FOURTH HUNGER GAMES

As stated in the novels, *Rue* derives from the flower *Ruta graveolens*, also known as the Herb-of-Grace, which is well known for its ability to tolerate harsh conditions. In European folk medicine, rue is said to improve appetite and to prevent the Black Death. In Rome (particularly around Caesar's time), it was used to induce abortion. Brushing against a *Ruta graveolens* plant can result in cuts and burn-like bubbles (much like tracker jacker stings, but without the hallucinations and death).

To rue means to feel sorrow over; repent of; regret bitterly; wish that something had never been done or never taken place.

The French homophone *roux* is a thickening agent in both Creole and Cajun cuisines in the Deep South. Rue's origins are in the same geographical location, and her death "thickens" or deepens the discord between District 11 and the Capitol while cohering the relationship between District 11 and District 12.

Another homophone, the German *Ruhe*, means *peace*.

SEEDER
DISTRICT 11 TRIBUTE IN THE QUARTER QUELL

Seeder, or one who seeds or plants seeds, is most likely derived from the District 11 specialty of agriculture. The name could also allude to her role in "sowing the seeds of rebellion" by being a part of the Quell plot—and possibly participating in the District 11 riots in *Catching Fire*.

SNOW, Coriolanus

The name *Snow* is fairly straightforward, as it's also a modern English word. Snow's primary characteristic is that it is cold, physically—just as the Hunger Games' Snow is cold emotionally.

"SNOW" was also the codename of a Welsh mole during WWII who specialized in bugging his enemies, something at which the Hunger Games' Snow also excels.

Colloquially, to "snow" someone is to intentionally deceive, double-cross, or con them.

Coriolanus was the name of a Roman emperor with philosophical parallels to the Hunger Games' President Snow. As a general, he successfully led the city's soldiers against an enemy tribe, the Volscians; however, after defeating them and thereby winning support from the patricians of the Roman Senate, Coriolanus argued against the democratic inclinations of the common people. After ruling in tyranny, Coriolanus was charged with misappropriation of public funds, convicted, and permanently banished from Rome.

Shakespeare's play about the exiled emperor, titled *Coriolanus*, opens in Rome shortly after the expulsion of the Tarquin kings. There are riots in progress after stores of grain are withheld from ordinary citizens. The rioters are particularly angry with Coriolanus, whom they blame for the grain being taken away. Coriolanus is openly contemptuous of the common people and says that the common people are not worthy of the grain because of their lack of military service. Faced with this opposition, Coriolanus flies into a rage and rails against the concept of popular rule, comparing allowing plebeians to have power over the patricians to allowing "crows to peck the eagles." He leads a new wartime assault against the city and is stopped only by a tenuous peace accord . . . which is broken by his execution. For readers who know the play, the name may also serve as false foreshadowing, given that Katniss chooses against assassinating Snow at the last moment.

TAX
ARCHERY INSTRUCTOR FOR THE QUARTER QUELL

Tax most likely comes from *taxes*—perhaps intended to evoke "No taxation without representation!"—the slogan of another rebellion, though there's no evidence Tax was involved with the rebel cause.

In the 1970s in the United States, there was actually a specific tax on archery equipment; this is probably a coincidence.

TEMPLESMITH, Claudius
THE ANNOUNCER OF THE HUNGER GAMES

A templesmith is literally a person who creates temples, which are houses of worship, but also places devoted to a special purpose or particular rite—such as the Hunger Games in Panem.

A NOTE ON DISTRICT NAMES

The best-known historical Claudius (Tiberius Claudius Caesar Augustus Germanicus) was the great-great grandnephew of Julius Caesar and the first Roman emperor to be born outside of Italy. Claudius constructed many new roads, aqueducts, and canals across the empire during his reign and took a personal interest in law, presiding at public trials and issuing up to twenty edicts a day. His death allowed Nero to become emperor. Emperor Nero is best known for his lackadaisical, inappropriate behavior during the Great Fire of Rome (thus the often-used phrase "Nero fiddles while Rome burns")—behavior reminiscent of the Capitol's preparations for the Quarter Quell, even as the rest of Panem begins disintegrating in riots and strikes.

THOM
DISTRICT 12 MINER

Thom is a shortened form of Thomas, meaning *a twin*.

Thomas the apostle, or "Doubting Thomas," is best known for disbelieving Jesus' resurrection when first told of it, then proclaiming "My Lord and my God!" upon seeing him alive again. He was the only apostle who may have gone outside the Roman Empire to preach. He is also believed to have crossed the largest area in proselytizing—making him a good fit as namesake for the Hunger Games' Thom, whose role in civil service for the government of New Panem takes him far outside District 12.

THREAD, Romulus
REPLACEMENT HEAD PEACEKEEPER IN DISTRICT 12 WHO WHIPS GALE

Thread may mean exactly what it sounds like, thread, and be an indication that the Peacekeeper has District 8 origins, despite Katniss' claim that most Peacekeepers are from District 2. However, it may also be a reference to the Fates, who spin, measure, and snip the thread of life, choosing the time and manner of each person's death. Romulus Thread seems to find the latter to be his purview as well, given his arbitrary interpretation of the laws for corporal punishment in District 12 in regard to Gale.

In Greek mythology, Theseus uses Ariadne's thread to find his way through the Minotaur's maze; for Katniss, it is Romulus Thread's mistreatment of Gale that leads her to a greater understanding of the depth of the Capitol's ills.

Romulus means, literally, *of Rome* and as Head Peacekeeper, Thread is the main representative of the Capitol in District 12. Romulus and his brother Remus are the mythical twins said to have founded Rome; Romulus was the more brutal of the two and eventually killed his brother over boundary rights. It is said that, as he slew his twin, he declared, "So perish every one that shall hereafter leap over my wall!" The Hunger Games' Romulus has Gale whipped for trespassing over the fence that borders District 12.

THRESH
DISTRICT 11 TRIBUTE IN THE SEVENTY-FOURTH HUNGER GAMES

Thresh's name is connected to the District 11 specialty of agriculture. To thresh is to separate grain from a plant, typically with a flail (a type of tool made from sticks and chain). It can also mean to convulse; to flail; to thrash; to beat. A thresher is a very dangerous piece of farming equipment. Like the names of other citizens in District 11, Thresh's name may be a comment on slave naming, as discussed in chapter eleven; he is named for his job specialization and does not seem to have a surname.

TIGRIS
CAPITOL SHOP OWNER AND FORMER HUNGER GAMES STYLIST

Tigris' name most likely comes from her tigerlike physical presentation, but Tigris is also the name of one of the two rivers that formed the Cradle of Civilization, where humanity is said to have begun. In the Book of Genesis, the Tigris is the third of four rivers that branch off the river issuing out of the Garden of Eden; for Katniss and her fellow soldiers, Tigris' shop proves to be a kind of Eden-like safe haven in the middle of a hostile Capitol.

A NOTE ON DISTRICT NAMES

TITUS
DISTRICT 6 TRIBUTE WHO "WENT CRAZY" IN THE ARENA AND RESORTED TO CANNIBALISM IN A PREVIOUS HUNGER GAMES

The name *Titus* is most likely taken from Emperor Titus. It was during Titus' short reign that the Coliseum—the stadium for gladiatorial games—was completed; the inaugural games lasted for a hundred days and were said to be extremely elaborate, including gladiatorial combat, fights between wild animals (including elephants and cranes), mock naval battles for which the theater was flooded, horse races, and chariot races. Titus died shortly after the inaugural games' end.

TRINKET, Effie

A trinket is a small showy ornament, a mere trifle: something that is irrelevant or easily replaceable, as Effie, with her superficial bluster, initially appears to be.

Effie is a nickname for a variety of names, primarily used in the United States and United Kingdom:

- *Euphemia:* This is the most likely option for the origin of Effie's name; it means "well spoken."
- *Elizabeth: Elizabeth* means *the highest authority is my oath*, and has been the name of many public officials and queens.
- *Florence:* The literal meaning of *Florence* is *prosperous*. The most prominent Florence is Florence Nightingale, who was a nurse in battle; Effie is technically supposed to aid and guide the tributes in the lead up to battle in their arena.
- *Margaret: Margaret* means *pearl*. This is the least likely source for Effie's name, although it does recall her (misinformed) statement that coal, under enough pressure, turns to pearls—implying that, put under enough "pressure," the District 12 tributes could be made to resemble that paragon of Capitol values, Effie herself.

235

TWILL
ESCAPEE FROM DISTRICT 8

Twill's name is likely derived from the District 8 specialty of textiles. *Twill* is a type of textile woven with a pattern of diagonal parallel ribs.

UNDERSEE, Madge

The name *Undersee* is most likely a play on the word *oversee*, meaning to supervise; while Mayor Undersee is mayor, and thus it is his job to supervise his district, he himself is under the thumb of the Capitol and Peacekeepers, making him an "under"seer.

Madge may come from the Madge Wildfire, a class of coal-burning trains in the British Railways era. Coal, of course, is the specialty of District 12. Madge is also associated with fire: she is the only female childhood friend of the Girl On Fire, and meets her death in the firebombing of District 12.

Madge's name shares a possible root with both Effie and Mags: Margaret, meaning *pearl*. In Madge's first appearance, she is dressed in white, the color of a pearl.

Madge is also the surname of bird expert Steve Madge (which seems appropriate, given that Madge is the source of Katniss' mockingjay pin), and mollusk expert Edward Henry Madge.

VENIA
MEMBER OF KATNISS' PREP TEAM

Venia's name may be derived from the famous Roman phrase *veni vidi vici*, or "I came, I saw, I conquered," which is most frequently attributed to Julius Caesar. It's also possible that *Venia* is derived from the word *venial*, meaning "forgivable"; it is the prep team, including Venia, who first show Katniss that the citizens of the Capitol are also, largely, products of their culture, and are worthy of forgiveness despite their complicity in the districts' oppression.

A NOTE ON DISTRICT NAMES

WIRESS
DISTRICT 3 TRIBUTE IN THE QUARTER QUELL

Wiress may be meant as a female form of the word *wire*, and thus be derived from the District 3 specialty of electronics/technology. Wiress' name may also be a portmanteau of "wire" and "mistress," suggesting that she is a master/mistress of electrical engineering. As Wiress is a part of the rebellion plot, she is technically a "resistance wire" (a type of electrical wire). The idea of wires being connective also has resonance for her character, since she, together with Beetee and Mags, is one of the first people Katniss is interested in allying with for the Quarter Quell. *Wire* comes from the Latin *viere*, which means *to weave together*, further suggesting the bond that she helps to forge between Katniss and the rest of the conspirators.

WOOF
DISTRICT 8 TRIBUTE IN THE QUARTER QUELL

Woof is the term for the threads that run crosswise in a woven fabric, at right angles to the warp threads, or for the texture of a fabric generally, and is most likely derived from the District 8 specialty of textiles.

Acknowledgments

Much like the Mockingjay in the Second Rebellion, *The Panem Companion* could not have succeeded without the help of people more skilled (in Book Publishing Things, not battle strategy) than myself.

The biggest thanks that I can give, and I'll say them a million times over, is to Meg Loeb, for spending nights with me making the original version of the "Map of Panem" and the "Etymology of Panem" and for parsing out Finnick Odair Feelings and Cinnalove. Thank you, thank you, Meg; you are the absolute best and I love you!

I also can't thank Savanna New and Adam Spunberg of Hunger Games Fireside Chat enough, for noticing the Panem map and inviting Meg and me to be on their very first podcast and for introducing me to Leah Wilson at Smart Pop Books to make *The Panem Companion* happen. Thank you so, so much! You're huge assets to the Hunger Games fandom and we're all lucky to have the Fireside Chat and your enthusiasm!

Massive thanks are also due to Shylah Addante, for her math skillz (with a z) and for her maturity and leadership in the fandom; the staffs of Down With The Capitol, The Hob, Victor's Village, and Mockingjay.net, for featuring the announcement for *The Panem Companion* and for their enthusiasm about the project and the map; Liz Soehngen, for explaining science ideas and why my own ideas are Not Real Science; and Eli, Puel, Mith, Ashley Irving, Dan Sabato,

Jenn Nguyen, and Katybeth Mannix, for fueling interesting content through essays, discussion, questioning, and enthusiastically engaged reading. Thank you to everyone at Smart Pop (Leah Wilson, Leigh Camp, Heather Butterfield, and everyone else!) for taking a chance on *The Panem Companion* and taking the book from a fan idea on a Livejournal blog to an actual, physical book—one that's in the Library of Congress and everything!

Thank you to the Hunger Games fandom, for being one of the loudest, most unabashed, most excited and energetic fandoms that I've ever seen, and for treating your source material with so much love and respect.

And a huge thank-you to my family for supporting me.

About the Author

V. Arrow graduated from Know College in 2008 with degrees in history and creative writing, specializing in twentieth-century pop culture and young adult lit. Under another name, she has previously published at Pop Matters, The One Love, Tommy2.net, and *The Hollywood Reporter*. She believes that pop culture affects, reflects, and informs all aspects of daily life in Western culture and that it is perhaps the most crucial form of media expression to analyze and discuss.

Endnotes

i. "A CONVERSATION: Questions and Answers, Suzanne Collins," Scholastic.com, accessed December 5, 2011, http://www.scholastic.com/thehungergames/media/qanda.pdf.
ii. Karin Zeitvogel, "Oil will run out 100 years before new fuels developed: study." *AFP*, November 15, 2010, accessed December 7, 2011, http://www.google.com/hostednews/afp/article/ALeqM5jv-QP6noOoD7u3wQqJG3xyvon-2Q?docId=CNG.c3a7214bcfe6083ee696ade4d9402691.6d1.
iii. E. Rignot et al., *Geophysical Research Letters*, March 2011, accessed May 13, 2012, http://www.agu.org/pubs/crossref/2011/2011GL046583.shtml.
iv. James G. Titus and Charlie Richman, *Maps of Lands Vulnerable to Sea Level Rise: Modeled Elevations along the U.S. Atlantic and Gulf Coasts*, accessed December 7, 2011, http://web.archive.org/web/20110602190057/http://www.epa.gov/climatechange/effects/downloads/maps.pdf.
v. Rob Young and Orrin Pilkey, "OPINION: How High Will Seas Rise?: Get Ready for Seven Feet," *Yale Environment 260: Opinion, Analysis, Reporting, and Debate*, January 14, 2010, accessed December 11, 2011, http://e360.yale.edu/content/feature.msp?id=2230.
vi. Michael D. Lemonick, "ANALYSIS: The Secret of Sea Level Rise: It Will Vary Greatly by Region," *Yale Environment 260: Opinion, Analysis, Reporting, and Debate*, March 22, 2010, accessed December 7, 2011, http://e360.yale.edu/content/feature.msp?id=2255.
vii. Ibid.
viii. Steven Dutch, "If You're Going To Sink California, Do It Right," Natural and Applied Sciences, University of Wisconsin-Green Bay, July 8, 1998, accessed December 6, 2011, http://www.uwgb.edu/dutchs/pseudosc/sinkcal.htm.
ix. Ibid.
x. Young and Pilkey.
xi. Jay Hambidge, *Dynamic Symmetry: The Greek Vase* (Reprint of original 1920 Yale University Press edition), (Whitefish, MT: Kessinger Publishing, 2003), 19–29.
xii. Richard H. Carson, "The Golden Mean: Context: The American Experience," *Planetizen: The Planning and Development Network*, January 27, 2003, accessed May 13, 2012, http://troymi.gov/futures/Research/Image%20and%20Feel/Golden%20Mean.pdf.
xiii. Susan Dominus, "Suzanne Collins' War Stories for Kids," *The New York Times Magazine*, April 8, 2011, accessed June 30, 2012, http://www.nytimes.com/2011/04/10/magazine/mag-10collins-t.html.
xiv. Al Gore, *An Inconvenient Truth*, dir. Davis Guggenheim, 2006: Paramount Classics, as quoted on "Sea Level Rise," accessed December 8, 2011, http://ninepoints.pbworks.com/w/page/9497558/Sea%20level%20rise.
xv. Young and Pilkey.

xvi. "Senate Vote #21 (May 3, 1921)," *govtrack.us*, accessed May 4, 2012, http://www.govtrack.us/congress/votes/67-1/s21.
xvii. Glenn Beck, as quoted in "Fear and Loathing in Prime Time: Immigration Myths and Cable News," *Media Matters Network*, May 21, 2008, accessed May 4, 2012, http://mediamattersaction.org/reports/fearandloathing/online_version.
xviii. Terry Martin, "The Origins of Soviet Ethnic Cleansing," *The Journal of Modern History*, 70, no. 4 (1998): 813–861, accessed May 5, 2012, http://www.jstor.org/discover/10.1086/235168?uid=3739664&uid=2&uid=4&uid=3739256&sid=21100771631831.
xix. Suzanne Collins, with Karen Valby and Gary Ross, "Team 'Hunger Games' talks: Author Suzanne Collins and director Gary Ross on their allegiance to each other, and their actors—EXCLUSIVE," *Entertainment Weekly*, April 7, 2011, accessed June 30, 2012, http://insidemovies.ew.com/2011/04/07/hunger-games-suzanne-collins-gary-ross-exclusive/.
xx. Shannon Riffe, "Why the Casting of The Hunger Games Matters," *Racialicious*. March 25, 2011, accessed June 30, 2011, http://www.racialicious.com/2011/03/25/why-the-casting-of-the-hunger-games-matters/.
xxi. David Freund, "What Our Experts Say: What is the Difference Between Race and Ethnicity?" *RACE—The Power of an Illusion*, PBS California Newsreel, 2003, accessed June 30, 2012, http://www.pbs.org/race/000_About/002_04-experts-03-02.htm.
xxii. Dalton Conley, "What Our Experts Say: What is the Difference Between Race and Ethnicity?" *RACE—The Power of an Illusion*, PBS California Newsreel, 2003, accessed June 30, 2012, http://www.pbs.org/race/000_About/002_04-experts-03-02.htm.
xxiii. Nancy Jervis, "What Is a Culture?" New York State Education Department, 2006, accessed December 31, 2011, http://www.p12.nysed.gov/ciai/socst/grade3/whatisa.html.
xxiv. Ibid. (Qtd: John Bodley. *Cultural Anthropology: Tribes, States and the Global System*, 1994.)
xxv. Dr. Grace Kao, "Group images and possible selves among adolescents: Linking stereotypes to expectations by race and ethnicity," *Sociological Forum*, Vol 15(3), Sep 2000, 407-430, doi: 10.1023/A:1007572209544.
xxvi. "What is White Privilege?" The White Privilege Conference. http://www.whiteprivilegeconference.com/white_privilege.html.
xxvii. Barack Obama, "Economic Speech in Kansas," Osawatomie, Kansas, December 6, 2011.
xxviii. G. William Domhoff, "Wealth, Income, and Power," *Who Rules America?*, 2012, accessed January 19, 2012, http://www2.ucsc.edu/whorulesamerica/power/wealth.html.
xxix. Ibid.
xxx. Dorothy E. Roberts, "Welfare and the Problem of Black Citizenship," 105 *Yale Law Journal* 1563–1602, April 1996, accessed January 19, 2012, http://academic.udayton.edu/race/04needs/welfare01.htm.
xxxi. Ibid.
xxxii. Ibid.
xxxiii. Sue W, "Four Things You Don't Know About Peeta," *Forever Young Adult*, May 12, 2011, accessed December 16, 2011, http://www.foreveryoungadult.com/2011/05/12/four-things-you-dont-know-about-peeta/.

ENDNOTES

xxxiv. Alexandra Guarnaschelli, "s04e01: Extreme Heat and Meat," *The Next Iron Chef*, 49:26–49:29, Food Network, October 30, 2011.
xxxv. Camille Dodero, "We Have Obtained a Copy of MTV's Standard Real World Cast-Member Contract," *The Village Voice*, August 1, 2011, accessed January 30, 2012, http://blogs.villagevoice.com/runninscared/2011/08/mtv_real_world_contract.php.
xxxvi. Camille Dodero, "Meet the Original JWoww and Snooki, Would-Be Stars of Bridge & Tunnel," *The Village Voice*, July 27, 2011, accessed January 29, 2012, http://www.villagevoice.com/2011-07-27/news/mtv-bridge-tunnel-original-jersey-shore/3/.
xxxvii. Dodero, "We Have Obtained a Copy."
xxxviii. Matthew Zoller Seitz, "'Deadliest Catch': Reality TV's first on-screen death," *Salon*, July 13, 2010, accessed January 30, 2012, http://www.salon.com/2010/07/13/deadliest_catch_finale/.
xxxix. Allex Conley, "Entertainment News: 'Real World' Star Sues MTV Over Alleged Rape: MTV 'Real World' Star Raped During Show?" *Newzy, via E! Online*, October 28, 2011, accessed January 30, 2012, http://www.newsy.com/videos/mtv-real-world-star-raped-during-show/.
xl. "Why Jersey Shore is NOT Okay," *Amplify*, October 14, 2010, accessed April 8, 2012, http://www.amplifyyourvoice.org/u/YoungStar_OneLove/2010/10/14/Why-Jersey-Shore-Is-NOT-Okay.
xli. Austin, Cline, "The Ethics of Reality TV: Should We Watch?" *About.com: Agnosticism/Atheism*. accessed January 30, 2012, http://atheism.about.com/library/FAQs/phil/blphil_eth_realitytv.htm.
xlii. Dodero, "Meet the Original Jwoww."
xliii. Cline, "The Ethics of Reality TV."
xliv. Ibid.
xlv. Dodero, "Meet the Original Jwoww."
xlvi. Marc Lynch, "Reality is Not Enough: The Politics of Arab Reality TV," *TBS Journal*, Middle East Centre, St. Antony's College, University of Oxford, United Kingdom. 2006, accessed 30 January 30, 2012, http://www.tbsjournal.com/lynch.html.
xlvii. Matthew Labash, "When A Kiss Is Not Just A Kiss: Reality TV Comes to the Arab World," *The Weekly Standard Magazine*, October 18, 2004, accessed January 30, 2012, http://www.weeklystandard.com/Content/Public/Articles/000/000/004/752xbofx.asp?pg=1.
xlviii. Dan Gillmor, "Time magazine's Protester cover reminds us of the value of Big Media," *The Guardian*, December 14, 2011, accessed January 30, 2012, http://www.guardian.co.uk/commentisfree/cifamerica/2011/dec/14/time-magazine-protester-dan-gillmor.
xlix. Jim Edwards, "These Time Magazine Covers Explain Why Americans Know Nothing About The World," *Business Insider: Advertising*, November 28, 2011, accessed January 30, 2012, http://www.businessinsider.com/these-time-magazine-covers-explain-why-americans-know-nothing-about-the-world-2011-11#.
l. Ibid.
li. "Timeline of the Iraq War," *ThinkProgress*, accessed January 7, 2012, http://thinkprogress.org/report/iraq-timeline/?mobile=nc#2006.

ENDNOTES

lii. "Amnesty International—People smuggling," Amnesty.org.au, March 23, accessed June 30, 2012, http://web.archive.org/web/20091023121433/http:/www.amnesty.org.au/refugees/comments/20601.
liii. US Department of Health and Human Services: Human Trafficking Resource Center, *Labor Trafficking Sheet*, accessed January 15, 2012, http://www.acf.hhs.gov/trafficking/.
liv. Geidre Steikunaite, "The Beauty Myth . . . and Madness," *The New Internationalist Blog*, March 9, 2011, accessed January 15, 2012, http://www.newint.org/blog/editors/2011/03/09/beauty-myth-and-madness/.
lv. Katybeth B (http://folkloric_feel.livejournal.com), in http://regendy.livejournal.com, "Heteronormativity and sexuality in Panem, or: The Curious Case of Finnick Odair," *Panem For Thought*, May 4, 2011, accessed January 16, 2012, http://panemforthought.livejournal.com/12223.html.
lvi. Katybeth Mannix, in http://regendy.livejournal.com, "Heteronormativity and sexuality in Panem."
lvii. Katybeth Mannix, in http://regendy.livejournal.com, "Heteronormativity and sexuality in Panem."
lviii. Elizabeth Soehngen (Dr.), personal interview regarding Annie Cresta by V. Arrow, February 5, 2012.
lix. Ibid.
lx. Sandra Santana and Felipe O. Santana, "Mexican Culture and Disability: Information for US Service Providers," ed. John Stone, CIRRIE Monograph Series, University at Buffalo, The State University of New York: Center for International Rehabilitation Research Information & Exchange, 2001).
lxi. Ibid.
lxii. Ibid.
lxiii. Ibid.
lxiv. Suzanne Collins with Rick Margolis, "'The Last Battle: With 'Mockingjay' on its way, Suzanne Collins weighs in on Katniss and the Capitol," *The School Library Journal*, August 1, 2010, accessed April 15, 2012, http://www.schoollibraryjournal.com/slj/home/885800-312/the_last_battle_with_mockingjay.html.csp.
lxv. Miles Geoffrey, *Classical Mythology in English Literature: A Critical Anthology* (New York: Routledge, 1999), 54ff.
lxvi. Allana Gillam-Wright, "Songs of Freedom," *Owen Sound's Black History*, 2004, accessed February 10, 2012, http://www.osblackhistory.com/songs.php.
lxvii. Ibid.
lxviii. "Finding Slave Records," *State Library of North Carolina*, 2008, accessed February 12, 2012, http://statelibrary.ncdcr.gov/genealogy/slaverecords.html#census.
lxix. "Slave Work Song: 'Shuck That Corn Before You Eat'," Teacher Resources E-Newsletter, The Colonial Williamsburg Official History Site, September 2003, accessed February 12, 2012, http://www.history.org/history/teaching/enewsletter/volume2/september03/primsource.cfm.
lxx. Ibid.
lxxi. Ibid.
lxxii. Sarah Bull, "The Hunger Games hit by racism row as movie fans tweet vile slurs over casting of black teen actress as heroine Rue," *The Daily Mail*, March 30 2012, accessed April 16, 2012, http://www.dailymail.co.uk/news/article-2122714/The-Hunger-Games-hit-racism-row-movie-fans-tweet-vile-slurs-casting-black-teen-actress-heroine-Rue.html.

ENDNOTES

lxxiii. Primo Levi, quoted in Alex Alvarez, *Governments, Citizens, and Genocide: A Comparative and Interdisciplinary Approach* (Bloomington: Indiana University Press, 2001), 21.
lxxiv. David Andress, *The Terror: The Merciless War for Freedom in Revolutionary France* (New York: Farrar, Strauss and Giroux, 2005), 178–179.
lxxv. "Maximilien Robespierre: On the Principles of Political Morality, February 1794," *Modern History Sourcebook*, Fordham University, 1997, accessed June 29, 2012, http://www.fordham.edu/Halsall/mod/1794robespierre.asp.
lxxvi. Steven D. Levitt and Stephen J. Dubner, "A Roshanda by Any Other Name," *Slate*, April 11, 2005, accessed December 23, 2011, http://www.slate.com/articles/business/the_dismal_science/2005/04/a_roshanda_by_any_other_name.html.
lxxvii. Steven D. Levitt and Stephen J. Dubner, "Trading Up," *Slate*, April 12, 2005, accessed December 23, 2011, http://www.slate.com/articles/business/the_dismal_science/2005/04/trading_up.single.html.
lxxviii. Ibid.
lxxix. "Baby Names 2011: Hottest Trends to Track Now," Nameberry, November 15, 2010, accessed December 23, 2011, http://nameberry.com/blog/baby-names-2011-14-hottest-trends-to-track-now?pid=1722 Acc 23 December 2011.
lxxx. H. J. RES. 57, accessed July 8, 2012, http://www.gpo.gov/fdsys/pkg/BILLS-105hjres57ih/pdf/BILLS-105hjres57ih.pdf.
lxxxi. Behind the Name, http://www.behindthename.com/names/usage/scottish.
lxxxii. "Cornelius Cardew," *Wikipedia*, accessed May 12, 2012, http://en.wikipedia.org/wiki/Cornelius_Cardew#Political_involvements.
lxxxiii. William Howard Russell, *The British Expedition to the Crimea* (Routledge & Co. 1858), as cited on Wikipedia, accessed May 6, 2011, http://en.wikipedia.org/wiki/Battle_of_Alma.
lxxxiv. *Cliff's Notes Guide to Antony & Cleopatra*, Accessed May 7, 2011, http://www.cliffsnotes.com/study_guide/literature/Antony-and-Cleopatra-Character-Analysis-Antony-Enobarbus.id-223,pageNum-104.html.
lxxxv. Tina Jordan, "Suzanne Collins on the books she loves," *EW's Shelf Life*, August 12, 2010, accessed October 17, 2011, http://shelf-life.ew.com/2010/08/12/suzanne-collins-on-the-books-she-loves/.
lxxxvi. *The Flickerman*, accessed May 12, 2011, http://resonancefm.com/archives/1448.
lxxxvi. Historia Augusta, *The Life of Aelius* (UChicago:Loeb Classical Library, 1921, 2011).
lxxxviii. *Aesop's Fables*, traditional.
lxxxix. Virgil, *Aeneid*, VII, Trans. Dryden.
xc. "Lavinia Andronicus," *Wikipedia*, accessed May 12, 2011, http://en.wikipedia.org/wiki/Lavinia_Andronicus#Characters.
xci. Jean Chevalier and Alain Gheerbrandt, trans. John Buchanan-Brown, *The Penguin Dictionary of Symbols* (New York: Penguin, 1997).
xcii. Hermann Gruber, "Masonry (Freemasonry)," *The Catholic Encyclopedia*, IX, (New York: Robert Appleton Company, 1910), accessed June 28, 2012, http://www.newadvent.org/cathen/09771a.htm.
xciii. Mike Marqusee, *Chimes of Freedom: The Politics of Bob Dylan's Art* (New York: The New Press, 2003).

247

ENDNOTES

xciv. Jeff Labrecque, "'Hunger Games': Suzanne Collins and Gary Ross talk casting Josh Hutcherson and Liam Hemsworth," *EW's Inside Movies*, April 5, 2011, accessed October 24, 2011, http://insidemovies.ew.com/2011/04/05/hunger-games-peeta-gale-statements/.
xcv. Karen Valby with Suzanne Collins and Gary Ross, "Team 'Hunger Games' talks: Author Suzanne Collins and director Gary Ross on their allegiance to each other, and their actors–EXCLUSIVE," *EW's Inside Movies*, April 7, 2011, accessed October 24, 2011, http://insidemovies.ew.com/2011/04/07/hunger-games-suzanne-collins-gary-ross-exclusive/.
xcvi. J.P. Sullivan (ed), *Apocolocyntosis* (Penguin, 1986) note 44, as cited on Wikipedia, accessed May 12, 2011, http://en.wikipedia.org/wiki/Marcus_Valerius_Messalla_Corvinus#cite_ref-3.
xcvii. William Smith, *Dictionary of Greek and Roman Biography and Mythology*, 1870: "Details on Octavia pt 1," scanned by the University of Michigan, Ann Arbor, Michigan, University of Michigan Library 2005. As archived on *The Ancient Library*, accessed May 12, 2011, http://web.archive.org/web/20110605011150/http://www.ancientlibrary.com/smith-bio/2336.html.
xcviii. Tina Jordan with Suzanne Collins, "Suzanne Collins on the books she loves," *EW's Shelf Life*, August 12, 2010, accessed October 17, 2011, http://shelf-life.ew.com/2010/08/12/suzanne-collins-on-the-books-she-loves/.
xcvix. Anthony Reed: Sargeant First Class, "Gender issues generic for Army Signal Command's G-staff," Army Communicator, Voice of the Signal Regiment: PB 11-00-2, Summer 2000. Vol. 25 No. 2, accessed May 12, 2011, http://www.signal.army.mil/ocos/ac/Edition,%20Summer/Summer%2000/TOPWOMEN.HTM.
c. Andrew Lintott, *The Constitution of the Roman Republic* (Oxford: Oxford University Press, 1999), pp. 37–38.
ci. Ibid.
cii. National Public Radio, "All Things Considered: Debbie Elliott, Chris Roberts," National Public Radio, December 3, 2005, accessed November 30, 2011, http://www.npr.org/templates/story/story.php?storyId=5038237.

Want More Smart Pop?

www.smartpopbooks.com

» Read a new free essay online everyday

» Plus sign up for email updates, check out our upcoming titles, and more

Become a fan on Facebook:
www.smartpopbooks.com/facebook

Follow us on Twitter:
@smartpopbooks

WANT MORE HUNGER GAMES?

THE GIRL WHO WAS ON FIRE
MOVIE EDITION

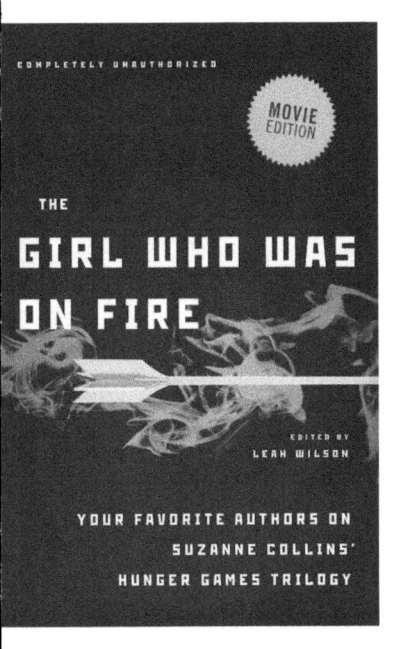

"*The Girl Who Was on Fire* is a MUST read for any Hunger Games fan…As touching and thought provoking as the series itself…[the] essays included will challenge you to think of the trilogy in a new and deeper way…the Hunger Games may be over, but thanks to *The Girl Who was on Fire*, the discussion continues." —**Down With the Capital fansite**

"Discussing the philosophy that lies beneath [*The Hunger Games*] film, the characters within, and allegories of society, Leah Wilson and sixteen writers of young adult fiction come together and provide much to think about with the work. *The Girl Who Was on Fire* is well worth considering for fans." —**Midwest Book Review**

"I thoroughly enjoyed every single essay…My copy is completely highlighted, underlined, written in the margins, and dog-eared. You don't know how many times while I was reading it I said emphatically to myself, 'Yes!!' as I underlined or highlighted a quote or passage." — **Book Nerds Across America**

Read a FREE EXCERPT from *The Girl Who Was on Fire* at:
HTTP://WWW.SMARTPOPBOOKS.COM/HUNGERGAMES

SARAH REES BRENNAN
JENNIFER LYNN BARNES
MARY BORSELLINO
ELIZABETH M. REES
LILI WILKINSON
NED VIZZINI
CARRIE RYAN
CARA LOCKWOOD
DIANA PETERFREUND
TERRI CLARK
BLYTHE WOOLSTON
BRENT HARTINGER
SARAH DARER LITTMAN
JACKSON PEARCE
ADRIENNE KRESS
BREE DESPAIN